YOU ARE INVITED

A GHOST STORY

SARAH A. DENZIL

YOU ARE INVITED
Sarah A. Denzil
Copyright © 2020 Sarah A. Denzil

Cover Design by Ebook Launch

Now I see the extent of our folly. We invited the monster in.—
Translated from Sister Maria Popescu's diary, 1946

Cath Fenwick, you are invited to the social media event of the 21st century.

You will make history.

You, out of thousands of entries, have been chosen because you are special.

This is the first day of your professional life and the best decision you have ever made.

Come. October. Carpathia.

Yours,

Irene Jobert

CHAPTER ONE

Alexandru muttered what I imagined was a curse word in Romanian as he shouldered the suitcase into his taxi. The boot lid came down with a slam that matched the volume of the man's grunting and groaning, before he sucked in a long draw of his cigarette, tossed it, and ground it into the pavement with the heel of his shoe. I quickly snatched up the flattened butt. He watched me gingerly holding the tip, and with a shake of his head—and an amused exhale—he continued to watch me throw it into the nearest bin.

I'd been in Brasov less than thirty minutes and already I was about to leave again. I had no desire to face the last leg of my journey, I wanted to sleep, and I found myself staring back at the ground.

"Is that your button?" I asked, pointing to the grey disc near my shoe.

His gaze followed mine to the tarmac and he cursed again. "Yes, that belongs to me." Then he slapped the fabric bomber jacket he was wearing and shook his head. "This is new! What happened to quality, eh?" He sighed, his greying beard sagging along with his jowls.

"It's an easy fix. Do you have a needle and thread?" He stared at me as though I had two heads. "That's okay, I do. It's in my suitcase though. Could you...?" I gestured to the car.

While he opened the boot, I scooped up the button and kept it safely between finger and thumb. Then I quickly rummaged in the suitcase for my emergency sewing kit.

"I'm not taking that case out again," he grumbled behind me.

"I've found it. Here, give me your coat and I'll fix it while you drive."

He removed the jacked and handed it over. "Careful. That is expensive coat. Christmas present from my daughter."

"Oh, I see. Don't worry, it'll be fine." I flashed him a reassuring smile. "I once made a tube top out of an old pair of jeans."

He paused by the open driver's side door, as though considering whether to ask further questions. Then he climbed in, clearly deciding not to bother.

Before following him into the car I allowed myself one last peek at the town I had no time to explore. Brasov was quiet around us as I hopped into the back seat. At the end of October, the tourist season was dying down. Only the most hardcore Dracula fans wanted to be in Transylvania for Halloween. Brasov, I thought, was far away from the vampiric nightmare of Stoker's imagination. The trees were heavy with amber leaves, the houses pastel fronted. Yet there was an atmosphere about the narrow roads, with the bruised contours of the mountains in the distance, that was tangible even on a clear, crisp autumn day like today. I imagined the isolation bad weather would bring, and the sweeping mists coming down from those blue peaks, touching the steeples and bulwarks of the Gothic churches.

On wide roads that felt out of place in such timeless scenery, there were tacky billboards for the "Dracula Experience". I imagined fairground ride attractions covered in fangs and blood, weary local actors donning black capes lined with red velvet, all run by young men with dark eyes that dart suspiciously from tourist to tourist.

But soon those busy roads quietened as Alexandru took us deeper into the Carpathian range, to the smooth winding roads of car adverts, flanked by forests and farms.

I reached into my bag for the welcome pack Irene had sent to me. *The Event* was printed on the front of the document in a bold font. Inside were photographs of the monastery's stark exterior—tall stone walls, lancet arches and stained-glass windows. A ruined infirmary built separately to the main abbey. Then there were a few pictures of the renovation. Irene Jobert and her mother, Adele, stood next to builders in hard hats, grinning like Cheshire cats. They were in the centre of the monastery, the open part, with the cloister around them. Above them loomed a tall cherry tree in full candy-floss bloom. I could just make out a separate wing behind them, opposite to the newly refurbished rooms. Its stones and arches were in silhouette; ink-tinged and macabre next to the smiling faces and pink blossom.

"Is it going well?" Alexandru regarded me with his dark eyes beneath bushy, white brows. Framed by the rear-view mirror, most of his mouth was obscured, but I imagined him frowning, unconcerned with such things I found myself troubled by, such as people-pleasing.

"I'll be honest," I confessed. "I'm distracted by the view." I placed the document down on the seat next to me.

There was a faint eye-roll visible through the rear-view mirror. "You here for vampire shit?"

"No," I replied. "Nothing like that."

"You are staying at Sfântul Mihail?" he asked. "The monastery?"

"That's right, yes."

"You know about the curse? The legend?"

I shook my head. "I don't."

He grunted. "Perhaps it's best you don't. How long are you staying in Transylvania?"

"A month," I replied. "Maybe longer."

His bushy eyebrows shot up. "So long? At the monastery? I did not know it was even..." He paused, searching for the word. "Habitable. It has been ruins for a long time."

"Not quite ruins," I corrected. "It'd been empty since the forties, but I believe the company I'll be working for has bought and renovated part of it."

"Well," he said. "The locals will not like that."

"Aren't you a local?"

"Yes," he said. "I mean the villagers. It is isolated around there in the mountains. They don't like outsiders in these areas. The closest village to the monastery is Butnari. Farmers who keep to themselves. Perhaps don't bother them too much and it will be fine."

"We'll be very respectful," I said, but I had to admit that a shiver ran down my spine.

Placing the button over the remnants of the snapped thread, I quickly sewed it in place and went back to staring out the window. The taxi wound along the serpentine road surrounded by tall spruces, thin silver birches, and the occasional high-reaching oak. They blurred at the edges. Green and gold like Christmas.

"The forest is beautiful."

"Yes," he said. "But they are cutting it down."

"Who?"

"Loggers." He shrugged. "They take too much."

"Your jacket is fixed now," I said, passing it through the gap between the front seats, placing it carefully down on the passenger side.

"Thank you," he said.

"How old is your daughter?" I asked.

"Twenty." His clipped tone made me decide not to ask any further questions.

For a time we fell into silence, while all around us the last dying light of the day set over the spectacular vista. Unfortunately, I'd arrived later than expected in Brasov, after an airport luggage-handlers strike had resulted in flight delays, which in turn resulted in me missing my connection from Bucharest. When I called ahead to inform Irene, which—because of her fame—was surreal to me in many ways, she'd sighed dramatically and told me to get to the monastery as soon as I could because the roads would be tricky at night.

Now that the light was fading, her words were on my mind, but Alexandru kept the car in control, not too fast, confident with the bends. Each road was a thinner echo of the road before. Soon the car had to work harder on the steep incline.

This was nothing like home. It was wilder. The forest sprawled and fought through the dark, roots and branches reaching their fingers and toes towards the road. But nothing like home had been exactly what I wanted. Hadn't it? A place as far away from home as I could find. An opportunity for change, to be a different person for a while. To leave the empty terraced house behind. My mind drifted back to it, to the room I now kept locked, imagining the dust collecting, the heavy air I'd longed to escape. My chest tightened with fear.

Alexandru broke the silence, pulling me from those thoughts. "You are not here for holiday?"

"No," I said.

"Then what will you be doing?"

"Writing. I'm meeting other creatives for a retreat that we're filming and streaming on the internet. We all have a social media following and those followers are also patrons, so they can pay for exclusive content."

Alexandru shook his head as though the concept seemed nutty to him. To be fair, I understood why. The strange world of social media influencing is not entirely accessible or easily understood by older generations.

"This is what you do for a living?"

I laughed. "Yes, I suppose it is."

"And your parents approve of this... trip?"

There was no way for me to answer his questions without lengthy explanations, so I simply made an *mmhmm* sound.

We were on a narrow road with a steep drop, but his eyes found me in the mirror for a brief glance. There was both warmth and hardness in his expression that reminded me of a father either about to scold his daughter or give her a life lesson. "What is your name?"

"Cath."

"Okay, Cath, I will tell you about the curse because you should know. But remember, it is a story, a legend. Truth and fiction combine in this story. A lot of it is not real. Do not let it frighten you. Do you understand?"

"Yes."

I saw his shoulders relax and decided that Alexandru was a decent man. "Good. Sfântul Mihail is an old building. At least two hundred years old but I forget the date. Lived in right up until the unfortunate event in 1946, just before the socialist republic began. The true part is, almost everyone in the monastery died one night. There was one survivor—the abbess. This place is not what you would call a monastery. You call it a nunnery, but we have no distinction between the two in the Orthodox Church. But all of the victims were women."

"That's tragic," I said, sitting up straight, one hand clenched around my emergency sewing kit. My eyes darted from the bouncing headlights of the car, to Alexandru's reflection in the mirror. Out there the darkness closed in, blocking out the precipitous drop. Enveloped in the night, we existed on our own plane, away from the world.

"Yes. Great tragedy." He glanced at me again, but I could tell he was mostly concentrating on the difficult drive. "Since then, villagers say the building is cursed. That the souls of the nuns roam Sfântul Mihail. But it is nonsense."

"Of course," I replied unsteadily. "Ghosts don't exist."

"You're not a believer. Good. Best to keep sceptical. The other part of the legend is a little... strange. Well, not so strange considering where we are." He hesitated again, and I saw the question in his eyes as he wondered whether to tell me the rest.

"Go on," I prompted. I almost wanted to add "I can take it" but I didn't.

"They say the bodies were bloodless with wounds at the neck. They say an argument ensued among the villagers. There were those who wanted them to be staked, or have their heads removed, because the old stories of the *strigoi* are still told in remote places."

"*Strigoi* is the Romanian word for vampire, isn't it?" I asked.

"Yes," he said. Again, his eyes appeared in the mirror, and again there was a hesitation, a warning. "You must understand that most Romanians are not this superstitious."

I nodded to show I understood.

"Well, I do not know whether the bodies were decapitated, but I know there are those who claim the ghosts walking the corridors are not ghosts at all."

CHAPTER TWO

The night robbed me of my first glimpse of Sfântul Mihail. It was through hazy yellow lights that I caught sight of old bricks and stained-glass windows. In the darkness, those walls could have been carved into the mountainside. They shared the same bruised blue of the silhouettes seen in the distance from Brasov. Alexandru cut the engine and the lights. It was a darkness I'd not known before. He flicked the lights back on.

When I opened the car door, the night chill tickled my extremities, and the strong breeze tugged at my loose hair. Even Alexandru rubbed his arms as he hurried to the back of the taxi. Before joining him I found it difficult to tear my eyes away from the ill-lit building before me. Now, with the wind and the rustling of the trees around us, the jagged church steeple barely visible against the night sky, and the clear dots of white stars suspended above, I could see how easy it would be to concoct a legend about this place. To imagine life continued beyond what we knew existed.

Stalking corridors. Pale fingers dragging against stone. I shivered. Up here we would be utterly alone.

I snapped out of my trance and walked around the car. Alexandru grunted as he pulled the suitcase from the boot.

"Thank you for the safe journey," I said, handing him the cash owed, along with a generous tip. He handed half of the tip back to me.

"For the button," he said. "My wife died, and I would not have done it myself."

"I'm so sorry," I said. And then I added, "Perhaps next time I'm in your taxi, I'll show you how to sew."

He laughed. "Teach an old dog new tricks, ha!"

I smiled, and then I gazed out along the narrow track back down the mountain. "It's a long drive to Brasov in the dark. Perhaps you should stay the night here."

I watched as Alexandru regarded the pale façade of the monastery, currently illuminated by yellow headlights. For the barest of moments he went still, his back held so straight it was stiff. It took that moment to understand the fear emanating from him, which made the hair stand up on the back of my neck.

"No thank you, I will drive." He reached into his pocket and produced a business card. "You must take care now, Cath. Here are my details if you need anything."

"It was lovely to meet you." I took the card. "Thank you for telling me so much about the history of this place."

"I wish it was a better story," he said, ducking into his car.

My heart lurched as he drove away. I thought of those narrow, winding roads, the precipitous drops down the mountainside. It was not a journey I would like to make by myself.

"You must be Cath."

The lilt of a faint French accent made me jolt from my thoughts. I tugged my suitcase and turned around to see a tall, slim woman standing in the large, arched entranceway. She wore shorts and a pyjama top. Her feet were bare, and her hair trailed loosely over one shoulder, tendrils of messy curls hugging the curve of her chest. A silk eye-mask had been pushed high up her forehead.

"Well, come on," Irene said. "It is draughty enough already inside." She rubbed her upper arms as I dragged my suitcase along to greet her. "Of course monasteries just *have* to be open in the centre. Who designed such a thing?" She glanced at me up and down as I approached. "Long journey?"

"Yeah. Felt that way at least!"

"You're here now. You can relax. Most of us have arrived but Nathan is coming tomorrow."

I pulled the suitcase over the threshold and joined her in the chilly corridor. Behind me, the large door thumped closed. Irene locked it with an old-fashioned key, the mechanism clunking into place as it finally hit me: I was sharing air with Irene Jobert, one of the most famous young women on the planet; an influencer with almost ten million Instagram followers; a cancer survivor; a model; a business mogul. My face warmed as I remembered feeling a tingle of excitement the morning I'd checked the post to find her invitation to The Event. Metallic card tucked in a black envelope, Irene's sloping hand liquid silver, like stardust on the night sky. I didn't understand why she'd chosen me out of so many, but chosen I had been, and now I was in Romania with her, standing close enough to smell her jasmine perfume.

"Are you hungry?" She ducked beneath another Gothic archway on our right and brought us into the next room. A laundry area or utility room, with two large washing machines and a huge fridge. I'm not an expert about which white goods are the most expensive, but these definitely appeared to be high-end. She pulled open the fridge door and offered me cooked meat and cheese. "This was where the nuns did all their baking. It was not easy getting electricity up here, believe me. We're lucky to have this fridge. Come on, let me show you the kitchen."

I took the packets of meat and the cheese and followed her through another doorway. The first thing I noticed was an abundance of white. From marble worksurfaces to the white tiled floor and walls. "Wow, this isn't what I expected."

"Wait until you step through to the dining room." She raised her eyes.

The dining room was adjacent to the kitchen but had an open plan feel thanks to the large archway. It was vast. There was a chandelier hanging low over a long teak dining table large enough to seat a dozen people. Beneath my feet, a mosaic of colourful tiles spread into a religious image, my toes resting on the halo of a saint I didn't recognise.

The mix of modern and traditional left me cold, but I had to admit it would be useful to have such a big space for cooking and dining.

"This used to be the refectory. It's where the nuns would eat their meals. Loup did a good job with the restoration because there was nothing but dust here eight months ago," Irene said. "Maman and I chose all the facilities. Modern comforts, but still the old, too. We did it well, didn't we?" She spread her fingers over one of the bricks, long nails catching the mortar.

"Loup?"

"The investment company," she said. "They had to bring solar panels up here for the electricity. The water system uses the old well as well as rainwater. It's completely self-contained."

"I had no idea so much money had been put behind this." I took the food back into the kitchen and began searching for a plate.

She pulled away from the bricks and rested on one of the barstools. "They were smart. Once The Event is over, Sfântul Mihail will be opened as an Airbnb. Knowing all the social media stars stayed here will make it extra valuable."

I found the plates in a cupboard next to the sink. "That is clever. Is your mother visiting us, too?"

"No. Just me. She's not really involved, but she did help with the décor." She stretched and yawned, revealing the strength of her toned muscles running along her upper arms. "The event begins officially tomorrow, and it's late. If I give you directions to your room, do you think you could find it?"

"Umm, yes, I suppose so."

"Good," she said, standing up and wandering back to the door. "Because I need my sleep. Oh, and do not forget to read the rules." She tapped a framed picture adhered to the one plastered wall in the kitchen.

I walked across to get a better view, all the while, Irene's fingernail continued tapping the glass.

Remain

Engage

Represent

"You must sleep here each night," she said. "Therefore, *remain*. At least one person must be *engaging* with fans at all times, either by providing content or using the message board to talk to them. We will take shifts for the night-time.

This is a global event. We must cover all time zones. And remember you are *representing* Loup, and me, and every participant in this event. That means all content must be appropriate. Nothing X-rated or political or religious. You understand?"

"Got it."

"Oh, and you should know that the internet connection is good, but the phone coverage not so much. You might not be able to make calls in the monastery. We had an aerial and a satellite dish put up, but we can't force the telephone companies to build towers." She shrugged. "You can email and send WhatsApp messages. The one other thing I recommend is not getting distracted. After all, you paid to come here. You won't make your money back if you don't follow the rules."

She tapped the glass again.

"I meant what I said in the invitation. This was the best decision of your professional life." She grabbed my shoulders and leaned closer. "Let me make you rich." And then she smiled, told me where my bedroom would be, and left me alone in the two-hundred-year-old monastery.

I WAS ALREADY USED TO RULES BY THAT POINT. ENTRANTS HAD to pay two hundred pounds up front to enter. Then, if chosen, there was a five-thousand-pound fee, not including travel expenses. All entrants had to have at least fifty thousand followers on Instagram, Twitter, YouTube or TikTok. I had sixty-five thousand followers at the time, more now. We also had to earn at least one hundred thousand US dollars per annum, after tax. I made over two hundred thousand.

And I was a nobody.

Irene Jobert had over ten million followers, a make-up company, a fan base—the Renees—and at least one corporate sponsor, the illusive Loup, who created this event. For four weeks, five social-media content creators would live-stream our retreat in the Carpathian Mountains. In order to see our content, users would pay for access. On top of that subscription fee, patrons could donate for special content. They'd pay, ask us to do whatever, and if it was a reasonable request, we'd do it.

It's the new world. The internet has created thousands of entrepreneurs making money from their hobbies; from Etsy artists, to lifestyle bloggers; from make-up artists, to writers. This world is about sharing: knowledge, skill, humour. But most of all, it's about monetising all of those things.

The truth is, I've never had a job. I finished my degree in English three years before The Event at the age of twenty-two and immediately wrote a book set in a fantasy world called Akarthis. When I self-published that book, I started to earn a bit of money through online sales. Those sales and the money grew every time I wrote and published another book, as did my number of readers and followers. When I started giving my followers the freedom to make suggestions for future stories, the Arkathis world grew in popularity again, with readers interested in the idea of having autonomy over their favourite characters.

But one day in the future, I might publish a book, and no one will buy it. Or I might find that the platform I rely on for my book sales has disappeared. One day it might all end. It wasn't greed that compelled me to join The Event, it was anxiety about an uncertain future and a need to make hay while the sun continued to shine in my direction.

You may be wondering why I, and the others, paid so much money to come here, or why we were prepared to sell access to ourselves. Well, that's the reason. But, still, when Irene placed her hands on my shoulders and told me she would make me rich, my stomach flipped with queasiness. What had I signed up for? Would it be worth it? How much of myself was I prepared to bare?

I WRAPPED UP THE UNEATEN CHEESE AND PUT IT BACK IN THE fridge. When the fridge door creaked shut, the sound reminded me of a movie monster waking from a deep slumber. It interrupted the stillness of the place, and I almost wanted to apologise to the building for my intrusion.

Back in the kitchen, I flicked off the light switch and shuddered in the dark, its shroud sudden and unnerving. What else could I expect from an old, supposedly cursed monastery? Then I wondered whether there were cameras in this room, watching me.

The Event had not started, and yet I already sensed onlookers out there. There'd been times between my house in Derbyshire and the airport that I'd considered asking the taxi driver to take me home. Four weeks of being watched by viewers. My every move monitored and critiqued. It made my skin crawl. So far I'd avoided as much scrutiny as possible, and now I was challenging myself to bask in it.

Irene had told me that my room was the sixth door on the left if I followed the cloister walkway, keeping the cherry tree on my right. My room was the farthest from the kitchen, closer to the old church at the back of the monastery. As I made that journey, my suitcase rolled noisily along, sandpaper on stone, a skateboard wheeling down the tarmac. I cringed with each step, body hunched over, balanced on tiptoes as though that would make any difference to the plastic wheels on the flagstones.

Rather than switch on the lights, I decided to use the light from my phone. *Do not let it frighten you*, Alexandru had said. I'd been game for the story while I was safe in the back of a taxi; but now I was walking where other feet had tread two hundred years ago, tingles spread up and down my arms and the back of my neck. I tried my best to ignore them. I peeked beneath the arches along the walkway, catching glimpses of the tree, and the old, untouched part of the building beyond.

Oh, it had been such a good idea at the time to encourage Alexandru's retelling of the myths about this building. After all, it was no lie to say I didn't believe in ghosts, because I don't. However, shadows in the corners, a bouncing mobile-torch illuminating a mere patch of corridor at a time, and my heart dancing around in my chest, resulted in possibly the most terrifying few minutes of my life up to that point.

Women had died in this place. For all I knew, I was walking where their blood had spilled, where their limbs had lifelessly trailed. Had it been international news? Had it been eclipsed by the rise of communism? Many names had been lost to history, including those of these nuns.

I counted the doors on the left and finally came to the sixth, opening it quietly, afraid I'd take the wrong one and wake another participant with a fright. My breath caught as I reached for a light switch. Eventually, after scraping my fingers against the bricks, I used my phone again and found the cord, illuminating more white walls and furniture. The sudden light made the place too sterile and modern, despite the lancet arches above the stained-glass windows. I closed the door behind me and dragged the suitcase into the centre of the room.

Tiredness hit me then, as well as a wave of unexpected homesickness; after all, coming here had also been a way to escape what I left behind. It soon faded. This room, the history of the place, the people I had yet to meet, and the strangeness of Irene's celestial presence, felt almost laughably bizarre. But despite the exhaustion creeping into every bone in my body, I rotated slowly, taking in every stone, every iron joint in the old window, every spot of coving, every cobweb, every panel of glass, every carved arch, every beam, and imagined the people who had lived here. I breathed in the air, scented with old must and new dust, and with that, there was nothing but the complete privilege of being in that place at that time.

Then I collapsed in the large, modern bed, and slept like the dead.

CHAPTER THREE

The dawn danced on my walls in irregular shapes of reflected emerald and scarlet. I sat up and listened. The monastery was as noiseless as it had been in the middle of the night. Not wanting to wake anyone, I moved quietly around my room, hanging my clothes in the wardrobe, folding knickers for the drawers, and placing toiletries around the sink in the small en-suite bathroom. Then I picked up the cardboard pill boxes from the bottom of my suitcase and stared at them.

Two packets for four weeks. At home, I'd leave them in the kitchen next to the glasses, and then every morning I'd get a glass, fill it, and take my pill. But I couldn't do that at the monastery, not in front of people I didn't know. During the application process I'd mentioned my mental illness to Irene, and she'd told me it was perfectly fine. But now that I was here, surrounded by strangers, in a place where legend says the dead walk... I wasn't at ease.

I swallowed one of my pills dry, and then I showered, dressed, and left my room. Part of me wanted to explore the building in the morning light, but I wasn't sure of the scope of the place, or whether I'd lose myself meandering through the passages. Instead, I slipped out of the same door I arrived through the night before, using the key Irene had left in a drawer in a small cabinet placed in the entry way next to the coats, and decided to stroll a lap around the place. It'd been dark last night, but I'd still had the sense that our rooms took up less than half of the building.

Up above the mountain, sunlight gilded every wall, while in the distance rolled a carpet of autumn leaves from the forest below. Tears formed at the corners of my eyes, from the biting wind, and the beauty before me. Humbled by it, I took my time to orbit the monastery, taking in every old stone and arched window.

It was mostly square, with the refectory poking out at a right angle on the south wing. The tall church loomed over the north. From it sprouted the tower with an empty belfry beneath its steeple. Next to the tower was the great, metallic aerial build for our retreat. It was a jarring contrast to the former ruin and a scar against the natural beauty. All along the renovated west wing of the monastery were sloping roofs, and on top of the shingles sat the solar panels, blinking and glimmering in the crisp morning. They were a blight on the monastery to me, but I supposed that was the price we paid for electricity. I walked along the wall of the church for a while, imagining the nuns filtering out through the great doors. Would they be chatty? Or serious? Chatty, I decided. Gossiping about the priest's delivery of the sermon, his lisp, one of the older sisters taking a nap in the back pew.

The way the nuns had died was sudden and violent. It was understandable that the locals would have started a legend to make sense of it all. A place so isolated from the world could be easily infiltrated by a stranger with a malign motive. A person obsessed with violence and terror.

But more than that, the place had an atmosphere to it, unlike anywhere I'd been before. Perhaps it was the way you could walk around one corner and sense a still quiet like none other, and yet around the next, the forest was alive before you, winds rolling down from the peaks, rustling through the trees. At times the walls shielded you from the weather, other times it thrust you into gusts of cool air.

I had to remind myself that the violence had been long ago, the local curse was simply a story. My rational brain understood those things, and yet my footsteps hurried back to the south wing, keen to direct my thoughts elsewhere. I slipped into the building and rushed to the kitchen, where I heard the sound of bread going into a toaster.

"Oh, hey. I almost locked the door, good job I didn't." She smiled and offered a hand to shake, still dressed in blue pyjamas, dark hair falling over one eye. "I'm Jules."

"Cath."

"Cool. Irene mentioned you'd be arriving late last night."

"I went for the cheapest flight. It ended up being a bad idea." I began opening cupboards searching for a glass, and Jules pointed me in the right direction.

"Are you a writer?"

"Yeah," I said, filling a glass with water. "But I write under a pen name, C. B. Finn."

She nodded, but I knew it meant nothing to her. That never surprised me. No one ever recognised my name when I told them.

"I like your blog," I said, referring to *Jules Chen Shows You How to Adult*, a popular blog and YouTube channel for millennials. "The financial advice is great. I have stocks and a pension now because of you."

"That's awesome." She grabbed her toast from the toaster and started buttering.

"Have you met everyone else? What are they like?"

As her knife scraped along the surface of the bread, she smiled as though she was in on a private joke with herself. "Well, Irene is *Irene*, you know? She's like a Valley Girl with a French accent. Then there's Dan Mendoza who arrived first. He's the fitness guy. Nice, too. Nathan should be here in an hour or two. He's British like you, right?"

"I don't know much about him to be honest."

Jules raised her eyebrows. "Really? I guess I don't know that much either. Except that he's a megastar and rich as fuck."

"Yeah, I heard that too. I've never seen his channel though, I'm not much of a gamer."

She bit into her toast. "Me neither. Reckon we should make pancakes?" Holding the toast between her teeth she wandered into the utility room and pulled open the fridge door. I decided to make my own and stayed in the kitchen. "Nope," she said from the other room. "Not enough milk. I know you Brits need at least ten cups of tea a day. My ex was from Bristol." She wandered back in, the silk of her pyjamas swishing. "Is that anywhere near you?"

I shook my head. "I'm from Derby."

"Maybe you're not far from Nathan. I think he's from Leeds," Jules said.

I decided to put the kettle on and add coffee into the pot for the later risers.

"He could be. All I know is that his gamertag is The Yorkie."

"Yeah." She laughed. "Always wondered about that. Isn't that a dog?"

"It's also a county. Yorkshire. Where Leeds is."

"Cool. Well I'm going to get dressed. There's a team meeting later." She smiled sardonically at the word *team*.

"Irene wants to brief us for the launch. We're just waiting for Nathan."

"That's going to be weird," I said.

"What?"

"Team meetings. It's like we're working in an office. I half-expect to turn around and see a watercooler."

She laughed. "I know, right? Anyway, I don't want to be in PJs for our first office meeting. I'll see you later, Cath." Jules sashayed out of the kitchen as my toast popped up, and I relaxed slightly. At least there was one normal person here, even if the others turned out to be strange.

After another hunt through the cupboards, I found strawberry jam, and popped a tea bag into a sturdy mug. Then I spent a few minutes searching for a quiet nook to eat. The kitchen was too modern and clinical, especially with the framed rules and the Loup logo above the door. It was at odds with the history of the place. Taking my tea and toast, I wandered through the open walkways and came to the cloister garth in the centre of the building. It was my first glimpse of the cherry tree, now covered with persimmon-coloured leaves and a deep russet bark. I was about to sit down on the lawn when I spotted a man talking into his phone. He set it down on the ground before lifting a leg, stretching out his arms, and holding what appeared to be a painful, contorted yoga pose. Dan, I supposed, a yogi and fitness instructor with thousands of followers. I knew of him but didn't follow his account. Consistent exercise had never been my thing.

He didn't see me, and I didn't want to interrupt him, so I slipped away and continued along the walkway. Finally, I settled on the first step leading up to the tower, placing the mug next to me on the stone. It was cold beneath my back-side, but I didn't mind. The solitude was too delicious. Loup hadn't touched this part of the building, helping to transport me back to another era.

The walls were still robust, but I could see dust crumbling out from between the stones. I thought of the bell, now gone, either removed by Loup or the nuns. After I ran out of toast and tea, my mind began to drift back to the murders. It was obviously my wandering mind that made me feel this way, but my scalp began to tingle. There was no one anywhere near me, and yet I felt the distinct sensation that I wasn't alone.

CHAPTER FOUR

We had convened at the kitchen breakfast bar by the time Nathan MacDonald burst through the door talking to his phone.

"Guys, guys, you're on Instagram Live," he said, rotating the screen to include us. "Irene Jobert, ladies and gents."

I watched Irene smile and wave to the camera before frowning as soon as he directed it elsewhere. We were supposed to be launching The Event together, but it seemed Nathan had other ideas.

"Oh shit, look at this place," he said, dumping a suitcase on the ground. "Not bad for new digs." For the first time, he regarded us all sitting around the counter and realised he'd walked into a meeting. "Wait, is this the launch meeting thingy? Hold on." He signed off to his viewers by sticking out a tongue and making a peace sign, then slumped down in one of the stools. He gestured back to the door. "Traffic was awful."

Jules rolled her eyes.

"We're in the Carpathian Mountains," Irene said. "There *is* no traffic."

Nathan laughed and fidgeted with the corner of his hoody. I immediately saw the chaotic energy that buzzed around him. He was slim, thin faced, with acne scarring partially covered by patchy stubble. Every now and then he ran his hands over his mousy hair, or pulled at his sleeve, or tapped on the tabletop. He was younger than the rest of us, I found out later that he was nineteen. Jules was twenty-six, Dan was twenty-three and Irene was twenty-four.

"I checked your flight details," Irene said. "Your plane wasn't delayed either. Where have you been? It's after three in the afternoon and you were due to arrive this morning."

"Dracula experience. I had to," he said. "What's the point in coming to Transylvania and not doing a vampire thing?"

"Well, us launching our first day on time is a good reason not to," Jules said, rolling her eyes again.

"This isn't a vacation," Dan chipped in. "We're here to make money."

I hadn't talked to Dan much at this point. He was tanned, athletic, obviously, with well-groomed dark stubble and brown eyes. It was easy to see how he'd accumulated so many followers with his good looks and soft way of speaking. But at this point, all I'd noticed about him was that his metal water bottle seemed attached to his hand.

"All right, all right. I'm sorry." Nathan held up his hands. "Let's get down to business then. What's the deal, Rene?"

A flicker of tension worked its way up Irene's jaw. Nathan's casual use of her nickname did not go down well. The strained atmosphere in the room made my stomach squirm with anxiety and I longed to be alone, working on the latest Akarthis story.

"First. Tech," Irene said. She opened a laptop and arranged the screen so we could all see it. "This is the website. The Event dot com." The launch screen showed an image of the monastery with a button to subscribe. Beneath the button were our faces and a promise: *Access the lives of those you covet.* "This, is what a subscriber sees." She logged into the site and showed us a page featuring six videos. The footage showed several places in the monastery, such as a small lounge, the cloister, the refectory, all empty apart from the kitchen. Irene smiled and waved at a camera in the corner of the room. "You will expect to find CCTV in the walkways, the snug, the utility room, the refectory and the kitchen. They are fitted with long range microphones so we shouldn't need to wear a mic. But there are no cameras or microphones in your bedrooms or any of the bathrooms."

"What about the church and the east wing?" I asked.

"None there either. Just the renovated part of the building." She used the track pad to click on each video and enlarge it. "Viewers can watch all the cameras together on this screen, or choose a feed. When we go live on the site, it works like Instagram Live. You'll see a ticker of messages. For the regular footage, there's a comments box at the bottom of the page so that the viewers can talk to each other."

"Cool," Jules said. "It's like they have their own micro-community."

"You'll also be expected to talk to the viewers using the comments box. If you're not on the live video function on the laptop, you can type in the comments box to chat. And, in addition to all that..." She hauled a box onto the counter. "After our meeting, I'll place these outside your doors." She began lifting out each item one by one. "Selfie stick. GoPro with a chest mount. A smaller body cam for inside the house. And a drone."

"Nice," Dan said. "We should get decent footage with the drone."

"Next fitness video?" Jules asked with a grin.

Dan picked up the drone and shrugged. "Would it be a problem if footage from The Event was used for things like that?"

"I'll have to check with Loup," Irene said. "I'd imagine there's a licence fee."

Dan pursed his lips and placed the drone back.

Irene continued. "I almost forgot. There'll be a delay of ten minutes between what the camera records, and what's shown on the website. However, when we want to do live challenges and interviews, we will have to reduce that time to zero, otherwise it won't work. I can override the upload. If you do anything stupid, like walk through the monastery naked—" Nathan wolf-whistled "—then you must tell me immediately and I'll erase it. But I won't do it for every little thing. Watch what you say. Think about what you do. If it's something you *don't* want hundreds of thousands of people to see, don't do it. Understand?"

"Yes, Fuhrer," Nathan said.

Irene simply smiled. "Get it all out of your system now, Nathan."

I watched the two of them and wondered if there was, or had been, a relationship between them. Jules caught my gaze and raised her eyebrows, which forced me to smother a grin.

"Someone needs to be online at all times," Irene continued. "That means sleeping in shifts, which I know won't be great for everyone. But it is what it is. This gives us a greater earning potential and means we can charge for membership in countries all around the world. Also, content needs to be uploaded at night. If you record a lot of decent footage during the day, upload at least half of it later, before bed. We will go on walks, exercise, talk, create and so on. These things can be added in the evening. I'll show the page to upload... Here. You've all got a username and password which will be in your welcome box with the other equipment."

"I'll be doing sunrise yoga each morning," Dan said. "It'd be great to have company."

"Sure," Irene said. "I can do that."

"I could try," I added. "But I've never done yoga before."

"Even better. It'll be more relatable." Dan smiled.

"Yes, relatable is important," Irene said. "We also want to be aspirational at times, but our content needs to appeal to everyone." Her subtle French accent was like water slipping over stones, sliding through syllables. "And don't forget to make the most of this location. It's like a haunted house with a ton of history. Use it but don't make it too cheesy. Play up on the fear if you like. That shit goes viral." She clapped her hands together. "I brought a Ouija board that we *have* to use at some point."

I noticed Jules raise her eyebrows. Nathan grinned.

"We have two hundred thousand subscribers to the regular channel, and ten thousand to the VIP channel who will receive extra content," Irene continued. "On top of that, we will receive donations from viewers, for live challenges. The money from the subscribers will be split between the five of us, with Loup taking a ten per cent cut. Donations will go to the individual the viewer decides to donate to. They'll see a button with your faces on. Cute or what? Also..." Irene pointed to a board on the wall. "There will be a friendly competition, too."

"Hell yes," Nathan muttered, staring up at our names on the boards. "Anyone else at eight million followers?"

"Me!" Irene said with a smile. "Also, Nathan, your gaming system is set up how you like it."

"You're a star, Rene."

"The launch begins in two hours. I suggest you get ready. We'll meet in the snug room ten minutes before it's due to start. I'll make a fire and put up decorations. We have a donation from Moet, but we need to keep the bottles visible at all times."

"Not a problem," Jules said, rubbing her hands together eagerly.

"Oh, I don't drink." Stupidly, I put my hand up as though in a classroom. Nathan's eyes finally rested on me and he laughed.

"Just hold one every now and then, okay?" Irene said.

I nodded, not sure what else to do or say, beginning to wonder why I was even there when all of these people were both successful and confident, and I currently felt like neither.

"Do we need body cams for the launch?" Dan asked.

"No," Irene replied, standing up from her chair. "There are enough cameras to catch everything. And I'll take my laptop so we can chat to subscribers via messenger, too."

"Actually, I have a question," Jules said, stopping Irene in her tracks. "I get the content stuff. I'll do my videos as usual, and write blogs, but what do we do in between? Do we have to constantly talk to the viewers? Because that isn't the relationship I have with my followers. I'm not like Nathan."

Nathan smirked. "I'm a one-off, that's for sure."

"They want to see you live," Irene said, ignoring Nathan. "They want to see us interact. Yes, we will have to talk to them and often do things they ask. If they want karaoke, we give them karaoke. If they want us to drink shots, we take shots." She shrugged. "Fun tasks for us, entertainment for them, *money* for us."

After Irene left the room, Nathan pointed at each of us and asked for our names. Then he left. Jules went to change before the launch, and I decided to do the same. Dan went to put in a HIIT session.

I hurried to my room, engulfed by the conviction that I didn't belong here. Consumed by thoughts of what it would be like to be seen. To be viewed and used as entertainment. At least in my bedroom there were no cameras watching me. For a heartbeat, I closed my eyes and reminded myself why I was there, the challenge I'd set myself. How I'd wanted to push myself out of my comfort zone and meet new people. Irene Jobert wanted to make me rich, and maybe I should stop worrying, and allow it to happen.

When I was alone, rather than put on a fancy outfit and do my hair, I opened my laptop and went to my reader's group. There were messages about the next Akarthis story, asking when it would be, what it would include. Several of the readers had offered suggestions:

Maya and Reeve have a baby.
Oslaf and Margrave kink!

I flexed my fingers and typed:

Origin story for Maya? Or a new character?

Almost immediately, the replies flooded in.

Origin story! Maya, please.
New character for me. Hope you're well, Cath.

I replied back to that one:

I'm good thanks. I'm in Transylvania right now, and the scenery is giving me inspiration.

The conversation went off on a tangent about Romanian folklore, but I felt better, less alone.

THE PROMISES MADE BY MY READERS IMBUED ME WITH THE confidence I'd been lacking. They'd be there with me. Watching. But I still found that butterflies danced in my stomach. The day had been a strange one. I still hadn't toured the entire building or found my bearings. We'd all eaten lunch at different times and spent most of the day in our rooms, unpacking or creating fresh content for the launch. I'd written a few hundred words for the origin story of Maya, my main character in the Akarthis world.

And now it all began. I'd agreed to come here, to share myself with the world, but at the same time, unease settled in my stomach.

Jules had put on a stripy top underneath black dungarees and had a glass of champagne in her hand. Her hair had been braided into two plaits piled onto her head, she wore no make-up and flashed me a relaxed smile. It helped to ease my discomfort, especially seeing someone else who didn't wear make-up or dress fashionably. She came closer to me and clenched her teeth together in mock trepidation.

"Ready for our big moment?"

"As I'll ever be." I picked up an almond from the selection of snacks set up along a small table, and then sat on one of the beige sofas. The nut was about all I could stand to eat as the nerves found a greater hold on me.

"God, I half think this whole thing will be a disaster," Jules said. "I'm impressed they've even got the internet working. Imagine if it went down."

"I guess this Loup company have invested a lot of money in getting things running," I said.

"Hmm," Jules answered, her attention now faraway.

Dan came in next and ran his hand over the fabric of one of the sofas. "Pretty nice in here." He unscrewed the cap of his water bottle, making a *sskssk* sound.

No number of beige sofas could detract from the overwhelming historical power of the room. There was a vaulted ceiling curving above us like a ribcage, while beneath our feet where uneven flagstones, worn down by ancient footsteps. Along the outer wall were three colourful windows above the sofas. I reached out and ran a finger along the lead moulding between glass panels. The pale face of a saint stared glumly back.

Dan saw me and said, "My room has a window depicting the crucifixion. When the light hits it just right it glows onto the opposite wall. It's cool but a bit creepy."

Irene bustled in with another bottle of champagne. "Ten minutes everyone. Where is Nathan?" Her large eyes moved around the room anxiously. She strode over to one of the cameras in the corner and nudged it slightly. "This has to be a good launch, or we'll lose subscribers. We need energy, drinking, eating, chatting." It could've been my imagination, but her eyes flashed towards me. The hint of a side-eye, the subtlety of judgement. With that I'd been deemed lacking. The plain girl who didn't belong.

"Haven't they paid for the month?" Jules asked.

"Yes," Irene said. "But there's a short period where

people can cancel." She shrugged. "Let's not allow that to happen. Be big, loud. But not obnoxious."

"Speaking of obnoxious," Jules whispered as Nathan walked in.

"Evening all," he said, snatching up a bottle of champagne from an ice bucket.

"Okay," Irene said, "I'm starting the live feed. There's no delay for now, so no one say anything they will regret."

"Stay woke everyone," Nathan added.

Jules sighed.

Irene began to count us down. "Five... four... three... two... one..."

Forkie: Naaathaaaaaaan. I love you from Norway.

Lu98: [heartemoji]

Reneeleanie: Irene! Beautiful. Say hello to me.

xXtoasterXx: [heartemoji]

OrIgInAlNeCkBeArD: Irene, will we see you naked?

TheTarg: When do the challenges begin?

Susu1376: OMG! #decorgoals #irenejobert #skingoals

Happyidiot: Irene, you're my inspiration.

Flexgirl: Dan! Will you be doing yoga?

Momofsix: Hey Jules.

AliceAkarthis: Hi Cath! Oh my goodness, it's so strange to hear your voice!

Notlyktheothergirls: [heartemoji]

69fart69: [angryfaceemoji]

Volk: If one of you kills the other and films it, I'll pay you one million dollars.

Motherofcats: Come to France!

Cheezemonkeys: Nathan, why do you have beef with Syd?

Forkie: @Cheezemonkeys fuck off.

Cheezemonkeys: @Forkie actual Nazi.

Reneeisagoddess: Say hello to Brazil, Irene. We love you! [heartemoji]

CHAPTER FIVE

Hundreds of messages came in all at once, scrolling in a ticker alongside our faces on the screen. Heart emojis floated up, fading at the corners of the laptop. We said hello to Norway, Germany, France, Brazil, South Africa. Nathan yelled out his catchphrases at random fans: *Never lick an onion*. I didn't understand any of them. I sat there with a plastic smile on my face completely overwhelmed, while Irene recounted her cancer survival story, Nathan thanked his fans and promised gaming content, Jules dished out advice on travel, and Dan answered fitness questions. Occasionally Irene said my name, but the messages disappeared so quickly there were times I missed what I was supposed to answer.

An hour in, and Irene moved the conversation to challenges for patrons. All they had to do was donate a small amount of money and we would complete their challenge, within reason, obviously.

Lu98: Dan, teach them all yoga. $3.
Fifi: I'll add $5 to that.

He taught us basic poses as further donations came in. The others were tipsy, and Nathan fell on his face, which resulted in fifty dollars of donations to him. I managed to stretch my muscles in the right places but couldn't hold myself as steady as Irene and Jules.

Reneeleanie: Karaoke!! $10.

Irene laughed and set up the machine. She tossed a songbook at me and my heart began to pound. Jules leaned over my shoulder.

"Let's do one together," she offered.

Relief flooded through me as we chose a Jonas Brothers song and waited for Irene to finish sincerely bellowing out Mariah Carey. I kept one eye on the laptop screen as she went through her performance, and watched the donations flood in. Ten dollars here, twenty there, even the odd one-hundred-dollar donation. Afterwards, she sat on the floor next to the screen and thanked each donor, blowing kisses to her fans. I knew that this was how other influencers interacted with their followers but seeing it happen in real life was a whole other bizarre experience.

Once we all went through the humiliation of karaoke, Nathan was challenged with telling the viewers what he thought of each person there. Cheezemonkeys informed him bluntly that he had to be honest.

"Dan's cool. Possibly a bit thick." Nathan shrugged.

"No thicker than you," Dan retorted, seemingly unbothered by the dig.

"Irene is hot," he continued. "But you'd get sick of her shit within a month."

"You would never even get a month, my darling," Irene said, grinning so wide it showed her teeth.

"Jules is so woke she's in 2021."

"And you're in 1982." Jules sipped her champagne and delivered daggers.

On the screen, the donations poured in. Many of the viewers praised him for being honest, for speaking his mind, and for calling out bullshit. Others jumped to the rescue of Irene, Jules and Dan, sending their own donations and vilifying Nathan.

"Don't worry everyone," Irene said. "Nathan has decided to be the bad guy. He's a boy *craving* attention. Well, now he has it. Shall we do the next challenge?"

"Wait, I haven't mentioned Cath."

My fingers tightened around the stem of my glass. I'd guessed that Irene was trying to move the challenge along before Nathan got to me. And from the delightedly mischievous expression on Nathan's face, I knew he had a devilish insult to throw at me.

Irene sighed. "Fine."

"Virgin," Nathan said.

A deep flush of red blossomed on my cheeks. My hand flew up to block my face from view of the cameras.

"Fuck you, Nathan," Jules said, putting one arm around my shoulder. "Fuck you. That was nasty."

Nathan laughed and shrugged. "They said be honest."

"Not cool." Dan shook his head. He reached across and yanked Nathan's champagne out of his hand. "I think you've had enough of this."

"Well, now you've pissed everyone off," Irene said. "But, Cath, you're getting donations now. And you're much too pretty to be a virgin."

It was a patronising comment, we all knew it. Part of me wondered if she'd said it to curry favour with the viewers. I glanced at the screen to see how they were reacting. The ticker was moving so quickly I could hardly read the responses.

Forkie: Woah, that was harsh.
Cheezemonkeys: LMAO!!!!!!!!
AliceAkarthis: We love you Cath. You're beautiful inside and out, unlike Nathan. He's a dick inside and out. $60.
Yorkiefan: No, Nath. Too far. $10 for Cath.
Reneeee: Aw, I feel bad for her. $10.
Susan87: Anyone else now shipping Cath and Nathan? LOL!

"Cath, there's a challenge for you if you're interested," Irene said.

I placed my glass on the coffee table and brushed my hair back. "What is it?"

Every one of my nerves jangled. Nathan's voice rang in my mind. *Virgin. Virgin.*

"Mayaforlife would like you to tell a ghost story."

Everyone's eyeballs shifted in my direction. The last thing I wanted was extra attention on me. But at least it would stop them from trying to figure out if it was true, if I actually was a virgin. And there was, of course, the perfect story ready and waiting. I nodded to Irene, and the room grew quiet.

"Actually, as I was coming here, my taxi driver told me the story of Sfântul Mihail and why it was abandoned in the 1940s. Do any of you know what happened?" I asked.

Everyone shook their heads apart from Irene.

"I know part of it," she said.

"I doubt you know everything," I continued. "Because the crime was so shocking, much of it was kept out of the press. And with communism on the rise, the murders were overshadowed." I waited for a moment, to allow the word *murders* to sink in. "You know that this building is at least two hundred years old, and you know that it was once a nunnery. Even back then when the nuns lived here, years and years ago, there were dark rumours about the building's origins, about this place, built and used as a holy sanctuary for those who had lost their way; those who needed guidance.

"And between these old walls, for many, many years, most of those women found the support they desperately needed. But what they didn't know was that there was an unwelcome guest among them. A malign presence waiting for an opportunity to strike.

"It was in the tower that the nuns often heard the terrifying sound. A low groaning that couldn't be human. A hidden evil, growling through gritted teeth, its hackles raised for a fight. No one in the nunnery wanted to ring the bells anymore. Only Sister Elena was fearless enough to climb the many steps up the tower and ring the bell. That was until the day her cold, bloodless body was found at the bottom of the belfry.

"The stubborn mother superior did not want a scandal. Despite the fact that Elena's throat had been ripped open, she had the death hushed up as an accident, claiming that the ill-fated woman tripped and fell. Shortly after, the bell was removed from the tower.

"But soon, several of the sisters claimed to see the silhouette of a tall man lurking in the cloister. His figure was seen in the dark annals around the monastery, in the surrounding forests, up the mountainside, skulking in the graveyard. The word *strigoi* was whispered among the most superstitious, and they hung garlic around the doors.

"For a while, the tall man didn't appear, and the sisters lived in peace. Their isolation had always been a blessing and a curse, but now they felt safer again. Some of the nuns decided to maintain a vow of silence, others grew fruit and vegetables, and every day they prayed, giving gratitude for their good fortune, and for God helping them stay protected against evil. The *strigoi* stayed away."

"What's a *strigoi*?" Dan asked.

"It's the Romanian word for vampire," I replied. "A summer went by, and then an autumn, and then a winter. The sisters aged. Mother superior died suddenly in the night and they buried her in the private cemetery east of the church. Her grave is covered in moss, but it's still there, and her bones are, hopefully, at rest.

"But her death signalled a change. The sisters grew complacent. They forgot to hang the garlic, and though they still prayed fervently, the presence of the *strigoi* was far from their minds. Until one day, their delivery from the village never showed. Sister Agatha decided to find out what had happened to Pavel, the young lad who usually brought them milk and cheese. She walked down the mountain path, calling his name, but heard nothing in return. She was about to go back, when she caught sight of a white wolf prowling through the trees. Sister Agatha began to run, but she wasn't quick enough. When she ran from the path in a panic, she tripped over Pavel's body and fell into the dirt. Her screams carried up the mountain to the monastery. When her sisters found her, she, and Pavel, were gristly versions of themselves, torn to shreds by lupine fangs."

"Fuck," Nathan whispered.

I resisted the urge to smile. "The sisters buried Agatha near their beloved mother superior. It was a lesson not to eschew the old ways, to be respectful of tradition. Yet they didn't see it that way, they forgot the garlic again. And when young Sister Maria was blowing out the candles for the night, she saw Sister Agatha walking back and forth outside the entry way to the building.

"'Sister! Sister' she cried. 'You're alive, I can't believe it.' Sister Maria flung open the door, a huge smile on her face. 'Will you invite me in?' Agatha asked. 'Of course I will. Come in, Agatha. Let me see you. How did you survive? Did you... did you have to crawl out of the grave? The... oh, my. I'm so sorry, sister.' But Agatha ignored Maria's questions as she floated over the threshold into the monastery. Agatha then paused by the door and faced the night. 'Come in, Master.' Maria's eyes widened as the tall man entered the monastery. His inhuman face would be the last she ever saw.

"One by one, the sisters awoke in joy at the face of their beloved Sister Agatha, and one by one their joy became terror as the tall man approached. One by one their blood painted the walls, the walls surrounding us now." I paused, and allowed that to sink in. Nathan's eyes roamed the room. He was so pale I thought he might be sick. "Alexandru, my taxi driver, told me that the monastery is cursed. The villagers nearby believe it is haunted by the nuns who once lived here. Others believe the dead walk, that this place is not haunted at all—it's occupied."

The story settled on the others like dust on furniture. Eventually, the sound of new messages brought Irene out of her stupor.

"You earned five hundred dollars with that story," she said. "Congratulations, Cath. You won today."

I glanced at the screen to see the messages about the story, as well as the donations still pouring in. But there was one that stood out to me immediately. I'm not sure the others noticed it, because the screen was moving so quickly, but a subscriber called Volk posted:

I'll give you a real horror story. If one of you murders another, I'll send you one million dollars.

CHAPTER SIX

The sunrise woke me, as it had the morning before, with the light from the colourful glass bouncing around the room. It made me feel as if I was trapped in a kaleidoscope for a moment. I sat up, still tired, but with a desire to appreciate this opportunity, as well as a few fresh ideas for Akarthis on my mind. However, there was also an uneasy feeling in the pit of my stomach, and that sensation started to spread over my body, making my skin tingle, the back of my head itch. It seemed to me that a change had occurred overnight. A different smell, drop in temperature or an object out of place. I couldn't put my finger on it at a glance. The gnawing discomfort could have simply been because I wasn't in my bed at home. No, that wasn't it. I was right the first time, because the packets of pills that I'd placed so carefully the night before on top of my cabinet were missing.

I swung my legs out of bed, hurried across the room, and began removing drawers, searching for my medication, pulling out all the carefully folded clothes. When I found nothing, I checked underneath. I checked my desk, under the bed, in the en suite. I checked the window ledge, behind the toilet, under the sink.

My pills were missing.

As that realisation hit, my heart began to pound. I couldn't be without them for four weeks. Getting better had been a long, rocky road, and the thought of going back to how I was when I was ill made me want to be sick.

Still in pyjamas, I hurried along the cloister to the old chapter house we used as a snug. Irene and Jules's voices travelled out of the room. I wrapped my arms around my body to protect myself from the morning chill, then I hesitated by the door.

"You made a mistake inviting Nathan," Jules said. "What he said to Cath went over the line."

"Look, he'll bring in subscribers. I needed at least one participant with a big following," Irene replied.

"Yeah but, him?"

"The others said no."

When I walked into the room, they both stopped talking and faced me. Irene was folded up on the sofa, barefoot, with a mug of coffee in her hands. Even though she was in her sleepwear, she had on make-up, her hair had been straightened, and everything about her gave off an air of togetherness. On the other hand, Jules sat in the armchair opposite, her hair mussed, crusts of sleep visible in the corners of her eyes.

"My pills are missing," I blurted out. "My anti-psychotic medication." I closed my eyes and took a deep breath. "For my schizophrenia. They've been stolen."

Out of the corner of my eye, I noticed Jules frowning at the word "schizophrenia".

Irene's eyes narrowed. "*Stolen?* That's not possible. Why would anyone take your meds? Maybe you lost them. We'll help you search if you like."

"I've checked every part of my room," I said. "The drawers, under the bed, the bathroom. They're not there."

"You can't accuse people of theft without any proof," Irene said. "I'll order you more if you tell me what you need. We can have a delivery in a few days. Will that work?"

"I don't know," I said. "I think it might mess with things a bit."

"But the new medication will kick in and all will be well?" she prompted.

"I guess," I said.

Nathan nudged my elbow as he came through the door. He held a plate of toast and was wearing a T-shirt emblazoned with a screenshot of a tweet by another YouTuber saying *The Yorkie is an edgelord*. "What's going on? It's like a puppy's funeral in here."

"Cath lost her medication," Irene said. "But it's fine. We get regular deliveries. She'll have new meds in a few days."

When he looked at me, his pale eyes beneath two hooded lids, he appeared completely and utterly bored, and yet I couldn't shake the feeling that it was all an act.

"Oh," he said simply. And then the conversation moved on. "Did you ban that weirdo that kept offering money for one of us to commit murder?"

"Yes," Irene replied. "He's gone." She glanced at me again. "Don't worry, I'll order those pills for you."

There wasn't much else to say, so I left.

I HAD TO GET OUT. DESPITE THE OPENNESS OF THE

monastery, its walls were oppressive to me now. I grabbed my notebook and a pen, strapped on a body cam and went for a walk. On the way out I remembered to take a bottle of water and a few cereal bars in case I was out for a long time. One of the others could chat to the live-streamers. It wasn't as if I would be badly missed.

Out there in the forest, I could be myself, without fear of being called a virgin, or worrying that every word I spoke and every thing I did sounded or appeared crazy, or being ridiculed for not being like them, oozing with confidence and self-possession. The mere thought that one of those people could have taken my medication was more than troubling to me, it was abhorrent. My crutch, the one thing keeping me together, had been stolen from me. Without those pills I was a different person. You could barely even call me a person; I was a shivering lump of paranoia who moved from catatonia to reckless impulsivity at the drop of a hat.

And the voice. The terrible voice that had plagued me in my worst moments could come back at any time.

I climbed and climbed, using every muscle in my body to distract my mind from spiralling into the first burgeoning of paranoia. Even though I knew the drug was still in my system, I couldn't stay calm. Nathan had stolen them, I was sure of it, but what if he'd had help? What if it was Irene? What if it was Dan? He was quiet, and often quiet people are the last ones you suspect, but the worst of the lot. Maybe it was even Jules. What if they all had a secret vendetta against me?

I realised I was already in the throes of paranoia, and I stopped walking and began to laugh. It was this place, it had to be. I'd been on edge since arriving, probably because of Alexandru's story. I just needed to relax.

Further up the mountainside, I stared down at Sfântul Mihail taking in the steeple of the tower, the tall church walls and the sharp gables. The imposing size of the place made me think of the story I told about the nuns. Out here I could imagine it all happening. Those minor details, the names, the events, they'd come to me in the moment. I'd been inspired by Alexandru, that's true, but there'd also been this sense of puzzle pieces clicking into place as I'd been talking. It'd been instinctual, like a lot of my writing is.

With this great vantage point, I sat and began jotting down ideas in my notebook, still working on Maya's origin story where she comes into her healing powers. I'd decided not to make her a sexy assassin or a tortured mage, those characters had been written so many times before. I'd wanted her to contribute to good. A character who makes a difference because they care.

But I had no time to explore these themes before a thin howl echoed around the mountain. The call prompted a jolt of electricity to work its way through my body, and I gasped. I put the pen inside my notebook and stood, squinting into the distance. It sounded again, and I realised that it was coming from up the mountainside. I rotated my body in the direction of the howl, the wind whipping sharp strands of hair into my eyes.

The pained, eerie call struck a chord with my emotions, which perhaps was because of the stolen medication. The animal was in obvious distress and a deep sadness spread down from my heart to my stomach. Could I walk away and leave it out here in pain? But I was no expert, and there was a chance the distressing cry came from a wolf. They were rare, but still existed in the Carpathians, I knew that much. If I hurried down to the monastery, perhaps I could get Irene to call some sort of local animal control, if one existed.

How long would it take for them to come? Were there rangers in this area? I remembered what she'd said about the telephone service. We'd probably have to send an email, which could take even longer, meanwhile, this animal had been hurt.

As another wounded howl echoed around the forest, my feet made the decision for me. I started walking up the hill, following the direction of the animal's call. I zigzagged my way through clusters of silver birches, their amber leaves almost touching across the divide. Even my presence among them made the drops of amber fall. If I hadn't had an urgent task, I would have stayed there for hours taking hundreds of photographs. But I didn't, I rushed through them to where the landscape opened into farmland.

There was a barbed-wire fence separating the forest from a flock of sheep. My eyes were drawn to the dead sheep first, the blood so vivid against the white wool, and then I saw what was lying next to it. A wolf. Bent and broken among the grass, its tongue lolling from its mouth, a pool of blood around its throat. My stomach lurched but I held down the water and cereal bars. It'd been dead for a while. So where did the howl come from?

I allowed my gaze to trail left until I saw the animal caught in the wire fence. Another wolf, but this one slightly over half the size of the dead one. It had to be the dead wolf's pup, but it wasn't tiny. It was the size of a Labrador, but skinnier. Its neck was caught in the wire and it was growling and struggling to get out. I took a few steps towards it before stopping to suck in a deep breath. How was I going to get this wolf out of the wire without endangering my life?

"It's okay," I said, as I approached. "I won't hurt you."

I was in so far over my head, and yet I couldn't bear to

turn back. I'd heard the desperation in its cries, the stringy loneliness echoing through the mountains.

When I was around four feet away from the wolf I tried to assess the situation. Its head was caught in the lower section of the wire, probably from trying to force its way underneath the fence to get near the sheep. Perhaps there'd been a hole here, but the farmer had replaced it to keep the wolves out. I crouched down and saw that a section of the wire had broken and pierced the wolf's flesh.

The wolf couldn't stay still, it wriggled and whined and snapped its jaws. A trail of bloody saliva dropped from its teeth.

"We're going to have to work together here," I said. "You need to not eat me, okay?"

I reached into my rucksack and pulled out the selfie stick Irene had given us. Perhaps I could use it to nudge back those broken pieces of wire and allow the wolf to get free. It was risky. I wished the wolf was on the other side of the fence, but I had to hope it would rather run away to safety than eat me. If I could get it free, it'd at least stop it from injuring itself further, and then I could make sure Irene told the appropriate authorities so they could keep track of it. I couldn't be sure, but I figured wolves are an endangered species and there had to be an organisation in Romania that checked up on the population in the mountains.

"I'm coming close. Don't panic." I kept talking to soothe myself as well as the wolf. Perhaps the sound of my voice would stop it from killing me. "I'm going to use this against the wire, here, okay?" A snarl rolled from the wolf's mouth as I pressed the plastic selfie stick against the wire. It was hard to get purchase as the wolf carried on squirming and growling, but I had a steady hand, somehow, and the selfie stick was sturdy enough to move the wire millimetre by millimetre.

Once the sharp piece of wire was no longer digging in the wolf's neck, it didn't growl with quite as much gusto. I moved around to the right side of the animal and worked on the other broken pieces of wire, bending them away from the wolf's flesh, gradually making the hole in the fence bigger and bigger. Once I saw that it was large enough for the animal to free its head, I retracted the stick and moved away, close to the birch trees, far from its sharp teeth.

Rather than back up from the fence, the wolf rushed through it, squeezing its lean body through the small space, in the same liquid way a cat gets through tiny gaps. I breathed a sigh of relief then, seeing that the wolf wasn't the slightest bit interested in me. In fact, I even dared to move a few steps closer to watch its behaviour. It's not every day you come across a wolf, not for me anyway.

But what broke my heart was where the wolf immediately ran—to the body of what I had to assume was its mother. It let out a whine and lowered its snout to the dead wolf. I stumbled out from the trees and stood near the fence, watching. As I moved closer, the wolf's head rose, and I saw its pale-yellow eyes for the first time. The grey of its fur was marred by blood, formed into a rudimentary cross on its chest. We both stood there, eyes fixed, until a force pulled me away. I stumbled back, confused, and tripped over my feet, landing on the grass, convinced that a hand had wrenched my shoulder. But there was no one around. Nothing moved, not the wolf, not the sheep, nothing.

At this lower spot on the ground a white shape caught my eye. It was far off in the distance, but I recognised it for what it was. On the left-hand side of the paddock was the edge of the same forest I'd hurried through to find the pup.

Between the trees stood another wolf, much larger than either of the others I'd already seen today. Its head was low, its back arched, throwing into my imagination the sound of its growl, the trembling of its hackles, the saliva dripping from its jaws. I hurried to my feet and ran.

CHAPTER SEVEN

I rene regarded me with disdain, the corners of her mouth pulled down. "Where have you been? You smell terrible."

On my way back to the monastery, I'd lost the path between the trees and ended up circling through the same patch of forest two or three times before I found my way again. Wandering so far up the mountain to the farmland had resulted in me staying out for hours. I'd stumbled back in the dark, mud on my hands and in my hair, heart still pounding after what had happened. With every step I'd imagined the large white wolf leaping from the undergrowth, ready to rip open my throat. In view for barely a moment, yet the sight of that beast had left a bad taste in my mouth, like rusted pennies. There'd been an intangible strangeness about its presence that I could feel even from so far away. The young wolf was just that, a skinny pup with a dead mother, but the white wolf was different. In fact, it was probably the white wolf that had killed the pup's mother, now I thought about it.

"I think I fell into animal muck," I explained. "I had a crazy walk. There was this—"

She held up one hand. "Shower and get online. You're late for your shift." She gestured towards the rota on the wall, leaning her weight against the doorframe.

"Okay, but you need to call the authorities about some wolves I saw. They're protected, aren't they?"

Irene threaded her fingers through her hair and paused. "I'll have to check."

"I'm sure you can find them on Google. Maybe you could email them? Or use your local contact?"

"Of course," she said. "You saw an actual wolf?"

"I saw two," I replied.

"Did you get it on camera?"

"Yeah."

"Wow. Okay, well upload it."

It was my turn to stay up late and interact with the viewers. In fact, I was the first to do this. But before I got started I took Irene's advice and got straight into the shower, washing away the mud and other delightfully smelling things I'd picked up on the walk. Afterwards, I pulled on my comfy clothes, padded into the kitchen and made toast. There were several dirty bowls and plates on the side from the dinner I'd missed, so I quickly rinsed them and put them in the dishwasher. By the time I took a laptop to the snug, nearly everyone had gone to their bedrooms. I realised it was after ten p.m. Jules had stayed up long enough to wish me goodnight.

"We should hang out tomorrow," she said as she left.

"Yeah, sure," I replied. "I'd like that."

I decided to upload the footage from the body cam as I was chatting to viewers. After spending so long away from the cameras in the monastery, I needed to provide content for the subscribers, plus I wanted to view the footage myself. On my way back from the mountain, my thoughts had been scattered and panicked, my fear too extreme, to dwell on one element of the day. There'd been a moment near the sheep field—as if there'd been a hand on my shoulder, yanking me away from the fence. Had another person been there? A farmer? One of the others out on a walk? And if someone had been there, why had they run away?

It took a while to go through the footage, skipping forward through my walk at the beginning. Every now and then I stopped to answer questions on the live stream, like: What is Irene like? Do you like The Yorkie in real life or is he a dick? How do you write so fast? Are you a virgin?

That one kept cropping up over and over again and I continued to ignore it, but every time I saw that word my stomach dropped. I had Nathan to thank for that. I ground my teeth, trying not to focus on him, to not allow my thoughts to spiral back into paranoia, back into the nagging feeling that he stole my medication.

When the wolf appeared on the screen, I leaned in, checking the surrounding area for anything I might have missed. There it was, panicking and whining, pulling its weight against the wires, hurting itself with each frantic tug. In the background, I saw the way the scenery fell into the distant mountains, and the trees carpeting the view in between green grass and blue peaks. There, in the trees, was a white shape. The large white wolf I'd seen after I freed the pup. It'd been there the entire time, watching.

It wasn't quite recognisable as a wolf on the footage, and no amount of zooming in helped at all. But, surely, it was the wolf. What else could it be?

Because the camera had been strapped to my chest, there was no way for me to see if anyone had been behind me, but I watched the footage from when I was tugged back, slowing it down, pausing it where I could to check for anyone else around. There was nothing, no one.

I had to admit to myself that I must have imagined the feeling of being pulled back. It made tears spring to my eyes. The disappearance of my pills had thrown me for a loop, and almost immediately set off unhelpful thoughts in my mind. First that someone had stolen the medication, and now that I was imagining things. Surely it was the stress of being in another country, not the beginnings of my illness coming back. I wiped away any traces of the tears, hoping that none of the watchers noticed them, and focused on editing the footage to make a compelling clip for the followers.

There was a fireplace in the snug. A small one big enough for a few logs, with a poker hanging from the alcove, and a ledge above it. On top of the ledge was a clock. The ticking caught my attention for a moment as the second hand moved over the twelve. It was after midnight and the monastery was silent. Even the sound of my fingers tapping on the keyboard sent shivers up and down my spine. I watched the usernames pop up in the chat box, already recognising the regulars, like Cheezemonkeys and Alice-Akarthis. It surprised me to see Akarthis fans online, and even a few donations from them. They already knew me well; I had a reader group set up, one that was free. Several were beta readers for the books, others I chatted with about non-book things. They already had as much access to me as they wanted, yet they were kind enough to play this game with me.

At two a.m. I posted the edited video and scrolled through the messages as they came in.

Lupo: Is the monastery haunted like you said in your story?
Cath: There's a local superstition about the monastery but I don't personally believe in ghosts. It's true that nuns were murdered here and that gives the location a heavy emotional weight.
Lupo: Who killed the nuns?
Cath: I don't know.
Lupo: Don't you want to find out?
Cath: I'm not sure how I'd find out. A local man told me the story and he didn't say who killed them.
Lupo: Online it said their throats were slashed.

The user dropped a link into the chat box that took me to a blog post about the murders.

Sfântul Mihail Monastery and the Deaths of Thirteen Sisters

It was a cold night on the mountainside near Butnari when the sisters opened their doors to a stranger. Several hours later, the women would be found dead, all of their throats slit. Only the mother superior survived.

Part way through reading the article, I heard a soft knock on the door of the snug. The interruption of silence caught me off guard, sending adrenaline surging through my body. But it was such a soft sound, not terrifying, not thumping, so quiet it was barely there. I stood, shook my head, trying to shake away that adrenaline spike, and headed towards the door. Perhaps one of the others wanted to speak to me but feared I'd fallen asleep and didn't want to wake me. I waited for a second to see if they came into the snug, but they didn't. My fingers reached for the handle and then hesitated, my breath caught in my throat. I waited another beat and then wrapped my fingers around the cold metal and twisted it to open the door.

The cloister was empty and dark. I leaned half of my body out, and, seeing nothing, quickly retracted into the snug, my heart beating loudly. It was natural, I told myself, to feel spooked in a place this steeped in bloody history. But I had to remain rational. I shook my head and went back to the sofa. While I was composing myself, a message popped up on the screen.

Lupo: What did you hear?

It served as a creepy reminder that I was being watched. I was on camera, of course, so the viewers had seen my fear played to them directly.

Cath: I thought someone knocked on the door. Must be my imagination though!
Lupo: There was someone on the other side of the door. I saw a shape on the camera.

I wanted to close the laptop and get out of that room, but I didn't. Instead I composed a message with cold fingers.

Cath: It was probably one of the others on their way to get a glass of water. I took a while to answer the door, so they must have walked away.
Lupo: Yes, I saw them walk away. Didn't see their face though. Didn't see any part of them, just a black shape.

I hated it then. I hated talking to this person who could be lying to frighten me, for all I knew. But the description of a "black shape" was so like the way I'd thought of the image of the wolf that I'd seen—the "white shape". Two opposing forces. It sounded like a theme I'd write into an Arkathis story, about love and hate, or good and evil. But this wasn't a story, it was real.

AliceAkarthis: Cath, that video! The wolf.

My heart calmed. I went on to talk about the wolf, telling the people in the chat all about the rescue mission. As I typed, the donations went up, and I was shocked by how much people were giving. They were willing to pay me as I talked to them. Yes, I'd published books, but I wasn't used to this kind of appreciation.

Eviee: Thank you for sharing this with us!
1378stu: [heartemoji]
Twix: I've gone from an Irene stan to a Cath stan.
Pigeon: OMG!! I'm donating. Gimme more content like this pls!
Georgie: Just bought your books. Hello from Australia.
Serra: [heartemoji]
Lupo: What killed the wolf?

CHAPTER EIGHT

There was a soft knock. My eyelashes fluttered. My hands balled into fists. I saw the outline of a man standing outside a door, waiting to be allowed in. They had to wait for the invitation, you see. Sister Agatha could never enter without one, and the tall man stood behind her.

"Cath?"

The whisper made my eyes open and I sat up, the laptop dropping from my knees. Someone caught it and placed a hand on my shoulder.

"I was just coming in to let you know it's my shift." Jules smiled and lifted the laptop.

"Crap, I fell asleep. What time is it?"

"Four a.m.," she said. "These shifts are going to be a nightmare, aren't they?"

I grunted my agreement as I untangled myself from the blanket. October nights were freezing cold in the monastery.

"Sorry, there are probably a few hundred unanswered messages now."

"No worries." She took my place on the sofa as I stood to leave. "Go have a rest, okay?"

I paused in the doorway, wondering whether to tell her about the strange knock on the door and the even stranger insistence by the viewers that they had seen a person out there. But then I shook my head and decided to go. At this point I hardly knew Jules and she hardly knew me. What kind of impression would I make if I told her such a crazy story?

That night, or rather that morning, I struggled to sleep. Even with the growing aches in my muscles from the hike, and the complete exhaustion from the late night, my mind refused to release the grip it had over me. I shivered down into the bedspread, twisted in the sheets, my mind racing with thoughts of wolves and ghosts and vampires. Outside, around six a.m., I heard a howl in the distance, and wondered whether it was the pup I'd rescued, or the white wolf. None of the comments on my video had mentioned its presence between the distant birches and I was beginning to wonder whether I'd been mistaken.

At seven, I dragged myself out of bed, put on leggings and a tunic top, and went to the kitchen to meet Dan and Irene. Jules was busy chatting to subscribers in the snug, Nathan was in bed. I was tired, but Dan needed people for his sunrise yoga and I'd volunteered.

Irene sipped coffee and mumbled a hello when I walked in. She sat hunched over her mug, with one foot resting on the seat of her stool, and tendrils of blonde curls falling over her frame.

Dan, on the other hand, was pacing back and forth, ready to go. He tapped the side of his water bottle with a finger. "Come on, girls. I need to get the best light. I found the perfect spot on the mountain yesterday."

We were about to leave when Nathan walked in clutching his phone. "What the fuck, Cath? Are you actively going after our fans now?"

His raised voice brought out a bloom of warmth on my cheeks. Despite his skinny frame, he was a looming presence in the room. I took a step away, shoulders slumping, my voice caught in my throat.

Irene slammed down her coffee cup to gesture wildly at Nathan. "Why are you yelling at her now?"

"Have you checked the live-stream message board this morning?" Nathan asked, holding his phone aloft. "*She* uploaded a video last night of her rescuing a *fucking wolf*. A wolf! What are you, Doctor Dolittle? Fucking Snow White? I mean... come on! How are we supposed to compete with this?"

Irene opened the laptop on the counter and clicked on the mousepad a few times.

"It wasn't as dramatic as he's making out," I said. "I just moved some barbed wire. I swear I didn't mean to go after anyone's fans."

I wrung my hands together. Everyone hated me already. I shrank away next to the kitchen sink, my heart hammering against my ribs as Irene and Dan watched the video. In the background I heard my shaking, tentative voice talking to the wolf. Nathan glared at me with his arms folded tightly across his chest.

"Holy crap," Dan said. "That was amazing."

Both Dan and Irene were staring at me with opened mouths, but I focused on Nathan.

"You're right. I shouldn't have uploaded it on the first day. I should've waited until we were further into The Event. It's not like I'm going to have much else to share over the next few weeks, so you'll all catch up."

My face burned with heat. Behind me the tap dripped rhythmically, like a beating heart caught in the room, or the steady sound of a metronome about to increase its tempo, cranking the tension.

"No, this is good," Irene said. "It's great content. You did the right thing. Nathan, stop being jealous, okay? You have your own fans to worry about."

"All I'm saying," he said, shoving the phone back in his pocket, "is that the more donations she gets, the fewer we get. If it's going to be this uneven, maybe we should talk about distributing them between us all."

Irene held up both hands. "Why don't we talk about this"—and then she lowered her voice—"another time?" Her eyes glanced at the cameras. I could see her point. Arguing about money wasn't the best way to entertain subscribers. "Now, come on. We're a team, no? Let's do yoga. Nathan, you're coming too."

DURING YOGA THAT MORNING, I STUMBLED MY WAY THROUGH A beginner's routine with all the grace of Bambi on ice, while Dan lifted and bent his body in impossible angles, and Nathan operated a drone to capture it all. We watched the footage back around the dining table in the refectory, analysing the meandering mountain vista, and the unfortunate close-ups of Irene's breasts and buttocks. Leave them in, she'd said.

I spent the rest of the day in my room, publishing Maya's origin story, and working on the next Akarthis novel. Wrist support strapped on, five thousand words written by one p.m., the story uploaded and sent to my mailing list. I tried to avoid the live-stream chat channel and my social media accounts. There was a good reason for Nathan's outburst. Overnight I'd accrued three thousand pounds in donations, and ten thousand new Instagram followers. That number kept going up during the day as the video reached Reddit, Facebook and TikTok.

But none of that mattered, not when Maya needed to find the boys with golden stars on their foreheads. They'd been transformed into trees, guarded by a huge white wolf. I'd taken inspiration from an old Romanian fairy tale along with my afternoon on the mountain.

At two, I took a break and went to make lunch. My wrists ached from the typing and my eyes felt strained from the computer screen. I'd expected everyone to have had their lunch already, but Irene saw me walk past the snug and waved me in. She was nestled among cushions, making me think of a pampered queen in a faraway land. Perhaps Irene could serve as inspiration for a princess in Akarthis. A beautiful young woman who on first meeting came across as shallow, but who had survived hardship in her youth, and for that reason had a harsher view of the world.

"Your video was amazing," she said, gesturing for me to sit, like a head teacher would a student. "Our numbers went stratospheric overnight, Cath. Well done."

"Thanks. It was luck."

"Yes," she said. "But could you imagine Nathan helping the wolf?" She laughed and flicked her hair back.

"No, I guess not. Did you contact the authorities? I'm concerned about it out there without its mother. I think it was starving," I said.

"Of course, don't worry about that. I emailed a local preservation society this morning. Listen." She leaned forward and began to speak softly. "Next time upload for the

VIP members first." She leaned back. "We need better content for them."

"Okay, no problem. Whatever you need."

"Well, now that you mention it. I don't know much about you, Cath, and that means the viewers don't either. You're quite private, aren't you?" The way she said it made me think that she'd run background checks on us before we'd arrived.

"I guess."

Irene pulled her feet onto the sofa and sat crossed legged, her hair falling over one side of her face in such a manner that made her features even more Gallic. She stroked the top of her bare foot idly, with perfectly manicured fingers.

"Where did you grow up? What was life like for you? Do you have a boyfriend? I would love to get to know you better."

Her questions ignited the same kind of creeping tension I'd experienced in the kitchen with Nathan's petulant voice filling the room. While she leaned towards me, I shuffled away, wrapping my arms around my body, searching deep down into myself for a way to answer her questions without revealing too much, and yet it was all blank. There was little more than an empty space in there. I began to speak, not sure where I was going with my words.

"I'm from Derby. It was fine, pretty normal. I don't have a boyfriend at the moment. To be honest, I don't have time because I'm always writing." I focused my attention on a small pink flower woven into the light beige fabric of the sofa. I wondered what spring would be like here in the mountains with fresh wildflowers budding in the meadows.

"What do you do for fun, Cath?"

"I write," I said.

Irene's eyes were like blue globes, wide and incredulous that *this* was the extent of me, and once again I found myself lacking.

Before she could ask me another question, I said, "You were a big inspiration to me. The way you and your mum started a new life in California, and the way you've always talked about your illness with such positivity. It really helped me during difficult times." I shook my head. "It had a big impact on how I see the world. I liked what you both used to say about the power of optimism."

I watched as her incredulity softened into pride. She smiled widely and took my hands in hers. "A strong will is everything. The way you think can change your life. I swear by it. My mother taught me to be grateful, always. Even when I had no hair and would throw up all day and night. When I was in so much pain I could hardly move, I would appreciate that pain because it meant I was still alive." She squeezed my fingers. "Eleven years in remission. I appreciate everything life has to offer."

She continued to talk about her years as a child suffering with leukaemia. I nodded along, half taking in her words, partly mesmerised by them. But there was another part of me, a strong one, and a fragment of myself that I didn't particularly like, that couldn't stop wishing, in an envious way, that my mother had imparted that kind of wisdom to me. All I ever received from her was hate.

CHAPTER NINE

A round four o'clock that afternoon, Irene gathered us in the refectory for a meeting. Her make-up and hair were perfection, with long curls framing her dewy face. She smiled and bright-red lips parted to reveal pearly-white teeth. She was wearing a pair of trainers that appeared to be brand new, and I wondered whether she'd been given them by a brand and asked to wear them. They weren't her usual glamorous style. Still, her polished appearance made me feel childish in leggings and thick socks.

"Put on your body cams," Irene said. "We're going to show everyone the monastery. As you know, Loup converted one wing, but the building is much bigger. We're going to show them the abandoned part. The scary, dark places." She lifted her eyebrows and gave us a fiendishly beautiful grin.

"Is it safe?" Jules said. "I walked part of it, and it's so old and crumbling. Are you sure we can go there?"

"I'm sure we'll be fine, as long as we're careful," Irene said, in a tone that made me wonder if she even knew the answer to Jules's question.

I noticed Jules glance at me as though hoping for my support, but I was so intrigued by the idea of seeing the rest of the building that I didn't speak up.

"I thought this was going to be a proper meeting," Nathan said. "I have an agenda item."

Irene lifted her chin. "Fine. Tell us."

"My chocolate has been stolen."

I watched Irene roll her eyes. "Don't be ridiculous. We have chocolate in the kitchen."

"It was taken from my *room*."

"Why do you have chocolate in your *room*?" Irene said, mimicking his tone.

"Because I brought my own. Proper Dairy Milk, in case you can't get it here."

"I notice you didn't share it with the group," Jules added. "Not like you, Nathan."

"You lot are the thieving bastards not me," he said.

"Yeah," Jules added. "We all arranged it. There was a heist and everything. We brought a battering ram, dynamite for the safe, ski masks, the lot."

"Fuck off," Nathan said. "It means someone was in my room. One of you went in, opened my suitcase and stole from me. Don't you think that's serious?"

"It wasn't when my medication was taken," I added.

He rolled his eyes. "Oh come on, you probably forgot to pack it. Who would want to steal psycho-pills. No offence."

My jaw dropped but before I had time to say anything, Irene held up her hands to calm everyone down.

"All right. I'll order you as much chocolate as you want, and we'll monitor the situation. If anyone is stealing for fun, to spice things up for the live-stream, you need to stop. It isn't funny."

That seemed to be the end of things. After we'd gathered

the equipment, and were filing out of the kitchen, Jules wandered closer to me. "I'm not sure about this tour," she said quietly. "I have a bad feeling."

"It must be safe," I said. "Surely Loup wouldn't have received planning permission if it wasn't."

She frowned, and, looking back, I remember wondering why she was so sure the rest of the monastery was unsafe. There'd been nothing to suggest it, apart from the fact it was old. It struck me then that she was scared for other reasons, using the potential danger as an excuse for us not to explore.

One by one, we filtered out of the refectory and walked along the walkway with the cherry tree on our left. It was a gloomy afternoon, and even in the open cloister garth the light dwindled. We naturally diverged into small clusters, with Dan, Nathan and Irene striding ahead, leaving me and Jules at the rear. I tried to reassure her that it would be fine, and that many old buildings exist for centuries without too much decay, but she shook her head. She opened her mouth as if to speak and then paused, and I had a feeling she was about to explain her concerns to me.

"Don't you think there's been this weird energy hanging over us the entire time?" she asked. As she spoke, her hands gestured wildly, fingers fluttering in the air. "I keep thinking about the curse you were telling me about, and the nuns who died here, and I can't shake the feeling that it left behind... I don't know, like a bad vibe. Do you know what I mean?"

I realised then that my story had rattled a few of the others and for that the onus was on me. The only person I'd meant to scare was Nathan, because of his unkind words to me.

"Honestly, I don't," I said, trying my best to reassure her.

"It's natural to feel spooked in a place so steeped with mystery and a bloody history. There are times when it messes with my head, but then I feel so grateful to be here. I just want to soak it all in. Do you feel like that?"

Jules nodded and I could tell she was mulling over my words. She took a moment to answer again. "I do. And I don't disagree about the history, but at the same time, my instincts are always screaming at me. They're telling me..." She trailed off, her eyes following the length of the arcade as we moved away from the refurbished wing and into a darker, foreboding east wing.

"What?" I prompted.

She lowered her voice. "That something evil lives here."

Despite everything I'd said previously, ice-cold needles prickled at my scalp, before the chill descended down my body, spreading over my skin. I clenched my jaw as Irene opened a creaking wooden door. One by one we ducked through the doorway into a long, dark room. Irene lit a candle to light our path, mimicking what the nuns would have done centuries ago. The rest of us used our torches, but mine cut out a few steps in, the battery dead. Jules sidled closer to me so that we could share.

"There's a night-vision setting on your body cams," Irene called out. "There's a switch on the side."

"Are we doing *Most Haunted*?" Nathan said with a laugh. "Holy shit, we are, aren't we?"

As we clustered inside the room, the light from Jules's phone caught Dan and Nathan. I noticed that Dan laughed at Nathan's flippancy, yet his skin was pale, and his eyes darted about the place. Irene and Nathan were their usual selves, but Jules and Dan were definitely afraid. Perhaps I was, too. Jules's comment about evil had disturbed me in an unexpectedly stirring manner. Adrenaline bounced around my body, my heart pumping.

"This is the dormitory along the east wing," Irene said. "Be careful. There are a few bits of old furniture lying around. We'll go through here, through the library and into the church from the transept."

"This is where the nuns slept," I noted. "How many nuns lived here?"

Irene shrugged. "I don't know, exactly. Perhaps fifteen to twenty. When Loup renovated our wing, they put up walls to separate the accommodation into rooms. The hardest part was plumbing in the en-suites." She let out a low whistle. "Cost a pretty penny."

"It's insane they were allowed to alter the ruins so drastically," Jules said. "You'd think a building like this would be protected."

"No one cares because it's cursed," Nathan said.

"Maybe you're right," she muttered.

Irene led on, her hand cupped around her candle. The others followed, while Jules shivered next to me.

"Do you want my hoody?" I offered, noticing she was in short sleeves. "I have a long-sleeve top on underneath."

"Are you sure?" she asked. "I don't know why I thought I could wear a tee."

I unstrapped the body cam and peeled the hoody away from my body. She pulled it on, flashing me a grateful smile.

"It's fucking freezing in here. Can we go now, please?" Nathan said, his eye-roll captured by torchlight. "Now that the Sisters of the Travelling Pants have organised their outfits?"

"This way," Irene said. "There's a beautiful old church around here with stained-glass windows and lots of light. You'll appreciate the... majesty of it all."

"You've got a way with words, my French friend," Nathan said, patting Irene gently on the arm.

"We just need to go through the library first."

Even Jules began to relax on our way to the library, intrigued to see something other than a long dark room. And as we walked, I realised I was coming to know and understand these people by simply being around them and observing the way they walked or the way they joked. Witnessing Dan's nerves, Nathan's sudden stillness as Irene paused to open the next door, Jules's superstition and intuition, as well as Irene's cool composure even when a draught extinguished her candle.

We were down to three torches. Irene shouldered the next wooden door open, and our footsteps echoed as we walked into the old library. I kept one finger trailing the walls on my left, but when I came across dampness, I decided to stop.

"How big are spiders in Romania?" Dan warily lifted his head to the ceiling.

"The size of your fist." Nathan flashed him a lopsided grin.

"Um, haven't you heard of the Romanian tarantula?" Jules said, somewhat gently.

"That's not a thing, is it?" Dan said. "Seriously?"

Jules replied with a solemn nod. "It's a thing, Dan."

He muttered a curse word.

There were no windows in the library. Despite it being the smallest room I'd seen in the monastery so far, our light failed to reach the corners. Along the walls were the skeletons of what it might have been. Empty, rotting shelves. A chair on its side. The books were long gone, but there were a few loose pages scattered on the flagstones, discoloured and dusty.

"I think it's through here," Irene said, nodding to the next door.

Finally, we reached the open walkway that ran alongside the church. I saw Dan's shoulders relax now that there was enough light for him to see any potential spiders lying in wait. But what the light revealed was not pretty. There was debris on the ground; broken glass, dirt, rubble. I realised, only then, that we weren't the first people to be there since the murders. Perhaps this place had been a spot for teenagers or drug addicts or homeless people to meet. But then I folded that thought away. Surely not, in this tiny rural community. Not up these mountains. Not when civilisation was many miles away.

We walked back towards our renovated, west wing, only to stop next to a set of double doors, wooden, like the others in the building, with large iron hinges and rusting locks. There were Romanian words spray-painted across the wood.

"What do you think it says?" Dan asked, a note of trepidation in his voice.

"It says, 'fuck off'," Nathan replied. "Come on, it's obviously the builders having a laugh." He pushed the doors open and strode into the church, before stopping dead less than two feet inside.

Irene followed him, continuing further within, followed by Jules and Dan. I was last, glancing over my shoulder as I trailed the others.

"Remember to change your cameras back to the regular setting," Irene said as she walked between the pews.

Though the ground was covered in debris, the dusty pews lined up like soldiers ready for a parade. I noted they were arranged as though a church service was about to begin, with rows on either side of the aisle. It gave me the strangest feeling that a group of nuns would walk in at any moment. History had never been so tangible.

I had to move around Nathan, who was still close to the doorway, his mouth slightly open, but with a cautious fear in his eyes, as though he was seeing the place through a different lens than the rest of us. Once past him, I allowed myself time to examine the somewhat grungy splendour before me. There were tall vaulted ceilings that were so high they must have gone up to the level of a second floor. The stained-glass windows were smashed in places, but still filtered the last embers of sunshine onto the altar, which was still draped with a cloth as though waiting for a crucifix to be placed there. There was even a lectern in the shape of an eagle close to the altar, waiting for a holy person to speak. The entire place was waiting, like a video game on pause. Waiting for the players to re-join.

I walked slowly through the chapel, listening to the echo of our footsteps. Aside from exploring, everyone was quiet in that moment, and, I cannot speak for them, only myself, but the church had a whole other ambience to our renovated wing. In here it was much easier to imagine the fear and agony those nuns experienced as they were murdered. To see the tall man with his teeth at their neck.

On shaking legs, I walked towards the lectern. I traced the carved eagle—gold paint flaking away—with my fingers. Resting in its holder was a bible still. The aged leather was cool to the touch but left a layer of dust on my fingertips. It, too, appeared to be waiting to be read, its words to be spoken. When I turned the pages, there was a brittle crackle, and almost seventy-five years of dust clouded up around me. But aside from that it was still in decent condition. I flicked through the book, enjoying the tightly scribbled notes around the text, words that I couldn't understand. It was in

Romanian, of course, but I enjoyed allowing my eyes to roam across each line, nonetheless.

"What did you find?" Jules had wandered silently over to me, and I suppressed a shiver of surprise.

"This old bible. It must have belonged to one of the nuns, or the mother superior."

"Or a priest," Jules added, leaning over my shoulder for a better view. "Cath, what is that?" She recoiled, as though the words were offensive.

I glanced down at the book in my hand and saw the splash of crimson across one of the pages. Though the mark was red in the centre, the edges had dried to be a burnished brown.

"It looks like blood," I replied at last.

Jules directed her face away. "I don't know what happened in this part of the church, but I don't like it here."

While she wasn't watching, I slipped the bible into the large baggy pockets of my long tunic. As I did, a strange sensation washed over me. It was as though I was now noticing the cold, or that a sudden chill had penetrated every part of my body at once. Yet, at the same time, there was a light and gentle touch on my shoulder, reminding me of the hand pulling me away from the wolf. Though I wanted to examine those feelings, and that strange touch in particular, it was gone almost immediately, leaving me with nothing but ice in my veins.

"What's wrong?" Jules asked, turning back to me.

I merely shook my head, not sure how I could put into words what I'd experienced.

CHAPTER TEN

We stayed in the church for another fifteen minutes or so, but I didn't have any more experiences of strange sensations or cold draughts. Having said that, it took me hours to warm up after walking back through the walkways. Along the way, the sun set, and the night air wrapped its cold fingers around our bodies. I heard the sound of Dan's breathing as we used our torches to light the way. And along with it, the cherry tree rustled a rhythm eerily like an inhale and exhale. It was in that moment I realised how easy it would be to imagine being followed; to create monsters in the darkness or to conjure the devil at the heart of Sfântul Mihail.

I'm not a believer for many reasons. My mother was not particularly religious, and my father had never been in my life and therefore had no influence on the person I grew up to be. Perhaps he'd been a man of faith, I don't know, and, in all honesty, it didn't matter to me. I had a feeling that science had the right of it when it came to those strangely mystical occurrences around the world. Yet, at the same time, I couldn't stop thinking about Jules's words on the feeling of this place. Because there was one thing I believed in strongly, which could be considered pseudo-science, or hogwash, or fantasy, and that was the idea that malice can be inherited. And not just malice. I believed any trauma of the past could slip down between generations. We are all constructed by our environments, the mistakes our parents and grandparents made bequeathed to us, perhaps we even profit from those mistakes. It's possible, though tenuous, that the same can be said for buildings. Does a building become malevolent because of the terrible crimes committed there? Or was the malevolence there to begin with? Does the energy remain? Or do we project our fears onto that building through rumours and curses?

Back in the snug, we unclasped our body cams and settled around the room. Nathan slumped into a tub chair, Dan and Irene took a sofa, and I sat next to Jules on the other one. Irene opened the laptop, no doubt to check on the live-stream. The room was quiet, with even Nathan unusually still after the tour. We hadn't lingered in the east wing, and we hadn't been to the ruined infirmary outside of the monastery either. Even though no one had vocalised it, we all knew none of us wanted to stay in that part of the building after the sun went down.

"So many comments," Irene said. "The tour was success-ful. Dan, people liked your fear of spiders."

"I'm not afraid of spiders," he said, with a hollow laugh. "Tarantulas, sure. Normal spiders..." He drifted off, no doubt still imagining a Romanian tarantula dropping from the dark arches above our heads. I wasn't afraid of spiders myself, but I could imagine that being particularly terrifying.

"Own it, man," Jules said. "Nothing to be ashamed of. I

was cacking my pants the whole time. The energy in that part of the building is totally different."

"Yeah." Nathan frowned. "I felt it too."

It surprised me to see Nathan admit to this. He'd arrived at The Event with such outward bravado that I never imagined hearing any vulnerability from him. But before I found myself endeared to this different side of him, I remembered my missing medication, the expression he'd had on his face when I'd told the group it was missing, and the way he yelled at me in the kitchen. I couldn't get those things out of my head.

"Do any of you talk in your sleep?" Nathan said.

We all shook our heads, though in truth, I wasn't sure if I did or not.

"What about you, Cath? Your room is next to mine."

"Not that I know of," I said.

Nathan's throat worked as he swallowed. "I heard a voice last night. It kept me up for hours."

Jules leaned forward on the sofa. "What kind of voice?"

He shrugged. "I couldn't make out the words but there was definitely a voice. A whisper."

"It could be the wind," I suggested. "These windows aren't exactly double-glazed."

"I guess," he mumbled, not convinced by my explanation.

"Huh." Irene shuffled in her seat, pouring over the laptop with her back hunched and a thumbnail between her teeth. "There are a few strange comments on here." She placed the computer on the coffee table in the centre of the room, angling the screen so that we could huddle around to see.

Lu98: Am I the only one who saw it?

Reenieleanie: Nope. Me too.

Forkie: And me.

SRoy: Fuck. That thing creeped me out big time.

Lupo: They aren't alone in there.

Lu98: The monastery is haunted.

Happyidiot: They should leave. Guys, if you're reading this, you should leave. This place is giving me the heebie-jeebies BIG TIME. And I'm a medium so I know my shit.

Cheezemonkeys: Fuck off medium. Scam artist.

Lupo: We all saw it though. There's another person living in the monastery.

Happyidiot: @Cheezemonkeys YOU. DO. NOT. KNOW. ME.

Lupo: Someone's going to die…

Forkie: @Lupo Wow, bad taste, man.

Lupo: One of you is going to get murdered. Will it be one of them killing another? Or is a stranger going to get in first?

Happyidiot: Lupo should go. That's disrespectful.

Lupo: I'll give a million dollars to the first person to commit murder.

Forkie: Not this again.

Lu98: @Lupo byeeee.

"I thought you'd banned the nutter offering us money to kill each other?" Nathan said, his knee moving up and down in agitation.

"I did," Irene replied. "Whoever it was made another account and signed up again." She shrugged. "I can't keep up with everything."

"Shouldn't Loup be monitoring this shit?" Nathan added. "Surely they can check IP addresses?"

"I'll raise it with them."

"Guys, what about the other messages? What are they talking about?" Jules frowned and rolled up the sleeves of the hoody I'd lent her. "They keep saying there was another person in the monastery."

"I guess they saw something unusual during the live stream of the tour," Irene said.

As soon as she said that, additional messages popped up.

Lu98: Time stamp 38:46 on Cath's camera. There's a dark figure standing in the corner of the dormitory.
AliceAkarthis: Stay safe, Cath!
Cheezemonkeys: There's a shadow in the chapel too. Time-stamp 46:20.
Lupo: Cath will be first.
Lu98: [angryfaceemoji] @Lupo

Though I tried my hardest not to let the words bother me, when I opened my mouth to speak, my voice came out breathy, like a distant call on the wind. "We'd better check the time stamps." The rest of the room went quiet, their gazes directed towards me, bringing out the familiar blush on my cheeks when I receive any sudden attention.

"I'll find the footage from your cam," Irene said.

She clicked through a few folders on the desktop and opened the file. Then she moved the pointer around on the timeline to a few moments before Lu98 claimed to have seen a figure. We watched it through first, and then Irene pulled the pointer back, and played it in slow motion, pausing exactly on 38:46.

No one moved. No one said a word. I fought back tears, either from shock, or fear, or the myriad of competing emotions wrestling inside myself, all as my eyes remained fixed on the computer screen.

There are moments that will stay with a person for the rest of their life, and this was such a moment for me. It was clear. At 38:46 there was the shape of a person in the dark corner, brought to life by the glowing green of the night-vision camera. Whoever it was wore shapeless clothes and faced away from us, but I couldn't imagine that particular shape being anything other than another human being. I'd been a few feet away from whoever this was without even knowing they were there.

"Take screenshots," Nathan instructed, breaking through the quiet. "And crop out that bit of us walking past. We need to keep this for evidence."

"Evidence?" Jules sounded incredulous as her brow furrowed. "For what exactly?"

"Trespassing," Nathan replied.

"Or ghosts," Dan said. I noticed that his arms were pulled tightly across his chest.

"We should check the other time stamp," I suggested.

"One at a time," Irene said, not impatiently. She took the screenshots and the relevant portion of the video, then she moved the footage on.

Timestamp 46:20 was the moment I took the bible from the podium. To my surprise, the camera lost connection at the moment I'd slipped the book into my pocket, meaning that my secret theft, if you could call it that, remained a secret. After buffering, the vision came back, and for a split second, there was a smudge barely visible, standing right in front of me, blocking Jules from view. I physically recoiled from the screen, a shaky breath exhaling from my lungs. That shape, that ill-defined, strange smudge, like a finger-print, was so close to me that we must have been touching.

Feeling wild eyed and terrified, I turned to Jules and she reciprocated my expression of horror.

"Did you see or feel anything?" I asked her.

"I wanted to get out of there," she replied. "And I felt sad. Very, very sad."

CHAPTER ELEVEN

I found myself stunned by what we saw on the footage. I knew that I would never forget the shape of that figure in the dormitory, or the smudged darkness of the shadow by the lectern. Yet it failed to change the course we were on, the unsteady hurtling towards disaster. Perhaps as I filter through everything that happened after, I'll be able to pinpoint the moment where I dismissed all of the fears those images incited in me.

After taking her screenshots, Irene called us into the refectory so that we could sit around the larger table and discuss what to do next. We were taking it seriously enough. There was the potential risk that a stranger had walked into the monastery to hide in those unused rooms.

"It's possible that the camera malfunctioned," Irene suggested. "It could be broken or the battery is running out."

She and Dan remained still, their features relaxed, whereas Jules pulled anxiously at a strand of hair and Nathan's knee kept jigging up and down, rattling the table.

"Okay, yeah, that's possible," Dan said. "If the issue is

Cath's body cam, the weird shape won't appear on the others. But to make sure we should check the footage from all of them."

Jules dropped her hair, her hands moving quickly as she spoke. "That's a good idea, but it'd take us hours to get through five different versions of the tour."

"Then we split it up." Irene shrugged. "We each take a different person's camera and check the footage for abnormalities."

"I don't know," Nathan said. "We should get the fuck out of here. There's a weirdo living in the empty wing of this building."

Irene sighed and tossed her hair over one shoulder. "We don't know that there's anyone there. Cath's camera could be faulty and picked up, I don't know, interference. It's an hour of video footage. If we all do it at the same time, we can have it done in an hour. We've all got our own laptops, yes?"

I was staring down at my fingers when I noticed that Irene was waiting for me to nod. I did, and we agreed to go back to our rooms and watch the tour. Jules and I swapped, which was good, because I wanted to see if her camera had caught the smudge in the church, too.

In my pocket, the weight of the bible pulled at my tunic top. *Sad. Very, very sad.* Was it possible that Jules had a psychic connection to the energy in this building? Or was she reacting to the morbid history of the place? All of my beliefs were beginning to be called into question. What we saw seemed to be actual evidence of... Of what? A shadow?

On the way to my room I forced my thoughts back to reality. This was the beginning of my illness, I could feel it, the way it worms itself into my thoughts and subtly changes them from rational to irrational. It pained me to dwell on the past, but I knew too well how paranoid and illogical I could become, and how difficult it could be to differentiate between reality and fantasy. Most of all I remembered *that voice* which had whispered in my ear all day and all night. Whispering like Nathan's night-time noises.

My nerves were getting to me, but I reminded myself I could counter them by not overreacting. The first step was watching Jules's video. I opened my laptop and was about to start the recording, when I decided to quickly check up on my private Facebook group for my readers. There I found a message from AliceAkarthis, who was simply Alice on here, and one of my oldest fans. Over the years she'd become a beta reader for me. We emailed a lot, and she moderated the Facebook group.

Alice: I think you should leave, Cath. I don't know if I believe in the ghosts or anything like that, but even I can see there's a bad vibe at that place. If it's not haunted then maybe there's an intruder. What if they want to hurt you? Remember the story you told? About the nuns inviting their sister in? What if she never left?

Cath: Guys, I'm okay. We're figuring out what's happening here in the monastery. Once we know for sure that this wasn't a camera malfunction, we'll decide what to do next. Alice, did you see anything on the other feeds?

Alice: Sorry, I don't know. I only watched yours. You had to pay extra to view the others.

Her comment set my teeth on edge. I hadn't realised the extent of Irene's monetisation of our event; that even switching to a different camera might mean a price hike to subscribers. I didn't want to believe Irene would be the orchestrator of such a money grab. Perhaps Loup had put pressure on her regarding the income. Whatever had happened, it made me view our retreat with a more cynical eye. Were all the gadgets gifted? Were we advertising everything in Sfântul Mihail? From the furniture, to the cameras, to the building itself, soon to become the next Airbnb that everyone wanted to rent?

Switching off from my paranoia, while recognising that it could be the lack of anti-psychotics in my bloodstream whipping up those outraged thoughts, I directed my attention to Jules's camera footage. The hour went by agonisingly slowly. I spent it hunched over my desk, eyes two inches from the screen, agitated fingers drumming against the keyboard. *What was I about to see?*

The answer was, very little. Jules's camera failed to pick up the figure in the dormitory and it cut out in the church at exactly the same moment mine did. But it seemed that mine had come back a few seconds earlier than hers, capturing that ill-formed, charcoal blur that I'd seen lingering between us. On Jules's recording there was nothing. Disappointment took hold of me and I closed the player and leant back in the chair.

To my alarm, I heard a voice: *You're not right in the head.*

"The others saw the shadows too," I said out loud.

You're the one who thinks it's a ghost. Aren't you?

"I don't believe in ghosts."

Are you sure about that?

My chair fell backward as I got to my feet. No. No, I won't accept *her* in my head, I won't have it. It's too soon for this. I've been without my medication for two days, that's all. How could *she* be back already?

And yet there she was, pitching a tent in my mind, settling in and getting comfortable, waiting for an opportunity to strike with the full force of her viciousness.

"No!" I shouted.

It was when I moved away from my desk that I saw it hovering outside my window, spying on me. A tiny dot barely visible in the night. It was one of the drones watching me, possibly filming me. I rushed closer, but it swung to the right, lifted higher, and merged with the dark sky.

In a panic, I ran out of my room and banged on Nathan's door. This had his grubby paw prints all over it and I was pissed off for a change. I wasn't going to let him terrorise me like this.

The door opened and he pushed his pale face through the gap between it and his room, hair dishevelled and eyes sleepy. He filled most of the space, but I could see his laptop open on his messy bed.

"Were you operating a drone just now?" I asked. Usually this kind of confrontation would make me want to shrivel away like a frightened hedgehog, but for once my body felt full of electrical sparks ready to ignite. I pushed my way into his room.

"Come in why don't you, Cath?" he said, rolling his eyes.

His room was chaotic. He hadn't bothered to unpack. Old boxer shorts and shirts mingled together in a pile next to his suitcase, where his unused clothes were folded, albeit in a shambolic fashion that he'd clearly rummaged through. There was a lingering sour smell in the air that I recognised from the changing rooms at school. Body odour. And yet the scent of sweet pine from the neighbouring forest breezed in. Nathan's window was open.

I faced him. "You never answered my question. Were you operating a drone?" Now that I was alone in a room with him, the sparks began to fizzle out, leaving me with a slightly deflated sense of bluster. All of that anger began to dissolve, flattening down to nothing, my hands beginning to shake.

"No. I was watching the video footage like Irene asked us to."

I gestured towards the window. "Why is that open?"

"I was hot."

"It's cold."

His eyes drifted towards the open window. If Nathan had been operating the drone, then surely the handheld remote would still be in his room, but all I saw on the windowsill was the remains of a joint. He'd been smoking weed. I should have noticed the way his eyelids hung low, as though they were too heavy to keep lifted.

"Here," Nathan said, the note of impatience in his voice slurred. "I'll show you the drone. It's right here on my desk still in its fucking box. Is that good enough for you Cathy? Does that fucking work for you?"

The fact that I was wrong sapped any of the remaining boldness from my body, draining the blood from my face at the same time. "Sorry. I... I'm sorry. I saw a drone outside my window."

He stroked the stubble on his chin. "It wasn't me. Don't tell Irene, okay? She warned me not to smoke while we're here. But that *thing* in the dormitory fucked me up. I needed to relax."

"It's okay, I get it." Which was the truth. And if I thought I could have smoked weed without it messing with my schizophrenia, I probably would have too. However, I didn't need extra paranoia on top of everything. "When I saw the window open, I jumped to conclusions."

Nathan brushed a few strands of his floppy hair out of his eyes and let out a long slow sigh. "Come on then."

I followed him as he walked out of the room, but I didn't understand what was happening. Confused, I lingered back until he beckoned for me to keep up.

"Let's go find the bloody thing then," he said.

"It'll be long gone now," I said.

"Not necessarily. It's after sunset and foggy. You can't see shit with those things in weather like this. If they got it back in one piece I'd be amazed. No doubt we'll find it in a broken heap because I doubt anyone here can fly for shit. Have you got your torch?"

"It's out of battery."

"That's okay, we can use mine."

Our footsteps echoed through the monastery as we traced our steps back to the kitchen. The place was quiet, with everyone in their rooms watching the footage of our tour. Nathan picked up his torch and took the key and opened the front door, leading me out into the gloom. There was low-hanging mist all around Sfântul Mihail, blocking out the mountains. It made the air moist, as if it had long stretching wet fingers reaching out to my bare neck.

It hit me in that moment. We were on a mountain, isolated, with weather that caused bad visibility, at a time when there might be a trespasser living with us.

"Shouldn't we just ask people first?" I suggested.

Nathan turned to me, switching his torch on at the same time. "Do you honestly think that the person driving a drone around the monastery, spying on us, is going to admit to it?" He shook his head. "No way. But there is something going on."

"Maybe it's the outsider?" I said.

"Maybe," he said, the torchlight catching the sharp angles of his face. He set off around the building, and soon became a pale figure in the dark.

CHAPTER TWELVE

S till in my tunic top and leggings, the biting cold nipped at any exposed skin, worming its way under my fingernails, seeping into the marrow of my bones. Despite being a couple of months away from snow, I could smell the approach of winter while we tip-toed around the edge of the monastery. Nathan led the way with his torch. I lagged behind until he stopped and waited for me to catch up.

"I've got nipples that could cut glass here," he grumbled, "and you're strolling around the place like we're going hiking."

"Sorry," I muttered. "It's this place... and what we saw earlier. What if we're attacked by that... *thing* we saw on the camera?"

I noticed Nathan's spine straighten. "That's pretty damn morbid, Cath, thanks." He sighed. "I shouldn't make decisions after a joint."

Despite our concerns, and despite Nathan's grumbling, we continued on through the darkness. I had to admit, I was beginning to change my opinion of Nathan. He didn't have to help me and yet he had, which meant my anxiety about being around him began to ebb away.

"This is the window to my room," I said, approaching a rounded triangle of amber gleaming through the glass. I'd left my interior light on and it emanated out, brightening the murky air around us. My heart pounded as I pressed myself closer to the wall and directed my gaze through the po-faced saint's depiction into the bedroom.

Nathan stepped closer so that we were side by side. "You can't see shit through this glass."

He was right. The opaque nature of the glass made it difficult to see. But not every part of the window was stained. The top third of the window was made up of regular, transparent glass, and I pointed at that section to show Nathan.

"It was through this portion that I saw the drone. It was directed right at me."

"I guess if you could see it, whoever was operating it could see you," Nathan said. "Why would they want to spy on you?"

I frowned. "I don't know. Maybe it was the same person who stole my medication."

"And my chocolate." Nathan let out a humourless laugh. "And you thought that was me."

Hearing him say those words made my stomach flip over. I'd guessed at the time that he knew my suspicions, but now that the suspicion had been voiced, it made me squirm in discomfort. Still, I managed to maintain eye-contact, hating the fact that I found myself making a stupid smiling face through the sheer uncomfortableness of confrontation.

"I... I didn't mean it like that. It was just that you'd been angry with me about the launch event and the ghost story and..."

Nathan held up a hand. "Whatever. None of it matters. I know I didn't take your pills so..." He shrugged. "But I'm not getting murdered by some freaky-deaky ghost stalker because of you. Let's find this bloody drone and get back inside where it's warm. I don't know about you, but I hope there's a cold bottle of leftover Moet because I want to get—"

Nathan rotated slowly, the torchlight moving with him. Through the hazy, yellow beam, I saw a dark column—at least, that was how it appeared for the split second it was in view—as shapeless as the thing we'd seen on the recording, tall enough to be human. Nathan's body jolted in shock along with my own amazement, and while he convulsed the torch slipped from his fingers, plunging us into the thick evening mist. We both fell to the ground at once, our fingers scrabbling for the small piece of plastic so necessary for our task. During those urgent moments, above the ragged noise of our breaths, I distinctly heard the sound of footsteps running away.

Finally, Nathan lifted the torch, fumbled with the switch while cursing under his breath, and managed to get the light back on. The silhouette was gone.

"Did you see it?" he whispered. "It was a person, wasn't it? A person."

I didn't answer because my voice had been stolen, perhaps by the cold air or the shock, I don't know. All I know is that I stood there unable to say a word. But if I had been able to speak, I would have said: *What kind of person has no face?*

WE CAME AWAY WITHOUT FINDING THE DRONE, BUT AFTER THE

shock of what we saw, neither of us wanted to stay out there. Our search had ended outside my window. The walk back to the front of the monastery was a swift one, finally injecting warmth back into my veins. Unfortunately, when we reached the door, we found it locked.

"Shit," Nathan said. "I left the key inside."

I stared at him in horror. "Why?"

He shrugged. "I put it back in the drawer. I guess it was instinct, I don't know. I'm high, all right."

"There are wolves out here," I said. "Not to mention rogue drone operators." I banged on the door. "Hello? Is anyone there? It's Cath and Nathan. Let us in."

Nathan joined in the banging, his fists hitting harder than mine and yet still eliciting a quiet, dull thud each time. The thick wood barely rattled no matter how hard we pounded it.

"We're like Sister Agatha," Nathan said. His eyes were so wide that the whites of them juxtaposed against the night.

"That was a made-up story," I said. "There was no Sister Agatha."

Nathan moved closer and roughly grabbed my shoulders. The sudden feel of his hands on my body made me flinch. He didn't notice. "That's not true. Sister Agatha is real."

At this point I began to worry that Nathan wasn't quite all there, especially considering the drugs and his evident fear.

"Nathan, no. It was a story I made up there and then. It's true that the nuns here died a long time ago, but I made up their names for the story."

His fingers dug deep into my shoulders. "No. I found the graveyard. I saw the stones. There was Sister Maria and Sister Agatha, though it was spelt differently. They were real people, Cath. They lived here, and they died here."

As his bulging eyes bored into mine, I had two competing responses, one was to run away from him, and the other was to laugh. It wasn't possible, surely, that I could accidentally guess the names of the real nuns. Maria, perhaps, it was a common name in many countries and had a religious connection. Agatha could be considered unusual for a Romanian setting. I'd said it because I had a memory of a famous fictional nun with the same name. It was one of those distant chimes that comes into the mind every now and then.

I shook my head. "You must be mistaken."

"I'm not, Cath. Go to the graveyard tomorrow. You'll see."

The door finally scraped open to reveal Dan in bare feet and shorts. "What are you doing out here?"

"Long story," Nathan said, barging his way back into the building.

I flashed Dan a guilty smile and followed through.

"Irene has set up a meeting in the kitchen. Did you guys watch the footage already?"

"Yes." I rubbed my arms vigorously, but it was like putting a scarf on a snowman.

"You okay?" Jules asked as we walked into the kitchen. "You look like..." She raised her hand over her mouth before she said it.

Nathan picked up the cue as he paced the length of the room. "What? Like we've seen a ghost? Yeah, we have. We saw one outside."

"We don't know that," I said, digging deep to find the rational within the irrational, no matter how much my para-noia screamed at me. "It could have been a person or a trick of the light." I walked over to the counter and picked up the kettle.

"It was a fucking ghost," Nathan continued. "It had no... no features. It was like this tall black blob." His hands gestured wildly, and even I felt a bit sorry for how desperate he came across. "Cath saw it too."

"I saw... I don't know what I saw," I said, filling the kettle with water. I placed it back in its base before flashing Nathan a sympathetic glance. "It didn't have much of a shape."

"Well, I heard footsteps," he continued.

"I did too," I admitted. "At least I'm pretty sure I did. It all happened so fast."

"You saw and heard something, but you don't know what it was?" Irene said. "That sounds familiar, no? It's what we've all been experiencing since we came. The figure on the recording, too. Sit down, Nathan, let's discuss this. And you, Cath."

"I thought I'd make us all a cup of tea," I said, pointing to the kettle as it began to boil.

"Fine, stay there then," she said, settling onto a stool around the breakfast bar, "whatever. Okay, did everyone watch the recordings of the tour?"

A chorus of yesses went around the room.

"And what did you see?"

The kettle boiled. I flipped the switch, opened the nearest cupboard and grabbed the mugs.

"Nothing," Dan said, going first. He was standing but with his forearms leaning against the counter. He leaned in Irene's direction. "I had yours, Irene. I swear I examined every second and the one weird thing that happened was the camera cutting out while we were in the church. Pretty sure it happened around the same time stamp as Cath's."

"I noticed this too," Irene said. "I was watching Nathan's camera, and it cut out in the church."

"I was watching Dan's," Nathan said. "I didn't see the figure, just the camera cutting out."

"I had Cath's," Jules said. "So I saw what we all saw. Like Dan I examined every second and I didn't notice anything new."

"Cath?" Irene prompted. "Did you watch Jules's camera?"

"I did." I took the first mug of tea to Nathan before passing the others around. "There wasn't a shape but the camera cut out."

Jules took a sip of her tea and added, "So, did the camera cut out for everyone?"

I nodded along with the others.

Irene sighed. "Then we have nothing to go on. We've seen nothing but shadows."

"Irene, all the cameras cut out *at the same time*," Nathan said. "Don't you think that's an unlikely coincidence? Maybe, just maybe, ghosts can interfere with electrical gadgets."

"In the movies," Irene said.

"Guys, I'm with Nathan on this one," Jules said. "I don't want to sound like a crystal healer or anything, but there is bad energy in this place. *Something* made our cameras cut out like that. Don't you think? If it isn't a ghost, what is it? Whatever it is, it scares me. And what we saw on Cath's camera scares me. There could be a stranger living with us in this building."

"I've spoken to Loup about what we've found," Irene said. "And we talked about a resolution. There is a food delivery coming tomorrow and I've asked for a police officer to come along with them and search the place. If the officer doesn't find anything, we stay, if he does, the person is arrested, and we finish The Event as planned. Either way, we stay. If anyone wants to leave, they forfeit the money they've earned so far."

"Hold on one fucking second," Nathan interrupted. "We lose our money? Isn't that illegal?"

She shrugged. "You signed a contract, Nathan. I suggest you read it first next time. Remain, engage, represent. Remember?" She nodded to the framed rules on the wall.

A heavy silence hung over us all. Nathan rubbed at his temples.

"All right," Jules said. "It's not like I can leave in this weather anyway. I'm gonna sleep on it."

"Me too," Dan said. "Thanks for the tea, Cath. I think I'm going to take some food back to my room and call it a night." He stood first and left the kitchen.

"Nathan," Irene said in a low, soothing voice. "You're on edge. Try to relax. Tomorrow will be better, I promise."

He shook his head, and for half a heartbeat I saw a much older person etched into his features, a changed man compared to the excitable boy who had arrived a mere forty-eight hours ago.

CHAPTER THIRTEEN

That night was not an easy one for any of us. Most of us didn't even eat, though I offered to whip up supper from the eggs and bacon we had leftover. Each one of us traipsed back to our rooms and locked our doors. I heard the sounds of the locks scraping, the clicks of them falling into place, and I realised that we had reached a lack of trust that might never recover. The thought made me uneasy, awakening the voice I kept locked deep inside me for ninety per cent of my conscious life.

You bring it all on yourself, she rasped.

I moved away from the door and said out loud to myself, "Tomorrow I'll have the medication I need, and you will be gone again."

I'll always be here. I'll always be with you, even if you use those chemicals to lock me away. Nothing you do will change it. I'll always be here.

"That's not true." A tension headache started to work its way through my skull, beginning with the front and radiating backward. "This is my illness. You're not real. I'm alone. I'm alone."

I sank onto the bed and leaned back, nestling into the pillows and closing my eyes. It was then that I fell into a troubled sleep, where I walked the length of the monastery, a cloud of pure terror hanging around me like that low-lying mist. The reddish-brown brick wall went by too quickly, as though I was in a car watching the scenery flash along. On and on I went until it opened out into the graveyard. Even in my dream I was aware of the fact that this was my first visit to where the nuns buried their dead. I saw grim-faced women digging holes for their fallen sisters. At the same time a string of competing thoughts told me that I'd been here before, that I knew what to expect, where to place my feet, and what to search for. Indeed, I walked straight up to a gravestone in the centre of the others, and slowly moved around it in order to see the epitaph.

It was old and unkempt. It leaned forward like a damaged spine, with lichen covering the sides, and water-marks at the base. A simple stone, with no embellishments, merely the smooth curve of the top edge, which I lightly ran my fingertips across, noticing the slightly damp texture from a recent rainfall. There was dew on the grass, too. The longer stems deposited their water onto the hem of my jeans, while the shorter stems clung to my trainers. I faced the front at last and read the inscription. For reasons I can't explain, it was in English.

They can no longer die; for they are like angels.
Beloved Sister. Daughter of Christ.
Maria Popescu Rests

Sister Maria. The woman from my story. I'd made up her name on the spot but Nathan had told me of how he'd seen her gravestone in the cemetery. I had clearly internalised his words for the next grave in my dream had inscribed on it, "Sister Agatha". I checked the dates, both were buried in 1946, which meant they were killed in the massacre along with the other nuns. I began reading the inscriptions for the others, all 1946. So many lives taken.

I found myself drawn back to Maria's grave. But this time, when I found her stone, there sat the white wolf, its teeth bared, its hackles raised. I backed away, all too aware of that mist of terror clinging to every part of my body. A pale hand gripped hold of my shoulder, but before I could turn my head to see who, or what, that hand belonged to, I was wrenched out of my slumber.

It was as if I'd been transported to another time. Part of me had expected to wake up in my room at home, in a bed I bought from a chain store, a television fixed to the wall, floral wallpaper and pale-pink carpet; instead I found myself back in the monastery, in itself jarring enough, but in addition, I found I was not alone.

My fingers clenched the bedsheets as I froze for several seconds. I could not tear my eyes away from the thin figure at the end of the bed. All I saw was a dark column, like the thing I'd seen outside the monastery. The figure moved towards me, reaching with a pale hand. I was convinced in that split second that the next sight would be of teeth, long and sharp resting on fat, red lips, but that is not what I saw.

"We invited the monster in. We invited it *in*."

My jaw dropped open, ready to scream, until I realised the person in my room was Nathan. He clutched my shoulders like he had outside the monastery, and as his fingernails dug in, his eyes became unglazed. I saw the fog lift. Slowly, Nathan understood where he was and what he was doing. He let me go, backed away and lifted a hand to his face.

"I'm so sorry," he said.

"It's okay," I tried to soothe. "I think you were sleep-walking."

"I haven't... This hasn't happened to me since I was a child. Cath, I'm so sorry." He rushed out of the room and I followed him, the night air cool against my flimsy pyjamas.

"It's okay," I said, but he was already rushing away.

The breeze from the open door brushed against my damp forehead. The nightmare, along with Nathan's sleep-walking, had brought me out in a cold sweat. I rubbed my eyes, trying to focus on what was real and what wasn't. My dream hadn't been real, but Nathan's odd behaviour was. The frightening tour of the monastery had obviously affected him more than he'd expressed. I decided to speak to him tomorrow to check he was okay. With that resolution made, I went to the door of my room, closed it, and locked it. As I heard the lock click into place, another realisation hit me: I'd locked my door before I went to sleep.

THERE WAS THE SOUND OF FOOTSTEPS WHEN I WOKE THE NEXT morning. Irene had made good on her promise, which meant delivery men and a police officer, or agent de poliție, were moving around the rooms. It was disconcerting to hear others in the monastery, but I was excited because it meant my replacement medication would have arrived, and I could finally get rid of my paranoid thoughts and the nagging voice in my head.

Even though the thought of seeing Nathan gave me butterflies, I made my way to the kitchen for breakfast. Irene was busy stocking the cupboards with chocolate and I hung close by at the counter to pass her goods from the boxes.

The radio was on with pop music filling the air, helping to alleviate the tension.

As I passed Irene packets of granola, Nathan walked in, saw me, filled a glass with water, and walked back out. Once the food was stored away, I sat down with Jules and ate a bowl of cereal.

Jules sipped on her coffee and bit into a slice of toast. "I had the worst dream," she said, chewing. "There was a white wolf below my window, howling and howling. When I walked to the front of the building it was there again, not letting me leave. The funny thing is, when I opened the door, it didn't come inside, as though it physically couldn't. Like a vampire."

"I had a nightmare, too," I said.

"What was yours about?"

But I didn't want to talk about the gravestones, or Nathan sleepwalking into my room. "A white wolf."

"You know, that's a real phenomena, people having the same dream. It's called shared dreaming." Jules put half of her toast down. "Probably because we're all feeling the bad energy here. Do you think the police will find anything or do you think we're all crazy?"

"I honestly don't know."

Irene interrupted. "I have a present for you, Cath, and it's going to make you very happy."

Two pill boxes flew towards me, giving me a mere second to react. I caught them clumsily before examining them.

"Medication for the... you know"—she made a face —"schizo-thing."

I turned the boxes over in my hands. "Are they what I asked for? I don't recognise any of the words on these boxes."

"Of course." Irene wafted a hand. "It's in Romanian but it's exactly what you asked for."

"Thank you," I said. Having my medication in my hands sent a wave of relief running through my body, already soothing the tense muscles I hadn't even noticed.

"And we have Nathan's chocolate, as well as milk, biscuits, fresh fish," Irene went on. "We're stocked up again. Today is a good day, no?"

From Jules's hardened expression and pursed lips, I could tell that she wasn't quite in agreement with Irene's statement. "We need to see if the police find any intruders before we jump to conclusions about what kind of day it is. Finding a vagrant on the property might put a damper on getting Nathan a chocolate bar."

Irene threw her hands up in the air. "Why are Americans so pessimistic?" And with that she left.

"Basic," Jules muttered. She sipped her coffee and calmed once Irene was gone. "I need to get out of this place, even for a few hours. Do you want to go for a walk?"

"Sure," I said. "I need to write this morning, but what about the afternoon?"

We agreed on two p.m. and then I left, not intending to go straight to my room, as I'd implied, but instead stopping at Nathan's. I found him pacing around with the door wide open. He was wearing a red dressing gown over a T-shirt and jogging bottoms. He was muttering to himself, but not like a person thinking aloud, more like a person talking to another person, pausing for a response. The sight of his waxy, pale skin made my blood run cold. I knocked gently on the open door.

"Nathan?"

He stopped dead in the centre of the room and rotated slowly on his heel.

"Hi," he said.

"Can I come in?"

"Okay." He took a step back and stiffly gestured for me to enter. Seeing this stilted version of him drew my attention to how different he was without the constant bluster and sarcasm.

"Are you all right?" I asked, hovering awkwardly near the door.

"Yeah, yeah. I'm cool." He scratched his head and his eyes glazed over.

"I wanted to ask you how you got into my room last night."

"What?"

"I locked it when I went to bed."

He frowned, rubbed his stubble and stared over my head for a moment. It was clear Nathan had lost interest, if I'd even had his focus to begin with.

"You sure?" he asked.

I glanced over my shoulder to see what he was staring at but saw nothing. "Pretty sure, yeah."

"Sorry, Cath. I don't know. I don't remember much about last night." He glanced down at my hands and saw the pill packets. "You got your medication?"

"Yeah."

"Cool. That's really good. Listen, I've got to play Fortnite for a few hours or my followers drop off, so I'll speak to you later, okay?"

I said goodbye and walked away, almost tripping over Dan on the way out. "Nathan was in your room last night?"

"Yeah, kind of, but it's not..." I smiled, trying to ease the uncomfortableness. "It's a long story."

"You said in there that your room was locked." Dan placed one hand in the pocket of his shorts and leaned his weight to the left. His eyebrows bunched together. "So he broke in? What the fuck? Do I need to get that cop?"

I wafted my hands to try and calm him. "No, don't do that. He was sleepwalking. I think I must have been mistaken about locking my door. It's a misunderstanding, that's all."

"Yeah?"

"Yeah."

Dan peered into Nathan's room, where he was now sitting at his desk, gunshot sounds blasting out. "All right then. See you later, Cath."

I lifted my hand to wave as he walked away, and then I headed to my room to check on the lock, because I knew I hadn't been mistaken. I'd locked that door.

AliceAkarthis: Nathan was in Cath's room at night! Was he creeping on her?

Cheezemonkeys: yeah that doesn't sound good...

Forkie: Get a fucking grip. He was sleepwalking it wasn't his fault.

AliceAkarthis: Her room WAS LOCKED. He broke in.

Forkie: ummm, can't you fucking hear? She said she might not have locked it.

Motherofcats: It does sound like a mistake.

AliceAkarthis: He's a perv. Pretty sure he broke in. He wasn't invited. It wasn't consensual.

Forkie: It WaSn'T cOnSeNsUaL. [laughingemoji]. Shut up feminist.

Gingerbreadman: None of you were there. Cath has forgiven him, maybe that should be enough for you.

Cheezemonkeys: Can't believe I'm saying this on the internet, but calm down you two. Nathan messed up but maybe let's not condemn him without knowing all the facts.

Lupo: Cath will be the first to die.

Forkie: LMAO @Lupo

AliceAkarthis: Reported

CHAPTER FOURTEEN

The sky was filled with glitter that afternoon. The sun's rays peeking through the clouds transformed every particle into a hanging star, and every leaf a falling sun. Beneath our feet we tread on a carpet of amber as we walked and chatted about the abnormalities we'd seen, the nightmares we'd had, and the lives we'd lived before coming to Butnari. Jules told me about her life in New York, the people she'd hired to help after her blog gained popularity, like the virtual assistant who'd stolen her passwords and siphoned money from her bank account.

"It left me closed up," she said. "I don't trust people now. She'd been my friend, you know? But that's what happens in this business. There was even a journo who took my content and published it on Buzzfeed without a credit."

"Did you get it taken down?"

She shrugged. "It wasn't worth the fight, so I rolled over and took it. I didn't have many followers at the time. There are times when it's not worth the energy, you know? I had a stalker for a while, too."

"Online?"

"Yeah. This guy slid into my DMs one day. The usual pervy bullshit. I'm sure you've had it too." She mimicked a sleazy accent. "'Hey bebe I like your eyes', that kind of thing. I told him where to go, blocked him, and then he kept making sock accounts and came back with creepy-ass comments. 'I dream of your smile' turned into 'answer me or I'll find where you live and cut your throat'." She shrugged. "It wasn't too bad until I started receiving letters."

"Jesus. What happened?"

"I told the police, got a restraining order, moved, and installed security cameras. God, this job is crazy, isn't it?"

"I've been pretty lucky with my followers. Most are friends."

Jules let out a *ha*. "Until they get too attached and then you find yourself looking over your shoulder at every turn. Sometimes I worry one of them will track us down here. Just turn up one night. Hell, maybe that's who the shadow is from the east wing."

We stopped for a breather and to view Sfântul Mihail sprawling out below. At that point we weren't far away from the field where I'd helped the wolf. Even though I knew it was rare to see wolves in the daytime, I still found myself on high alert, especially when dark clouds rolled over the sun, eradicating the last of the glitter from the sky.

"Do you think they'll find anyone?" Jules said, nodding towards the monastery.

"No."

Her chin angled in my direction and she regarded me with narrowed eyes, perhaps intrigued by why I seemed so sure of myself. "You don't?"

"No, I don't. I know that things have been strange for the last few days, but it's an old, badly lit building, and the night-vision setting on those cameras isn't the best. It could have picked anything up."

"You don't think it's a trespasser?"

"Where's the real evidence for it? There's been nothing but weird shapes on a night camera and a few strange noises."

"You don't even think it was a ghost?" she asked.

I shook my head, briefly considering the way that first glimpse of the shape had made me feel. A significant moment; an image I would never forget. All of that was true, but I'd begun to rationalise every crazy detail. It was a coping mechanism for me, one particularly helpful when I was feeling paranoid.

"What we saw on my camera scared the crap out of me, but I've started to think about it all in a different way. We're on edge, and our minds are on overdrive. Maybe my schizophrenia gives me an alternative view about what's actually going on. During my episodes, I heard things that weren't real and for a time it fucked me up." I laughed without humour. "I even thought I was being *haunted* at one point, which is ironic now. The thing is, it took me a long time to accept that it wasn't real, but I did. And once I accepted it, I suppose you could say that I learned to look at the world through a different lens. Before then I would've been open to the idea of ghosts. In fact, I was obsessed with them. I'd listen to every podcast I could find about the supernatural, wanting to hear people's stories and I believed every word. Until I started to hear that voice, and I realised that it's our minds that are haunted, not our lives."

"What do you mean?"

I rubbed the tops of my arms as fog rolled in from the mountain, trying not to dwell on the voice that had whispered its poison into my ears when my life was in turmoil and I was at my weakest.

"Our mind is made up of tiny electrical charges. It has a plasticity about it that means when we're growing up, it moulds into new shapes, and those electrical charges change along with it. There are so many ways that synapses can go wrong. A fever can lead to hallucinations. Our eyes have blind spots that are filled in by the mind, and not always accurately. Stress can change the way we process what we're seeing. Illness, too. I'm not saying that everyone who has a supernatural experience is mentally ill, but the fact is, we can't always trust what we see or feel."

"Thinking about it like that makes me feel cold all over." Jules let out a small laugh. "Or maybe it's the fog." She paused for a moment and I waited for her to speak again. "It takes the magic out of the world. If our thoughts are all electrical charges, where are our souls?"

It was in that moment, as I watched the mist wrap itself around Jules's slight body, that I knew I had to include those words in a book. Perhaps not the bit about the electrical charges, at least not in a medieval fantasy land like Arkathis. But all this time, I'd been waiting to figure out what my main character, Maya, wanted, and now I knew. She wanted to understand what it all meant. Where, or what, our souls were.

"What is it?" Jules asked.

"Nothing," I said, not confident in my ability to explain my epiphany. "Maybe we should go back and find out what's been going on."

"Yeah," Jules said with a sigh. "We can't hide out here forever. Plus, the fog's coming in thick and fast. I can barely see the monastery anymore."

There were moments on the way down when we had to

hold hands to stop ourselves tripping over stones. As we walked to lower ground, the mist obscured our vision. It was exactly like the night before when Nathan had helped me search for the drone. I half-expected to hear the phantom footsteps from that night. The thought kept clawing at my stomach. Eyes in the dark. Being watched. Unless... unless it was in my mind. We'd never found a trace of the drone after all.

My strong, rational assertion that ghosts didn't exist wavered as we approached the monastery. Both Nathan and I had seen the shadow and heard the footsteps. No, that was what we thought, not what we *knew*. Nevertheless, my mind pulled me back and forth. Was it time for me to stop rationalising everything and accept that there were supernatural occurrences here? Or was it still important to remember how my mental illness could twist so many things and make them seem beyond what they truly were.

It was all real. All of it. I'm real and I'm never leaving you.

The sound of her voice in my mind made me inhale sharply.

Jules glanced across at me with a question on her expression. "You okay?"

"Yeah," I lied. "Stood on a stone."

Because of the fog, we ended up approaching the monastery from the back of the church. Somewhere along the way we'd drifted from the path, but once we saw the graveyard, we knew we were close. The sight of those leaning slabs of stone took my mind back to my nightmare, and a creeping sensation tip-toed across my skin. I remembered the way the terror of my dream had spread over my body, like walking neck deep into cold fluid, like water but thicker, heavier. That weight came back, clinging to my bones.

Yet I still found myself heading over to the graves, intrigued by the promise of those names. My heartbeat quickened. I thought of Nathan's pale fingers gripping my shoulders, and the earnest expression on his face. Would the epitaphs match those in my dream, and along with it, the story I told on our second night here? We were facing the backs of the tombstones, which meant I had to walk among the graves to find what I anticipated would be there. I shivered as we tread over the patchy grass, letting out my breath with a trailing vapour that hung there among the mist before vanishing.

"What is it?" Jules asked, perhaps sensing my fear.

Once we were in the centre of the old graveyard, I pivoted slowly until I faced the stones. There was one near to us with its slab leaning forward, pushed over by time, marked by weather, lichen growing over the curved edge. The first name I read was Sister Maria Popescu.

Now, it has to be acknowledged that Maria Popescu is one of the most common names in Romania. Before coming to the Carpathian region I did some research and it's possible that I internalised the name, and thus it happened to be the name I reached for when I made up the ghost story on the spot. Additionally, the shape of the grave, the watermarks, the way it leaned, were all typical of old graves that had not been tended to after the person's death.

But what I can't explain is how I guessed the names of two other nuns: Sister Elena, written on the stones as Sister Elena Kowalski, and Sister Agatha, or Agafya Baranov. Two nuns of different nationalities who also died in 1946. I checked when I got to my room and Agafya is the Russian form of Agatha. There was no way I could have also internalised those names, was there?

The inscription on Maria's grave was in Romanian. I took a picture of it with my phone, and ran that picture through a translation app. The words were exactly the same as in my dream.

While waiting for Irene to brief us all on what the police officer found, I decided to upload my recordings from the body cam I wore on the walk with Jules. It wasn't worthy of VIP access material, but I wasn't comfortable with following through on that promise to Irene anyway. When it was done, I opened up my readers' Facebook group to chat.

Cath: New vid up. I'm 15k into the next Akarthis story. I should finish it tomorrow. [kissemoji]

Alice: Cath, the guys watching you at the monastery overheard you talking to Dan in the hallway. Did Nathan go in your room??

Cath: You guys heard that? He was sleepwalking. It's NBD.

Alice: You sure? It seems kinda stalkerish. What if he took your pills?

Cath: I don't think that was him…

Alice: Then who was it?

SaraB: You need to stay safe there, Cath. Those other people are energy vampires. They're using you for likes and views. ESPECIALLY Nathan.

Nicky: Sara's right. You're being too nice, Cath. I don't trust Jules.

Cath: Are you guys all subscribers?

Alice: Of course we are!

Nicky: How could we not support you?

Cath: You're all so sweet. I'm fine, I swear. There've been a few weird coincidences and strange things going on, but I think it's mass hysteria or hallucination or something.

Alice: We saw the shadow too.

Nicky: The place is legit haunted.

Beth: THE GRAVESTONES!

MikeS: Have you guys watched the video? Cath's story mentioned the same names on the gravestones! Sister Maria and Sister Elena. WTAF?

Alice: There's a bad vibe going on there, hon. I know this is a living for you, but you should go home.

Sam: Maria and Elena are common names in that part of the world. Just sayin'.

Cath: Unless the police find evidence that convinces me to go, I think I'm going to stay. Nathan, Jules, Irene and Dan aren't as bad as you think. They're all decent people, I'm sure of it.

Alice: Hmmmm......

Cath: Listen, I'm thinking about doing another sponsored 10,000 word writing day. You guys up for it? I'll run polls and see what you want Maya to do next. Whatever I write I'll email directly to you guys so you're not paying twice. What do you think?

A knock on the door pulled me away from the laptop screen.

Irene pushed her head through a narrow gap between the door and the wall. "Cath? We're having a meeting in the refectory."

"Did the police find anything?"

"That's what we're going to discuss."

CHAPTER FIFTEEN

"The police didn't find anything." Irene got straight to the point, barely waiting for us to sit down in our chairs. "And if you don't believe me, ask Dan. He walked around with the officer for most of it, and they found nothing. Not even any evidence of an intruder, like old food packets or somewhere to sleep."

"What about our missing items? Cath's pills, my chocolate?" Nathan asked.

"We didn't see any sign of them," Dan said. "No empty pill packets, no chocolate wrapper."

"Hold on a moment," Jules said. "None of that means we didn't see a person on the recording. There could've been an intruder who left, taking the evidence with him. What if there's a rando coming in through some hole or secret passageway to spy on us? Like, some pervert who wants to see us naked. Did you show the police the cam footage? Did they see what was recorded on Cath's camera?"

"They did." The corner of Irene's mouth lifted. "I sat down with him and went through every single frame. Look, it wasn't so bad on the second viewing and I believe it may have been a regular old technology malfunction. All the cameras cut out when we were in the church. Obviously, the batteries were beginning to fail."

Out of the corner of my eye, I saw Nathan shake his head, but it was Jules who reacted. "Are you kidding? We all agreed it was a person."

"I dunno, Jules," Dan said. "I watched it again and, honestly, I think we were all on edge after the creepy tour in the dark. And then the viewers told us about this ghostly apparition, which made us biased about what we were seeing. Watching it again, there's just a dark blob. It was probably a trick of the light."

Jules frowned and folded her arms across her chest, sharp brown eyes focused on Irene. "Are you covering up anything, Irene?" She kept her voice low, accusing. "Is there something you're not telling us in order to keep us here?"

At first Irene remained motionless, calm even, until her eyes widened, and her hands flew out towards us. She muttered in French, and then said to Jules, "How dare you! I did everything you wanted. I had the police come, watch the footage, search the monastery. There is no one here. The place is safe."

Jules's frown deepened but she remained silent.

"If you want to go, go!" Irene gestured wildly towards the door.

"I want to get paid like everyone else here," Jules said. "Unlike most of you, I actually need the money."

"Good for you," Irene mocked. "Poor Jules. Poor little Jules needs money. Well, unless you've been through cancer you don't know suffering. Disease is... it's the worst thing in the world. Money matters less after you've been through what *I* have been through."

"Oh, right. *That's* why you created your make-up line,

because money doesn't matter to you. Got it." Jules stood, her chair scraping back against the tiles, and walked through to the kitchen.

"Are you leaving?" Irene shouted as Jules's shape melted away.

"No," she called back.

"Fucking drama queen," Irene said.

"Maybe I should check she's okay," I said, beginning to stand.

"Wait." Irene held up a hand, freezing me in place. "We missed our late-night shift last night. I amended the schedule and, Nathan, it's your turn tonight."

Next to me, Nathan's body went rigid and I heard him inhale sharply. He didn't say anything, though, simply rubbed his eyes.

"We should all be together this evening. Let's meet in the snug. Maybe we can talk this through with the viewers." Irene's eyes fixed on mine. "I don't know what you and Jules did today, but the comments are all about you two. What does shipping mean?"

Dan answered. "It's when fans want two people to get together. Romantically."

"*Ohh!*" Irene leaned across the table and took my hand. "You're gay? Why didn't you say?"

I pulled my hand away and tucked it under the table. "I'm not gay."

She raised her eyebrows. "Okay, well, whatever. I promised my fans a make-up tutorial and I'm going to do it. As a special treat, there will be party food in the snug tonight. Oh, and you all need to use those drones for some-thing cool. The company that gifted them wants to see as much footage recorded by them as possible."

The others began to leave, but I knew I needed to ask the

question that had been on my mind all day. I cleared my throat, but they ignored me; I waved, they ignored me; finally, I asked loudly, "Was anyone using a drone last night? There was one outside my window."

Dan shook his head on his way out. Irene mumbled a no before checking her phone. Nathan shrugged.

"You know it wasn't me," he said.

One by one we made our way out of the refectory. I listened to the rustling of the cherry tree and our footsteps clacking on the flagstones. There was an iron fist over my heart. The meeting had left a sour taste in my mouth, particularly the way Irene had spoken to Jules.

There was movement to my right. When I turned my head, I noticed Irene and Nathan walking along the cloister garth together. Nathan's voice travelled to where I was standing outside my door.

"Shouldn't we have been paid by now? It's been nearly a week. I was led to believe that the donations would filter into our bank accounts right away."

"I'll raise it with Loup," Irene said. "I'm sure it's nothing to worry about."

"You're way too lenient with them. Rene. This shit needs to be sorted out. Otherwise you're the one who's going to get it in the neck."

The two of them walked away, and I decided to check on Jules. I stepped away from my door and walked back towards the snug. Jules had brought a name sign to hang over the handle. It was purple, with yellow stripes along the J. I knocked softly on her door and waited. After a moment, she opened it but didn't invite me in.

"We're all supposed to meet in the snug later to provide quality content for the subscribers." I rolled my eyes. "We need to perform for our audience again."

Her impassive face failed to recognise the jokey eye-roll. "Thanks for letting me know." She nodded and was about to close the door, but I persisted.

"Are you all right? You seemed upset at the meeting."

Jules stretched her lips into a smile that didn't meet her eyes. "I'm fine. I mean, I'm going to stay, but I don't feel good about it." She paused and I sensed she was holding back. "You know in the movies when the teenagers continue to camp in the woods even though weird things are happening? And you know how you watch those movies and scream at them to get out?"

"Yes."

"What if we're the kids in the woods? We've been warned. We saw the ghost, and don't try to tell me otherwise, it was a fucking ghost. We *saw* it."

"Jules—" I started.

She shook her head. "No, don't say it. You have to believe it's real. You're more haunted than anyone. It was your camera that picked up the shape in the dormitory."

"The thing is," I said, "when we watch those movies, we know the kids are being haunted and we know the ghost is real because it's a movie. But this isn't. It's real life. We don't know for sure. It could all be smoke and mirrors."

"How?"

"Coincidence, hypersensitivity, the heaviness of history affecting our judgement. Do you think if we hadn't heard the building was cursed that we'd be this afraid?"

She ignored my question, and softly uttered, "I hope you're right, Cath," as she closed the door. "I hope you're right."

As I went back to my room to write, her words were never far from my thoughts.

THAT NIGHT, WE PLAYED MUSIC SO LOUD IT SHOOK THE BATS out of the belfry and drifted up to the top of the mountain. The snug vibrated with energy as everyone else let off steam, eating and drinking to excess, while I shivered in the corner of the room, unsure and forgotten.

Nathan was back to his old self, removing clothing for donations, calling himself a cam girl and Irene his glamorous assistant. There was so much dancing that one of the sofa cushions split under the weight of Irene's high-heeled boots. Dan pulled out the feathers and they belly danced beneath floating wings.

Jules drank with a frown on her face, sinking deeper and deeper into the sofa. She was sullen and quiet, not the Jules I'd come to think of as a friend. But I understood that her thoughts had grown dark. The sight of her so blue twisted up my gut.

I wanted to fix everything that had gone wrong in the monastery, but I saw no solution. For most of my life, I'd tried to fix things, especially for other people. If a button needed sewing back in place, I'd do it, if someone was cold, I'd lend them my coat.

But there were difficulties that required more than making someone a cup of tea or sewing on a button. Most of my life had fallen underneath the umbrella of one of those challenges, and I'd consistently failed to see a way out. Now, here I was, unable to see a solution to a problem—a person —in need of fixing. Here I was again, seeing someone I cared for alone and upset, unable to help them.

"Would you like a hot drink and a chat in the kitchen?" I gestured towards the others. "I don't think they'll even realise we're gone."

"We're supposed to be here providing *content*," she said bitterly.

"Well, maybe we can provide our own version of it," I said, scooping up one of the laptops. "Come on."

Back in the kitchen, Jules sat on a stool with a bottle of beer, while I placed the laptop down. I quickly set up the coffee machine, thinking that coffee might be better for Jules, and then I typed a message into the message board.

This is Jules and Cath! We will answer all your questions!

AliceAkarthis: Hi Cath! When's the next Akarthis story?
Cath: I finished it today. I'll read over it and publish it tomorrow, and then we can do the 10k challenge.
AliceAkarthis: YAY!
Cheezemonkeys: Seen any more ghosts?
Cath: No. We think it was a shadow after all.
Lu98: What do you guys think of the others.

Jules snatched the computer and spun it around.

Jules: Nathan is a prick. Irene is really into money. Dan is shallow. Cath is naïve.

I sat there staring at her message. The replies began to flood in.

Lu98: Ok wow. NGL, I think I like you less now.
Jules: Do I give a crap?
Lu98: Yeah, probably, you just replied.
Momofsix: looooool. You asked her to spill the tea.
Cheezemonkeys: She's not wrong through. They are all those things.

Lu98: Cath, how do you feel about that?

"How do you feel, Cath?" Jules laid her cynical, narrowed eyes on me.

I moved the laptop closer and typed my reply.

Cath: I'm not as naïve as everyone thinks I am. I'm not the things people keep suggesting. No one here knows me.

AliceAkarthis: Stay safe, Cath. None of these people are your friend. #fuckjuleschen

Farkas: Irene is a narcissist, Nathan is an attention seeker, Dan is an insecure frat boy, Jules is lying to everyone, and Cath is going to die.

CHAPTER SIXTEEN

I'd slammed the laptop closed after that. It marked the end of the night for me and elicited within a deep embarrassment about who I was as a person. And yet, I still cleared away the mess in the kitchen while Jules took her cup of coffee back to her room, silently, her head bowed, and her shoulders slumped. I think she recognised how her actions had marred the friendship we'd built. Her words had been like a sharp implement against a swatch of fabric, tearing through layers of woven threads. Perhaps it sounds silly to talk in that way, because we hardly knew each other, but she'd always been my ally at the monastery, and it saddened me to see what she truly thought of me.

There were squeals of joy coming from the snug. The pop music drowned out the sound of the dishwasher. A door opened and Nathan staggered in, his face a queasy shade of grey. I was about to ask him if he was all right, when he leaned over and vomited onto the tiles, it flowing into the cracks, a vile sour stench filling the room. My stomach churned, but I stood there silently, watching. He lifted his head and wiped his mouth, eyes distant, as though he didn't even know what was happening.

"Are you okay—"

He put a finger to his lips. "It's okay, Rene, I won't tell anyone."

"Tell anyone what?" I asked.

"You know," he said, and winked. With that, he walked out of the room.

Quietly, I followed him, but as I walked past the snug, I peeped in on the others for a moment. Irene was sitting on Dan's lap, their heads together, noses touching. She leaned even closer, her lips closing over his, and Dan's hand slipped up her dress. I promptly walked away. Nathan was nowhere to be seen, probably back in his room. I thought about reminding him he was supposed to be talking to subscribers tonight, but then I decided he was too inebriated anyway.

By the time I'd cleaned up Nathan's vomit, Irene and Dan were gone. The snug was a mess, with feathers, spilled alcohol and party food strewn all over the floor. I closed my eyes and leaned against the wall.

This is all you're good for, she said. That voice again. *This is who you are. You're the person who cleans up the mess that other people make. This is all you have to contribute.*

"No," I said out loud. "It's not like that."

Keep lying to yourself, see if I care.

"I'm not lying."

Oh, sure! You're not lying. Good one, Catherine.

"That isn't who I am," I said, as I bent down to pick up the debris. A plastic bag rustled as I snatched it from the floor and threw it into a bin liner. "I can't control them, but I can control me. They might be messy, that's their choice. It's *my* choice to be otherwise." Bottles and cans jangled together. The feathers tickled my palms. "Everyone thinks I'm naïve. Everyone thinks I'm innocent. They're wrong."

Yes, they are.

"And you can shut up! Shut up!" I dropped the bin liner to the floor, my heart racing. Every nerve drawn tightly, and tightening still, like the twisting of a violin tuner. I put my head in my hands and leaned forward. "You're not real, you're in my head because I had a break from my meds. You're not real. You're not real."

It took a while, but the voice stopped.

I DIDN'T GO TO BED THAT NIGHT, INSTEAD I TOOK MY LAPTOP to the refectory table and worked on the next Akarthis story. Keystrokes echoed in the long room. There was the faint odour of Nathan's vomit filtering in from the kitchen, mingling with the wood and stone earthiness in the room. As I was writing about Maya discovering that her twin brother Stefan had betrayed her for the Sword of Light, I found myself distracted by the messages on the live stream.

Forkie: K, so… Cath's a nutjob.
Reneee: Who cares about Cath? Irene and Dan are probably going at it right now.
FuckJobert: Irene Jobert needs to respond to my messages. I have an ISSUE with her make-up.
AliceAkarthis: [heartemoji] Take care Cath.
RuRu: Nutjob is such an offensive term.
Luce99: Dan, how could you?
Cheezemonkeys: Who u talking to, Cath?

On and on they went. Nathan was supposed to be

communicating with these people but instead he'd thrown up on the floor and left. It was me, here, alone, with thousands of judgemental people who had seen me having a psychotic moment. I wanted to leave. I was close to quitting then and there, but I didn't, I closed the chat screen and wrote a battle scene where Maya stabbed her twin with the Sword of Light.

At five a.m., I uploaded the story. In the distance, there was a feeble howl. The music had stopped by then. There were no other sounds at all. No movement in the monastery. After everything that had happened, I should've been on edge, but I had a few rare moments of peace as I placed my cheek on the teak tabletop and drifted off to sleep. There were no dreams that night, merely the cool surface of the wood.

A hand on my shoulder woke me. The air was richly scented with coffee, then a mug was placed down on the table next to my sleepy head.

"I owe you an apology," Jules said, standing above me in her dungarees. She'd showered, dressed and brushed her hair.

My neck muscles complained when I sat up straight. There were aches and pains in my entire body after sleeping at such an unnatural angle. I couldn't find a response, so I sipped on my coffee instead, craving the caffeine, but wincing at the bitterness.

"God, weren't you scared to stay up on your own last night?" Jules said, her eyes drifting around the room. "I couldn't have."

"It was fine," I said.

She shifted from one foot to the other, a hand placed in her dungarees pocket. "I'm sorry about last night. There's a lot going on and I acted like an asshole. But there's no excuse for it so I want to say I apologise, I'm an idiot, and I hope you can forgive me."

"If you put a teaspoon of sugar in this coffee, I'll think about it."

"I didn't mean it, you know," she said, wandering through the open archway to the kitchen. I heard her moving around, opening a drawer, then a cupboard. She re-emerged a moment later with the sugar.

"Yes, you did," I replied. "I guess there are worse things to be called."

I noticed her mouth move from one side to the other as she contemplated an answer. "I should explain, then. I don't think you're a naïve person, not after our conversation yesterday. There's a very shrewd person inside of you who gives great advice." She sat down opposite me and paused to open the sugar cannister. "But I think you're naïve if you believe you can be this kind to these people and expect anything in return. I know what it's like to be screwed by a friend. My assistant knew everything about me, and she used it all to her advantage. I see you doing everyone a kindness, like making cups of tea and cleaning up after the others, but I think it's stopping them from respecting you." She leaned across the table and stirred a teaspoon of sugar into my coffee.

There was a moment of silence, as her words hung between us, where I realised that I agreed with her, but I didn't care. I held her brown eyes with my own. "I know."

"You do?"

"Yeah, and it's okay."

"But they'll take advantage of you."

I shrugged.

"You don't care?"

"No."

"Why?"

"Because I need to atone."

Jules reacted by pulling her head back, like an animal recoiling from a bad smell. Not repulsed, simply befuddled. "I don't understand."

Before I could say anything else, Irene stepped in, grinning from ear to ear, her silk dressing gown floating behind her. She was humming under her breath and carrying a croissant on a side plate.

"Bonjour," she said, her eyes glistening. Still humming, she disappeared out of the refectory. I heard the tap run and then her humming faded away as she headed back to her room.

Jules raised her eyebrows. "Wow. That bitch got laid."

THE STORY I'D POSTED AT FIVE A.M., AFTER A TENSE EVENING, had been lambasted with terrible reviews. I'd watched in dismay as my review average plummeted and one star after one star filtered in. *How could you kill Stefan? You made Maya a killer? Fuck you, C. B. Finn. Wow, guess I hate Maya now. So stupid. Trash. I'm never reading C. B. Finn again, she's a garbage human being.*

I told myself, as I read them, that it was water flowing over a stone. Then I went for a walk up the mountains with a steak packed in my bag. The young wolf was out there alone without his mother, and he needed to eat. Perhaps he was so close to the monastery last night because he was hungry. There were no sightings of the wolves, or anything else for that matter. I felt alone, truly alone, without the sensation of being watched. I left the steak behind a rock and hoped that the white wolf didn't get to it first.

The party had done what it needed to do. It had cleared out the tension and paved the way for a new start. After that morning, the group fell into a routine, albeit one marred by my private troubles.

It was Irene who mentioned the missing steak that first night after the party, but when no one explained it she didn't press. Dan had a protein shake for dinner anyway, which meant the rest of us still got to eat our slabs of meat with garlic butter that Irene made herself. Nathan made a joke about vampires, we all laughed politely, and the whole day disappeared into one of those mediocre moments often forgotten.

We had more of those kinds of days. I completed my sponsored 10k write-athon with aching wrists and a fuzzy brain. The exhaustion kept *her* out of my head, which was good. Dan and Jules both took their night shifts entertaining the international followers, neither of them noting anything strange or noticing any unpleasantness on the chat screen. Irene facetimed with her mum a few times, doing Q&A sessions with the subscribers. Irene's mum was almost as famous as she was, because of a viral photograph of Irene going through her chemotherapy. It was strange seeing an older, coarser, bleached-out version of Irene.

Nathan's joking voice and loud video games could be heard through his wall. He didn't sleepwalk into my room those nights. Aside from the steak, nothing went missing. The weather was pleasant, if a bit cold, and reflected light woke me each morning.

We went into our second week as babes, coddled by the good fortune we saw for ourselves. We were young. We were alone without the pressures of society on our backs. We were being paid for the things we loved to do. We were all so, so wrong.

CHAPTER SEVENTEEN

Our second week at Sfântul Mihail began with yet another meeting, but this time away from the cameras. No one in the house had received any of the patron donations from viewers, and Nathan was getting antsy, threatening to leave.

We went to the church for the meeting, shivering in the draughty space. Jules was wearing my hoody, but I didn't mind. I had on a thick jumper with sleeves that reached my fingertips. It felt good to hide myself away from the others. It was fair to say that I'd been quiet over the last few days, keeping myself to myself, writing in my room in an attempt to repair the damage caused by my last Akarthis story. Irene even pulled me aside to note the dip in my patron money.

I'd been nervous to go back to the church, in fact we'd all expressed concerns about it, but once we were there, we soon got down to business, and the conversation about money stripped the mystique from the place. There's nothing like a financial analysis to make even the most mysterious locations feel boring.

Nathan paced the space, his trainers crumbling bits of broken plaster underfoot. There were broken frescos all around us, the faces of saints glaring down at us from heaven. "What I want to know," he said, "is who the fuck is Loup? You've told us jack shit, Irene."

"They're an investment company," Irene said with a shrug. Frustrated, and muttering to herself in French, she opened her laptop and typed furiously into the search bar on the Google page. "That's the website, if you'd bothered to actually do your research."

"I did," he said. "The website is practically empty. No contact details, no 'about' section, nothing. A stock image of an office and a vague description about investments."

"Let me see for a minute." Jules reached out for the laptop. "This is kinda weird. Did you meet with them?"

Irene nodded. "I met with the CEO and he asked me to keep his identity anonymous and promised me that they'd be in the background helping out. He set up the renovation and funded everything. His systems are organising the payments. That's it. Everything else is about us."

"But you always have to check in with them," Jules said. "It feels like Loup is running the show, not you, Irene. Their logo is on the wall in the kitchen!"

"Because they paid for the kitchen!" Irene snapped.

"Let's all calm down." Dan lifted his hands and slowly lowered them towards the floor. He was lounging on one of the pews, wearing shorts over running tights. "Everything has been organised well so far, right? I mean, the electricity and running water, the Wi-Fi. They've already put in a ton of money in upfront. They aren't trying to scam anyone here."

"They want this to work," Irene said. "Think about it. If

we leave, this fails. If they don't pay us, we leave. You forget I'm a participant, too, and I want to get paid as well."

"Three days," Nathan said. "If I don't have my money in three days, I'm going."

Irene shrugged. "Then so be it."

Everyone was so concerned about the money that no one flinched as we sat in the older wing of the monastery. It was almost as though the abnormalities picked up by my camera had never existed. Even Jules seemed distracted. She frowned and was distant, but she no longer brought up bad vibes like she had during our tour. Instead, her expression was determined, fixed on a task I knew nothing about.

———

IT TOOK ME A WHILE TO MUSTER THE COURAGE TO GO BACK TO my reader's Facebook group after the disaster that was my last Arkathis story. But I finally decided to face the music.

Cath here, wanted to stop in and say hi. Hope you're enjoying the live stream from Romania.

My heart was pounding. What if they threw me out of my own group and never bought one of my books ever again? Worse, what if they decided my story was so offensive that they'd spread the word, take me down on Twitter, and destroy everything I'd built as a writer?

The messages began to filter in.

Why did Maya do that? Stefan could have been redeemed! Never thought I'd read such lazy writing from you.

I quickly typed:

Guys, Maya had to make a difficult choice, but it was for the story. She can't always be good!

I hated it.
Maya's an unredeemable bitch now.
She's a full-on murderer.
Why didn't you ask us what we wanted?

I responded:

I can't ask you every time. I need to be able to make creative decisions on my own, otherwise I won't want to write ever again.

It sucked, Cath.
Cath sucks, lol.
If those are the kind of stories you want to write, I'm out. I'm done.

I leaned away from the computer, reeling. A flush of heat wormed its way up to my neck and a flash of anger took hold of me.

I've danced for you all too many times. If you want to leave, go right ahead.

WTF? I've bought every Akarthis story, and THIS is how you repay your loyal fans?
Nice to see how much you care about your readers, NOT.

Every part of my body tingled. I knew I should stop, but I couldn't.

I owe you all, NOTHING.

YES YOU FUCKING DO! WE ARE YOUR READERS! WE'VE
BEEN HERE FOR YOU.

The final blow:

Either buy my books, or don't. This is over.

It'd been worse than I'd imagined. It'd severed everything, and it was all my fault. The wound was deeper than I
could've anticipated, because it meant that I was finally
alone, completely and utterly, in life and in my work.

Those people, Alice and my other first readers, had been
like family. The first people I talked to in the morning, often
the last at night. There was no one else to like my
photographs on Instagram, or comment on my posts on
Facebook.

Nothing meant more to me than Arkathis.

Not school.

Not family.

Not friends.

Because none of those things had truly existed for me.
I'd never been popular among people my own age, always
too quiet and serious. I'd never had much of a family, just
me and Mum. University had been a string of lectures with
the eyes of my peers watching me warily, never wanting to
get to know me. But my stories, my words and my readers
had been my life. How could one story, a mere twenty thousand words, bring it all crashing down? Had they always
been so fickle? Did I owe them? If I did, *what* did I owe
them? Or did they owe *me*? I pushed the laptop away and
tried not to cry.

Can I come back now? she said in my mind.

Even though I knew it wasn't real, I conceded. It was time.

———

IT'D BEEN A SHAKY START TO THE WEEK, FROM THE MONEY issues, to the dissolution of my reader group, to the tension between me and Jules. There was no desire in me to write Arkathis stories, so instead I started reading a book about Romanian fairy tales. I found them dark and disturbing. Many featured beautiful young women punished for not being good wives and bending to their older husband's will, or crones never able to have children, or enchanted animals and dark witches.

Those old stories made the sweeping forest around the monastery an ever darker, dangerous place. It made me feel impossibly alone out here among the shadows and wolves.

My mind was fractured. It took all of my willpower to force myself through each story. As I read each word, I noticed an itch at the back of my mind. That nagging voice reminding me that I was alone, and that it was all my fault. Rather than fighting my schizophrenia, I leaned into it, believing every word. I took my medication in the morning like a good patient, yet I'd lost hope that the voice was going to leave. No one came to my door to demand I gave subscribers additional content.

I decided to open the bible I'd taken from the church. The one I'd hidden from the others. I'm not sure why it took me so long to examine the pages within. Perhaps because it felt like stealing when I'd placed the book in my pocket, or because the Romanian language meant nothing to me. Either way, it was the first time I'd cracked the spine since standing by the lectern I'd removed it from.

It occurred to me that I could use the translation app on my phone to read the notes that had been written in the margins. I almost slapped my forehead out of frustration. Why hadn't I thought of that any sooner? I grabbed my phone from the bedside table, settled into my pillows, and found the app. Then I took the bible and began flicking through the pages. I took photographs of the scribbled notes, working as quickly as I could, keen to discover more. I'm not sure why I was suddenly so eager, the massacre of the nuns had intrigued me from the beginning, but I hadn't been obsessed with it before now.

My fingertips drummed the duvet as I waited for the app to translate the messages, but, finally, when the results came back, my shoulders slumped. Most of the notes had been scribbled in such a chaotic hand that the app failed. It had translated half of the words, but it was almost impossible to work out any real meaning.

-- *invited --- ------ in*

Mother ---- save --- -----.

Our Father --- ------ --.

Remember what that boy said to you in the dark? We invited them in.

She had a point. Nathan had ranted about us inviting something into the monastery, but I didn't know what he'd meant then, and I failed to see a connection now.

I skipped through the page, skimming them by eye to see if anything jumped out to me. There were several pages missing towards the end, which I thought was odd. Then I noticed the name written on the inside flap of the back cover: Maria Popescu.

CHAPTER EIGHTEEN

I t was my turn to talk to subscribers that night, but I wasn't alone for a change. Jules had decided to join me, and we were streaming a slasher movie called *Massacre on Dread Street* chosen by the patrons. Several of our reactions to the gore had already been made into GIFs.

Jules squirmed as blood splattered the camera and a blonde woman in her underwear pleaded with the killer. The effects were low budget, which made it gritty and authentic.

"You've not been around much recently," she said, pulling her bare feet underneath the weight of her body. "Are your stories going well?"

"Actually, I've taken a break from writing and I've been reading instead." Yes, trying to read Maria Popescu's bible, not that I'd uncovered anything interesting. "I have this book of Romanian fairy tales. I finished it this afternoon."

"Was it good?"

"It was interesting. They were all pretty twisted, like the old versions of the Disney stories."

"Cath, you need to tell me these old versions right now. I love your brain."

I told her about "Aschenputtel", the original version of "Cinderella" and how one of the stepsisters cut off part of her foot to try to fit into the slipper and fool the prince. And the 1740 version of "Beauty and the Beast" where the Beast begged Belle for sex every night. And how in "The Little Mermaid", the prince marries a completely different woman, and Ariel goes back to the sea to do good deeds for three hundred years in order to gain an immortal soul.

Jules simply stared at me blinking. "Cath, you need to speak up, girl. You have such interesting things to say."

I laughed. "Well, I've tried shoehorning fairy tales into everyday conversation, but it never works."

"I want to listen to what you have to say. I want to know what your life is like outside here, outside Irene Jobert's ridiculous event."

Jules continued to watch me, rather than the television screen, and I saw her piqued curiosity. *If you tell her about where you came from, she'll think less of you*, said the nagging voice of paranoia in my mind. I believed the voice, of course, I had internalised it for many years. The truth was, I didn't want to tell any of these people about my life, especially the ones watching us. When Irene had begun to pry, I'd found it easy to distract her. Jules was different. Jules wasn't self-obsessed and her interest was genuine.

"I mostly write," I said, with a dismissive shrug of my shoulders.

There was a moment where Jules's expression went blank as she seemed to contemplate whether to press further or leave the conversation as it was. Her eyes narrowed and I realised she was going to press. My throat closed over as I reached deep within to see if I could pull out a convincing lie.

You're a terrible liar.

But that was when the door opened, and Nathan walked in.

He was wearing nothing but boxer shorts. Even though his eyes were open, I could tell that he was sleepwalking.

"I can't rest," he said.

The pallor of his skin, the waxiness of it, made me move away from him in repulsion. He leaned over me, his hands reaching for my shoulders again. That was when I saw the scratch marks all over his arms.

"Nathan, what have you done to yourself?"

"Cath, I can't rest."

"I'll wake up Irene," Jules said.

"Okay, I'll take him back to his room."

He was obedient as I guided him out of the snug. I threw a blanket over his shoulders to protect him from the breezy walkways. At the cloister garth, Nathan stopped and wandered towards the cherry tree. Even when I took his hand he refused to move, instead staring at the russet leaves. I said his name three times, but it had no effect on him. It was a cool night, not so cold that I would shiver in my leggings and long-sleeved top, yet in that moment, I began to tremble. The temperature dropped. I worried for Nathan wearing so little, but even when I pulled on his arm, he would not move. His skin was as cold as ice, his body as rigid, his breath a fog emitting from his lips. There was a wheezing sound coming from his lungs. I began to panic, considered whether to call for help, but felt ridiculous for not being able to make a man walk.

Before I could act, the spell appeared to be broken, and Nathan turned away from the tree. My feet hopped across the grass to keep up with him. He muttered under his breath. Nothing that I could make out, really, apart from a few yesses and nos. We came to his door, but he walked straight past it and into my room, where he collapsed on my bed and went to sleep. There was nothing else I could do other than cover him with the duvet and take myself back to the snug.

Jules and Irene caught up with me along the way.

"Cath, will you talk to her. She won't delete the footage of Nathan sleepwalking."

Irene held up her hands. "I don't see the problem. It's a man wearing boxers, what is so shocking?"

"He's basically unconscious," I argued. "He can't consent to what we just saw. Seriously, stop it from airing." I lowered my voice. "You wouldn't want the world to see you so vulnerable."

Irene scoffed. "The world has seen me bald, ill from the chemo, throwing up into the toilet. Do not talk to me about vulnerability."

I noticed Jules's jaw tighten and her lips purse. The tension been the two of them was growing with each day, and it made my abdomen ache with unease.

"Watch the footage," I said. "I think you'll agree with us when you see it. He wasn't in his right mind."

"Yeah, he was completely out of it. Cath's right. We should stop it before it goes on the live stream and then ask Nathan tomorrow if he wants it uploaded," Jules said.

Irene relented, and pulled the recording, barely in enough time. My skin itched. The subscribers would have seen the door begin to open and then nothing.

"We should post an explanation online," Jules said. "Blame it on technology."

"Very well." Irene typed furiously, and with that we were

back online. In the background of the snug, the slasher film continued.

———

JULES AND I SLEPT IN THE SNUG THAT NIGHT, SEEING AS Nathan was in my room. We avoided talking about him while we were there in front of the cameras. In the latest of hours we both fell asleep while the messages rolled in.

YaBol23: That was weird...

JoJobert: Guess the cameras cut out.

YaBol23: Yeah, RIGHT as someone was about to come in. #tin-foilhat time.

Forkie: That's because that place is haunted as shit.

Lu98: What if they're faking it. For views.

SimoneB: Oh God. @Lu98 is dead on.

YaBol23: Holy shit. That's messed up.

While I checked the comments the next morning, Jules typed messages on her phone. She lifted her head and smiled. "Just catching up with my sister."

I returned the smile.

"You're not much of a phone person, are you?"

"What do you mean?"

"Well," she said, "you don't check your phone much. Don't you have people at home wondering how you're doing?"

"We're online most of the day," I said, gesturing to the laptop. "Everyone knows we're doing okay."

Jules folded one leg over the other and placed her phone down on the coffee table in the centre of the room. That

same inquisitive expression I'd seen the night before spread
across her face.

"But we haven't been okay. You found a wolf on the first
day here. We had to call the police because we thought
there might be a stranger living in the monastery. We've all
been arguing about petty shit. Nathan sleepwalked into your
room. And no one has called to check on you?"

She knows...

I closed my eyes for a split second, no longer wanting to
see her searching gaze.

"Hey, Cath," she said. "I'm sorry, that was..."

"It's fine."

She knows you're alone.

"If you need anyone to talk to..."

"I don't." I met her gaze then. It burned through me, and
through her. I saw the way she retracted. Saw the fear.

But she still said, "You do know that I'm your friend,
don't you?"

She isn't.

I nodded, as though it was enough. Then I hurried out
of the room, away from her, from the prying lens of the
camera, from the people around the world watching me.
Dan waved from underneath the tree, but I ducked down
and kept walking, ignoring the confused expression on his
face. I raced along the walkway noticing that the door to my
room was still closed and I carried on and on until I came to
the church. I didn't go in, I continued along the cloister path
until I came to the door to the library. There I went in, stepping in among the dusty shelves.

You belong here, said the voice. *With the mice, the dirt and
the spiders in the corners. In the cracks along the bricks, nestled in
the mortar, deep down between the flagstones where the dirt*

gathers. This is you. This is what you are made for. Live with the bats and the rats and the white wolf in the woods.

I clamped my hands over my ears as I continued through to the dormitory. But I couldn't shut her up.

Be the shit, the scum, the lichen. Be the woodlouse, the worm, the beetle.

"Shut up!"

Not until you admit who you are, she said, always talking, always in my head.

My feet made me circumnavigate the long room. Pacing and pacing. I was not fully in my mind, I was somewhere far away. Just as Nathan had wandered into the snug, muttering to himself, no longer conscious of his actions, I stumbled around and around the dormitory until I found another door. That door took me out into a narrow corridor, this one dark, enclosed and away from the open cloister. I entered a smaller room adjacent to the dormitory. I had no idea what it was, but I felt as though I'd stumbled into the depths of Sfântul Mihail.

One grimy window let in the scantest amount of sunlight. I stepped into the centre of the room and spoke to the darkest corners.

"I know who I am." The tears began to fall down my cheeks. "I know I'm alone."

No, not that, replied the voice. *The other thing.*

CHAPTER NINETEEN

The small, square room reminded me of a prison cell. I opened out my arms and could almost touch both sides. There was a shelf on the wall, empty apart from an old pen. I took it and placed it in the pocket of my pyjama bottoms. There was more furniture here than in the dormitory. A rusted metal bedframe rested against one wall, while on the opposite side was a desk and a chair. In my mind this was either the mother superior's bedroom, or a place for a priest to stay.

I took a step towards the chair, tentatively wrapped my fingers around the wooden frame, and dragged it away from the desk. Then I sat. It was cold there, and I wrapped my arms around my body. I huddled forward and started to rock back and forth. There's no knowing how long I stayed like that. All I know is in those moments I was alone. The voice in my head had gone. I felt her absence deep in my bones, and it was a relief. But at the same time, I was still on edge from the scattered thoughts flashing through my mind and the shaky breaths coming from my lungs. My body rattled all over, but I ignored my fears and got to my feet.

I walked back into the dark corridor and placed my hands on the wooden door leading into the nun's dormitory, listening to the complaining creak of the hinges when I pressed my weight against it. Whoever slept in the small room with the desk would have to go through the dormitory first. Then surely it must be a place for a mother superior because a nunnery wouldn't want a man walking through private accommodation for the nuns.

It was as I entered that I saw the echo of our own accommodation within that protracted space. I pictured the walls being inserted in by builders, splitting up the line of rusting beds along the outer wall. My fingers brushed over the metal frames. White paint peeled and dropped to the stone floor. I inhaled must. If age had a smell it existed in that room.

A sense of peace spread over me. It was sudden, startling in itself. There's no real way to explain the change in my mood, because it wasn't as though I'd forgotten the voice in my head, and the horrible things she'd said to me. Perhaps I'd come to realise that those words weren't real, or perhaps my mind had become so broken that I'd compartmentalised the paranoia into a separate entity. Whatever happened, a modicum of inner strength flowed through my body, allowing me to stay.

It was above the fifth bed that I noticed it. I walked over to the wall and let my fingers trace the residue left by an old crucifix. I felt the cold again. Felt its grip on me. There had never been a stillness like there was in that dormitory. It pained me to move, because each step broke the silence. For reasons unbeknownst to me, I knew that this bed had once belonged to Maria Popescu. She had slept here, but did she die here too?

There was furniture in this room that I hadn't noticed

before. Just one chest of drawers. Perhaps it was shared by the nuns. I walked towards it and reached out, my fingers hovering by the handles. I wanted to open it. *Someone* wanted me to open it. I was being watched.

Now. Let me explain what was happening to me, because it isn't easy to justify my thoughts. There is no doubt that I was not alone in that room. But you may wonder why an individual who has continually professed not to believe in the paranormal could be completely certain she was not alone. You may think I'm a hypocrite, even, but I had spent the last twenty minutes or so talking to the nagging paranoia of my mental illness and alongside that voice came the conviction that I was not alone. Even though she had provided me with a reprieve from her vicious words, I knew that presence remained, nestled inside my skull, waiting for me to be vulnerable again.

Another possibility was that the historical energy of the place had a leftover effect, making me feel as though I was being watched. Did it make it less real to know there was no physical manifestation? Or was the fact that the building had a tragic history enough to make the presence real? If trauma could be passed down through generations of people, could it occur in buildings too?

Or perhaps it was the ever present, overarching sense of the cameras. Of the viewers. Even when I was in a space not inhabited by CCTV, like my bedroom, I imagined that they were still there. It was like a spider crawling over your skin, and the lasting memory of that sensation. It would take time away from spiders for that memory to fade away.

The last explanation was that there was a ghost in the room with me, standing behind me, watching. If it was an actual spirit, it was the shape from the body cam, the hand on my shoulder pulling me away from the wolf, the smudge standing between me and Jules in the church. It was the hand nudging the door handle outside the snug. The thing Nathan was transfixed by in the cloister garth. The footsteps running away from us in the mist.

While I was in that room, I heard it breathing.

That's right, I did.

As I'd walked to the dresser and wrapped my fingers around the pull handle, there was the sound of a rasping breath behind me. It quickened as the drawer opened, as though their heart was racing. Part of me expected it to speak, but it remained silent, allowing the scraping of the wood to be the one jarring sound that echoed along the empty space.

It was one of those old-fashioned tall-boy dressers. My mother had used one of these. It was a worn-out thing she'd bought at an antique fair decades ago, built of cheap wood, plywood drawer bottoms sagging like a pig's belly. When I opened the drawer, I half-expected to see her mess of clothing in there. Knickers and odd socks piled together in a tumble. There was nothing like that. Instead, I found a wooden crucifix. When I pressed that crucifix to the outline on the wall, it was a perfect match. I lifted it closer to my eyes, and that was when I saw the stain.

A long time ago, this had been Maria Popescu's crucifix that she kept on the wall above her bed. I lowered myself to my knees and pressed my palms together for a moment before getting back to my feet. It was an odd thing for an atheist to do.

I took the crucifix back with me. On the way, I stumbled into another hidden corridor, discovering the old wash-rooms for the nuns, a small office behind the church, and, finally, the entrance to the belfry tower. This time I decided to walk the steps up to the top. It was dangerous, I knew that, but I couldn't stop myself. I needed to see what the Carpathians looked like from the very top. Had the nuns visited this part of the building often? When did they ring the bell? Why did they ring the bell? Did one of them raise the alarm during the murders? I supposed that I would never know the answers to those questions, but I couldn't stop thinking about them as I walked, step by step, up the tower.

When I heard the scurry of vermin at my feet, I almost lost my footing. I clutched the old, rickety rail next to the wall as I paused to calm my heart. Despite the shock, I resolved to keep going all the way to the top. The stairs continued to spiral upwards. I had one hand on the railing, and the other wrapped around the crucifix. Unsteady breaths slipped through my lips.

By the time I reached the final level, I was sweating through my clothes and my nostrils were clogged with dust. But the window to the outside world was worth it. The fresh air filtering down from the mountain, untainted by the pollution of a city, was like a tonic to the mildewed stench of the east wing. I walked over to the window and gazed out below, with one hand wrapping tightly around the ledge. To my left, the mountain sloped down to grassy meadows where livestock grazed. I saw the roofs of Butnari tucked into the dales and a sense of relief washed over me. We were not alone. We were still in the world.

There was a scattering of forestry there. I smiled at the scene, because it's impossible not to smile at pure, unaltered beauty. I was happy. Despite everything that had happened, I was at peace. But that happiness did not feel like my own. It felt borrowed.

My eyes continued to roam until a blot on the landscape caused part of that happiness to wane. Still on my left, on the edge of the woods, was a small white figure. A crouched animal. Even from this height I recognised the shape, and size, of the white wolf. The taste of pennies in my mouth. My blood ran cold for a moment, but the sight of the wolf did not completely eradicate my sense of peace, merely disrupted it. I closed my eyes to steady myself. While I stood there with my eyes closed, there was a pull. The wolf waited patiently for me. For me at my most vulnerable. I would reach that point; I knew I would. My mind drifted to dark thoughts, like whether I would survive if I jumped from that height or whether I'd die, or if I'd survive but with a grave injury. The thoughts made my skin tingle with excitement, a sensation that frightened me. When I finally opened my eyes, the wolf was gone. Had it ever been there? I gently shook my head and told myself to calm down.

Then I moved to look to my right, to where the graveyard lay. Those old stones bent towards the monastery, pushed forward from decades of strong mountain winds. There it was—the uneasy resting place of the murdered nuns.

Behind the graves stood a person dressed top to toe in black. Their head was shrouded by a dark fabric covering, which fell into place with a shapeless tunic that draped down to and over the feet. I was no expert on religion, but it was exactly the kind of outfit a nun would wear. I closed my eyes, telling myself that I was seeing exactly what my paranoid mind wanted me to see. When I opened my eyes again, the figure was also gone.

CHAPTER TWENTY

There was a buzz of excitement going on in the refectory. I'd missed lunch, but Jules had set aside and refrigerated a portion of pasta salad for me. There were two empty bottles of wine on the table and the others were red-faced and grinning despite it being barely five p.m. Irene's favourite pop music blared out from the portable radio set up in the kitchen.

"We got paid," Jules said by way of explanation. "We didn't get all our donations, but it's over half."

"That's great."

"What've you been up to?" Dan asked. "Saving wolves on the mountains?"

I smiled thinly. In truth, I wasn't sure. I'd become dazed walking back from the tower. I'd wandered around the perimeter of the monastery, and spent some time exploring the infirmary ruins and its crumbling walls. When I'd found my way back to my room, Nathan had gone. I'd hammered the crucifix to the wall above my bed before sleeping for an hour or so. As soon as I woke up, I made a start on a new book all about Maria Popescu. I was convinced that I knew who she was and what'd happened to her here in the monastery. For most of the day I'd been experimenting with her notes in the bible, handwriting out the words as best I could to try and translate them using my phone app. The results had been pretty unsuccessful.

"Writing mostly," I said. The words made me feel nauseous with shame. I'd been avoiding my usual work ever since the terrible reaction to the latest Arkathis story. There'd been an email waiting for me in my inbox from Alice, my most loyal reader, and I hadn't had the courage to open it.

Irene wrapped an arm around my shoulder. "We missed you."

Her syrupy voice paired with that lilting accent set my teeth on edge. She hadn't missed me, none of them had. But I recognised that I needed her, so I quietly asked if we could speak privately. She agreed, her expression bunched in surprise. As we slipped out of the room, Nathan and Dan were too engrossed in a conversation to notice, but Jules's eyes followed us.

"What is it?" she asked, as I led us through to the utility room. The washing machine was on, which was good, because it meant the others wouldn't overhear if they wandered into the kitchen.

"I'm not sure the medication you bought is working." I balled my sleeves into my fists as I spoke, my body rigid with tension.

"It's not? How do you know?"

I let out a small sigh. "I just know. I think I might need to see a doctor. Can I travel to Brasov to see one? Or maybe to Butnari?" Even the thought of seeing a different doctor made me anxious, but I knew I couldn't go on, not with the voice steadily chipping away at my sanity.

"Are you sure?" She leaned over me and placed a hand on my shoulder.

"I'm sure."

"Perhaps I can get a doctor to come here," she said, as though thinking aloud. Her mouth moved from left to right, mulling over private thoughts. "Yes, I'm sure I can."

"Would a doctor come all this way?" I asked. "I don't understand the healthcare system here. I have travel insurance, but I don't know what it would cover."

"Let me handle it. I'll find you the best doctor who will take care of everything."

"Thanks, I really appreciate that," I said.

As I started to make my way out of the room, Irene called my name and I stopped.

"Your fans online need to see more of you," she said. "You were so great at the beginning, but now you've hardly posted, and you spend too much time away from the cameras. Cath, we need your content. I know you're not yourself right now, but I believe in you, and I think you can push through this."

Her words made my stomach twist with guilt. "I don't know. I feel—" I stopped myself before I began to cry. The voice inside my head finished the sentence for me... *alone.* Then she screamed it. *ALONE!*

Irene came over to me, a placid smile on her face, eyes so knowing that it was easy to imagine her with all the answers. "I know you can do this because I've been through it myself. My life is strange and wonderful. My parents were, are, rich, and I could've had whatever I wanted, but instead I was sick. There was no hope for me until I made hope exist. Do you know how I did that?"

I shook my head.

"By sharing my illness with the world. Once you share it,

the power of it goes away. I want you to do the same thing. I believe in you, Cath."

Before I could speak, the door to the utility room opened and Dan stood in the doorway. "Sorry to interrupt, guys, but Nathan's acting weird again."

Irene muttered a few words in French and left with Dan. A cold sensation wormed its way down my spine. Even though I couldn't hear the breathing this time, I was certain there was a presence there. I didn't follow Irene right away, instead I walked over to a dark corner next to the laundry basket. I saw nothing, of course, but it did strike me as colder than the centre of the room.

Back in the kitchen, Nathan was sitting at the breakfast bar smiling. It doesn't sound so strange, but he was staring at nothing and nodding to himself. Jules was standing by the entrance to the refectory.

"Is he sleepwalking again?" I asked.

"He was talking to me and everything was normal," Dan said. "But then he kept staring above my head, as though there was a person behind me. I couldn't get his attention at all in the end."

"I think he's having a psychological break," Jules added. "None of this is normal. Maybe we should call the emergency services."

"What for?" Nathan's voice in the room surprised us all. Jules visibly flinched. "What are you talking about?"

"You spaced out, Nath," Dan said. "You started talking to the wall."

"I did?" He glanced around himself, eyes trailing the stones as well as each of us in turn. "Sorry, guys. I haven't been sleeping much. Cath's sleep talking keeps me up at night."

"I don't know if I—"

"Oh, you do," he said.

"But you slept in *my* room last night. I was in the snug," I added.

"Yeah but I'm talking about before," he said, scratching his chin.

"You seem okay now, though," Irene said. "Do you want us to call anyone?"

Nathan shook his head. "Nah, I'm good. But I might get a kip. Dan's on the late shift, right?"

"That's right," Irene said. Her eyes narrowed. I could see her weighing up a decision, but I wasn't sure what it was. Jules watched her too, her expression unreadable. "Have a good night's sleep. Bonne nuit."

"Auf wiedersehen," Nathan said with a wink before leaving the room.

When the door closed and Nathan was gone, Irene shrugged. "I'll have a doctor come out in the next few days."

"There's something not right with him," Jules said in a low voice. "This place is getting to him."

"Maybe it's the pressure of this event," Dan added. "It's getting to me, too. These night shifts, Rene. Can we cool it with them?"

"I'll talk to Loup," she said.

Jules rolled her eyes. "Whoever the fuck Loup is."

Irene clearly didn't want a discussion because she glared at Jules before she left. The door slammed after her.

Dan sighed. "I guess I'd better get the laptop out. Rene's supposed to be doing yoga with me for the first hour."

"I don't know how you put up with her moods," Jules said. "I can't stand drama whores."

"Hey, she's been through a lot, you know," Dan retorted.

"I know," Jules said with a sigh. Her lips twitched as though she had more to say but didn't feel comfortable enough to say it. Dan left, and I found myself alone with her again. We were on opposite sides of the room, and neither of us were able to make eye contact.

"I'm sorry," she said eventually. "I kept prying about your personal life, and I shouldn't have. I didn't mean to upset you."

"It's okay," I said. I waved a hand to try and lighten the mood. "I'm oversensitive."

"If you want to talk…"

"Thanks."

"You want me to get you that pasta salad?"

I smiled. "That would be nice."

She wandered into the utility room. I sat down at the breakfast bar, my stomach rumbling.

"What do you make of Nathan's funny episodes?" she said, walking back into the room with a Tupperware box. "It's giving me the heebie-jeebies."

"We're in a stressful environment and he said he's not getting much sleep. It's probably exhaustion."

"Do you think he's dangerous?" She took a plate out of the cupboard and set it onto the counter.

That's a word that no one with a mental illness ever wants to hear. Paranoid schizophrenics in general get a terrible reputation, which I can understand. Mental illness can occasionally be a factor in violent behaviour, whether it's a lone wolf terrorist who kept himself to himself, or a homeless person convinced that the random person doing their Christmas shopping is actually the devil. I get it. I understand why it puts people on edge, but I hate that it does, and I hate that I'm one of the people making others nervous. Especially when ill people tend to harm them-selves before they harm anyone else.

"I know he's acting strangely," I said. "But... violent? I can't see it."

Jules raised an eyebrow. "He's been quite shouty at times."

"Yeah, but he's not that aggressive with it. He's made me feel a bit uncomfortable every now and then, but I don't think it's anything to worry about. Do you?"

She shrugged. "No, I don't think so either. But I don't know whether I agree with you about what's happening. I don't think Nathan is exhausted, I think he's haunted."

CHAPTER TWENTY-ONE

The doctor came two days later. It was the Friday of the second week, and we'd noticed that subscribers were getting bored with our content. Not even Dan and Irene's budding relationship was gripping viewers. Jules and I went on a few walks, but we didn't see any wolves or potential ghosts. At one point, Irene suggested that I speak to the doctor with the cameras on and talk about my mental illness, but I said no. Since then I'd avoided her, afraid that I'd let her down. Every day I failed. I'd upset my readers with my work, not provided interesting content for our live stream, and struggled to keep my mental health in check.

But what I enjoyed over those two days, was writing about Maria Popescu. In my story she was a young girl from a small village on the Ukrainian border, deep within the mountains. Her father was a sheep farmer, and her mother had died of breast cancer when she was ten. Maria was in love with the blacksmith's son, and he was drawn to her gentle nature. She wasn't a beautiful girl, but she had a smile that could light up a room, strong hands and lustrous dark hair. They started a relationship before he joined the army and participated in the invasion of the Soviet Union. She never saw him again, but she was pregnant with his child.

That was all I had written so far.

At night, I stared at the crucifix. Once, I heard the howl of a wolf. The white wolf, not the young wolf, I was sure of it.

Nathan had spent most of his time playing games in his room. I heard the sound of gunfire through the walls at all hours of the day and night. Previously, I'd often heard him talking to his followers as he played, but over the last few days it had been nothing but gunfire and game music.

The morning the doctor was due to arrive, I found myself chewing anxiously on a thumbnail. The idea of having a new doctor to talk to made my anxiety so acute that it brought out that voice in my head again.

They won't understand you or what you've been through. They'll prescribe you the wrong medication or send you to a psychiatric institution in Romania that you'll never leave.

During my research of Romania, I'd seen the footage of the orphanages from the 1990s and it'd chilled my bones. I was afraid of the healthcare system here, even though it was thirty years on. She knew that, of course, and she understood to needle that fear.

When the doctor arrived, he ran into the monastery from his car, hooded coat pulled up over his head. Torrential rain and wind rattled the windows. We'd been listening to it dripping in the walkway all morning, puddles accumulating on the flagstones. Once the doctor peeled away his sodden raincoat, I saw that he was a portly man in an ill-fitting suit, around fifty or so. Irene greeted him, of course, while the rest of us pretended to be doing other things. I cleaned the kitchen counter, my hands shaking with nerves. Nathan sat on a stool with an untouched cup of tea. Jules and Dan were sorting through laundry in the utility room. The atmosphere was electric. A new person had entered the building for the first time in a week.

"I thought perhaps you could do your consultations in their bedrooms for privacy. Cath, can you show Dr Dumitru to your room?"

Nathan and I locked eyes when I put down the cloth and made my way out of the kitchen. Was he as terrified as me? Prior to Dr Dumitru's arrival, Irene assured me that he had been a general practitioner for over two decades in Brasov. But it was still strange to see a doctor in my room. It was supposed to be a safe haven from everything that made me feel exposed and vulnerable.

And alone.

I clenched my jaw, willing the voice to stop.

"It is strange to see a monastery used this way," he said as we made our way past the cherry tree in the cloister. "But I see you have all modern comforts. Not a bad way to live."

"There are solar panels on one of the roofs," I said, "and a water system that uses the old well. Sorry, I didn't fully understand how it works myself. I can't explain it properly."

"Impressive." He nodded his head enthusiastically.

"Thank you for coming such a long way," I said, showing him into my room. I sat awkwardly on the bed while he took a chair by the window.

"I don't come to the mountains often enough," he said. "On the way back I might stop, take a walk. Breathe in the fresh air. If it stops raining."

"It's stunning here," I said.

"Yes." His eyes caught the view through the coloured glass. "But lonely, perhaps."

I believe the polite smile faded from my face when he said that word. I was sure he noticed, but he merely cleared his throat and began. "Ms Jobert said that you've had problems with your medication."

I passed him the pill packet. "I was taking Abilify but my medication went missing. Irene told me this was the same thing."

The doctor rotated the packet in his hands. "It is aripiprazole, the same kind of antipsychotic you were taking. You shouldn't have had any issues transferring. Did you miss a few days?"

"Yes."

"Can you tell me about your symptoms?"

I explained the paranoia and the voice. At first, I was reluctant to tell him about the ghost sightings both from the others in the monastery and the people subscribed to the live stream, but I decided it was important that I did. He nodded his head, occasionally frowned, eyes directed towards the cardboard packet in his hands.

"Any side effects?"

"I've lost weight," I said. "I usually gain weight on this drug and have to cut down on my portion sizes. I must admit, I have missed a few meals. There's a lot going on here and at times I'm distracted."

"Have you had any thoughts about harming yourself or others?"

I thought back to the moment at the top of the tower when I was standing overlooking the mountains, the white wolf in the distance. There had been a moment where I'd considered jumping, but could I say that moment belonged to me? I'm not sure I could.

"No."

"Hmm." He crossed one leg over the other while he was deep in thought. "There isn't much I can do. I think this might be because you had the gap after losing your medication. I think you will feel much better in a few days."

"Do you think I should leave?"

"Do you?"

I was taken aback. His question put me on the spot. Part of me wondered whether I should leave, in case I grew sicker and frightened everyone. On the other hand, I truly had nothing to go home to. The thought of being ill by myself in that terraced house made me feel even worse.

"No," I said. "I don't think I should."

"Listen, you must monitor yourself. I think you can do this well. You are a smart girl. Perhaps Ms Jobert can call me if you think you are struggling, and we could talk again then. Okay?"

"Okay. Thank you."

———

THE DOCTOR'S VISIT LEFT ME WOBBLY. UNSURE OF everything. Myself. The things I'd seen and heard while living in the monastery. What you need to understand, is that I knew I couldn't trust my own thoughts, and yet the illness was chipping away at what was real and what wasn't, meaning there were times I *did* trust those thoughts, even though I wasn't supposed to. And, well, there were further complications to what was going on that I can only show you rather than tell you.

But the fact is, after the consultation with the Romanian GP, I wasn't satisfied with the outcome. It was at this point in time when I probably should've left the mountains altogether and got on the first plane home. Anyone of sound mind reading my account would tell me to do so, and probably have done so before this point. I did not, though, as you will discover. I stayed. I did this mainly because of my burgeoning obsession with Maria. By now I longed to complete her story.

After Dr Dumitru left, I sat for a while, worrying about my mental health, then I faced Maria's crucifix and imagined her kneeling before her God, praying... praying for what? Atonement.

I snatched up my laptop and the story continued. Maria Popescu was pregnant, and her boyfriend had entered the Second World War with the Romanian army, who joined the Axis at a slightly later date to Germany's other allies. I wondered what her blacksmith's son would be like. Perhaps he was a young idealist caught up in propaganda? Or a dejected youngster searching for a scapegoat? Or perhaps he was poor and needed a wage to send to his family.

Maria could not bring a child into the world as an unmarried teenage girl. When she told her father, he was outraged. I wrote out a quick plan. Maria would be sent her here, to Sfântul Mihail, where they could help her birth her child, and then help her get rid of her child. I imagined how she'd kneel to her crucifix each night and pray for absolution for the mistakes she had made.

My fingers flew across the keyboard. I was so sure I was right about everything, that this was the life Maria had lived. It was almost as though Maria was inside me, guiding me.

But she wasn't the voice in my mind, no. I knew that because writing about Maria was the one thing that kept the voice out of my head. It silenced those thoughts. Jules had to come to my room and take me to dinner because I'd forgotten to eat. Dr Dumitru had left by then. I hadn't even heard his car leaving the monastery. Nothing had consumed me as much as Maria's story. Not Maya and the Arkathis world. Not the land of unicorns I invented when I was six, or the island of talking cats from when I was ten. Nothing.

Maria and I had merged into one being. I even had the desire to be her. In a way, it was better than being myself.

Maya4Lyfe: Who was that older man in the monastery?

ReeeeneJJ: Irene, your lipstick gave me a rash. Why can't I contact customer support?

Burgerboi: They didn't explain the old guy! Why? What are they hiding?

Forkie: He went into Cath's room, then Nathan's. Why them?

Pigeon: Looked like he was carrying a doctor's bag.

Forkie: Cath and Nathan because they're both nutters.

Twix: That's a nasty way to talk about mental health.

Otso: Told you, didn't I? One of them will be dead soon.

AliceAkarthis: @Otso reported. Stop saying that shit.

CHAPTER TWENTY-TWO

I rene wanted to perform a séance for Halloween. It was finally the end of October after what had felt like the longest twelve days of my life. It was late, completely black outside, and we were all in the snug together after dining on the vegetable stew I'd made everyone. Now Irene was determined we would make a fuss out of the fact that we were in Transylvania for Halloween. But what disturbed me and the others about that was the fact that Irene had packed a Ouija board specifically for tonight. As she unfolded it on the coffee table, Jules stared at the piece of cardboard with such a scowl, that deep ridges lined her usually smooth forehead.

"Absolutely not," she said. "We've literally just got back to normal after all the weird shit that happened and *now* you want to tease out the spirits. Have you lost your mind?" She lifted her hands and pressed her fingers against her temples.

Irene made a guttural sound in response. "It's what the subscribers want to see. Don't be such a scaredy cat. What do you think will happen?"

"People died here," Jules continued. "It's not right."

"Hey, I'll give it a go," Dan said. He was stretched across the sofa, bare feet dangling over the cushions. Irene sat next to him, one hand idly resting on his leg. As time went on, they had become like one person, with one mind and one opinion. "It's a bit of fun, Jules. Take that stick out of your ass for once."

There was an uncomfortable silence, I think each one of us was shocked. It was usually Nathan who came out with that kind of crass insult, not Dan. He'd always struck me as fairly reserved before then.

"I think Jules is right," I said. "Perhaps it isn't respectful to the dead."

You might get to speak to Maria, said the voice in my mind. *You'd like that, wouldn't you? Seeing as your only friend is dead.*

"Nathan, what do you think?" Jules asked.

We all faced him, and he rubbed the stubble on his chin. No one knew what he'd said to the doctor, but in the end he'd decided to stay. All Irene said was that he was fine to continue participating and the doctor wasn't concerned.

He shrugged his shoulders. "It's a bit of fun, right?" As he was talking, Irene pulled the laptop onto her knee and started typing. "If it's what the paying customers want to see..." He trailed off and his gaze moved around the room.

Jules shook her head in disappointment. "This is crazy."

"Look." Irene rotated the laptop screen and placed it on top of the Ouija board. "The patrons are already donating."

Nathan leaned forward to inspect the computer. As always, money was a draw for him, not that he needed more of it.

"I won't take part in this," Jules said, moving towards the door.

"Then you won't receive donations." Irene shrugged and

flipped her hair over one shoulder. I saw no tension in her body. No suggestion that any of this conflict bothered her whatsoever. I could never tell whether she truly was *that* relaxed, or whether she had issues with showing her emotions.

As Jules made her way out of the door she hesitated, her eyes fixed on me. I realised she expected me to back her up again, and for the second time I hesitated. The moment dragged. The sensible side of me, the side that was still grounded in reality, knew that I should go with her and not partake in this childish game. Yet, I stayed. It was too tempting to give in to my curiosity instead. Jules's arms dropped to her side in dejection. She shook her head slowly. Being a disappointment to another person is a heartache, but there are times when selfishness controls our decision making. This was one of those times.

Jules went back to her room alone. Irene's satisfied smile could not have been wider as she put the laptop onto a free sofa cushion and then placed the planchette on the board.

"Candles, we need candles. Dan, will you get them from the laundry room?"

He kissed the top of her head as he left. I remained standing awkwardly at the back of the room, sensing Nathan's eyes on me. His lips were slightly parted as though he was going to speak, but he didn't.

When Dan came back with the candles, he lit several and spread them around the various surfaces in the snug. Irene switched off the overhead light, and we sat down on the floor around the coffee table, nestling into the rug that covered the flagstones. Next to me, I heard Nathan swallow loudly. He placed an index finger on the board, tracing the space between "yes" and "no".

"This is so juvenile," he whispered. He turned to me as though he needed affirmation. "Isn't it?"

"Yeah, it's harmless nonsense," I said. My voice was shaking slightly, betraying the lie I told. "Ghosts don't exist."

I exist, said the voice. *If I exist, then ghosts exist. Deep down you know it's true.*

I waited for the sound of the rain and thunder, but there was none, only an oppressive stillness as we all quietened down. A crack of thunder and lightning would turn our game into absurdity. It would be a scene in a movie. What did add a layer of surrealness was the flickering candlelight and the way a slight breeze bent the flames. Of course, in a movie, the candle flames would flicker and flicker until suddenly being extinguished in a dramatic, terrifying moment. My heart fluttered at the thought of us being plunged into darkness. I hoped it wouldn't happen.

Irene settled on top of a cushion before she began speaking in a low voice. Her accent was working for her, slotting into that trope where anything other than an American or British accent makes the English language sound almost exotic.

"We sit where many have been. We sit where many have been killed. Now we reach out to the spirits. It is Halloween, a night where the veil is lifted between the living and the dead. Will you respond to our polite request on this sacred night?"

My eyes widened in surprise at her opening monologue. It came across as rehearsed. I knew that Irene understood how to milk whatever opportunity came her way, but this seemed manufactured down to the letter. That logical, inquisitive side to me, the one working in polar opposite to my schizophrenia, had its suspicions raised.

"Everyone place one finger on the planchette."

We did as she asked.

"Is there anyone willing to talk to us?"

Dan let out a nervous giggle. Out of the corner of my eye I was vaguely aware of the messages coming in from viewers. The screen was awash with floating heart emojis and comments. Thousands of people were watching us. The ticker zoomed on. Hearts. Angry faces. Laughing faces.

Nothing moved but the candle flames. Nathan's back remained rigid, his bony finger pale on the plastic counter. I felt cheapened by our surroundings, the camera feed, Irene's phoney speech, Dan's delight, the flimsy cardboard and the garish alphabet. It was all wrong and I wanted to leave, but I didn't.

There was no surprise when the planchette began to move beneath our fingers. Of course it would. You can't play with a Ouija board without one of the players moving the planchette. A small window in the middle of it revealed the word "yes".

"Who are we talking to?" Irene asked.

I eyed the messages on the screen.

Susu1376: #halloween just got real.

Fifi: OMG

Reneeleanie: Oh my days, Irene Jobert at a séance!! Let me be dead. LOL.

Cheezemonkeys: This sucks.

Burgerboi: Lame.

Sassquash: IRENE JOBERT IS A FAKE!

The messages were coming in so fast that I couldn't keep up, even though I wanted to read those written about Irene.

Akarshit: Maybe Cath's writing career could speak to them.
Lu98: #dead
Forkie: savage.
Susan87: LMFAO

The moving planchette pulled my attention away from the laptop quickly enough to not let the insult sink in, though it would plague my thoughts afterwards. It moved quickly beneath our fingertips and my first instinct was to snatch myself away, but I didn't. Whoever was controlling it began to spell out words.

I
U
S
E
D

In my mind I was seven years old at the one birthday party I'd ever been invited to. Katie Lynch's house had been much bigger than mine and I remembered her telling us all about their cleaner. She got a Ouija board out when her mother was in the kitchen drinking wine. I hadn't wanted to do it, but I did. Michelle Flannery had pushed the planchette around the board to fake that her grandad was contacting us and then cried until we all comforted her. Several years later, one of her grandads came to see her perform as Desdemona in our English class's performance of *Othello*. I always wondered whether he was the grandad she'd cried about that night, or was her other grandad dead? I wanted to ask her, but I'd stopped myself. Those girls hated me already, there was no way I was adding fuel to that fire.

T
O
L
I
V
E
H
E
R
E

Dan's breath whistled through his teeth. "It's one of the murdered nuns."

"Then why isn't she speaking Romanian, idiot?" Nathan snapped.

Happyidiot: STOP RIGHT NOW. I'm a medium. You do NOT mess with this shit.
Forkie: Nobody, absolutely nobody, asked you to speak to your fucking ghost.
Lu98: Fuck off, guys, this is awesome stuff. WHO IS IT??

"There may have been nuns from different parts of the world," Irene pointed out. "Priests and nuns are often sent to serve in different locations."

"I was right then," Dan said pointedly to Nathan.

"Do you want to say anything to us?" Irene asked.

When the counter moved it *swooshed* across the board.

G
E
T

O

U

T

Dan let out a long, elongated "fuck". Irene was quiet. Nathan gasped. The comments came in fast.

Forkie: Ok, I don't believe this shit now.
Happyidiot: Told you.
Cheezemonkeys: That is one angry ghost.
AliceAkarthis: Can't believe you're involved in this nonsense, Cath. Reply to my email.
Sassquash: Irene is lying about this like she lies about everything.
Otso: I told you they weren't alone there.

"We don't wish you any harm," Irene said. "We're not here to upset you."

It wasn't the Ouija board that raised the hair on the back of my neck, it was the tickle of a breeze behind me. I felt the sensation of a person leaning over my shoulder and breathing down my neck. In fact, I checked over my shoulder to make sure Jules hadn't walked in without us noticing. She hadn't.

"What is it?" Nathan asked.

"Nothing, just a draught."

"It's the ghost," Dan said. He was sweating.

I didn't reply.

The planchette moved. I was aware of the fact that I was moving it this time.

M
A
R
I
A

D an stood. "I can't do this." He shook his head, eyes burning at Irene. I sat there taken aback by his sudden intensity. "This is sick. You know I didn't want to go along with this."

"Grow some balls." Irene rolled her eyes dramatically. "You're a grown man for God's sake."

Dan yanked open the door. "We're over." He slammed it behind him, causing the candle flames to extinguish.

The screen provided a dim light in the room and Irene reached across for the gas lighter and began relighting the candles.

"He'll be okay, he's just being ridiculous right now. Shall we continue?"

"No," Nathan said.

"Yeah, I don't think we should," I added. "It doesn't feel right."

"Fine!" Irene folded the Ouija board, slamming the cardboard sections together. The planchette went flying, falling beneath one of the sofas.

"Babies. You're all babies."

Her bare feet slapped against the stones on her way out, and a few moments later I heard the shuddering of a slammed door. When she was gone, I couldn't help but glance at the computer screen to see if we were still being watched.

Lu98: Wow, that drama was better than the séance.
Burgerboi: Right?! Ha!

I closed the laptop with a snap, sank down onto a sofa cushion and sighed. Nathan stayed cross-legged on the floor. Both of us were in silent contemplation.

Finally, he said, "I thought we were the unhinged ones."

Despite everything, I laughed.

———

It was my shift to stay up late, and it was the last thing I wanted to be doing. Negativity filtered out from the subscribers. It was clear that the viewers were as on edge as everyone in Sfântul Mihail. I kept seeing the same names over and over again, people who were staying up almost 24/7 to watch us. We weren't entertaining anymore. We weren't providing them enough content, or at least enough *interesting* content, because according to them, we were basic.

Most of the hate wasn't aimed at me, though I had noticed the fact that many of my regular readers had dropped out of the message boards. I wondered whether they'd cancelled their subscriptions after the latest Arkathis story. Only Alice continued to post every now and then. The vast majority of the hate was aimed at Irene, which surprised me. She was by far the most popular out of all of us, but perhaps that was why she also attracted so much negative attention. The more followers you have, the more haters you accumulate.

Still, the messages were concerning to me, mainly because of how coherent they were. These weren't random death threats or vitriolic, jealous messages, they were specific.

I've been selling your make-up for six months and have made less than ten dollars.
Irene, your eyeshadow gave me a rash!
What's happening, I'm hearing weird things about you, Irene.

What was going on with her and why were people bashing her make-up line? I made a mental note to raise the issue with Irene. Perhaps, with her gone, the company had been testing new materials that weren't up to the same quality standards.

My heart felt raw that night. I was alone, still not quite myself, still plagued by the paranoid voice in my mind, still obsessed with Maria Popescu's fictional life. At the same time, my stomach roiled with shame. I knew that I'd moved the planchette during the Ouija board séance, spelling out MARIA. At least, it had to have been me. I was projecting my obsessions, even on a subconscious level. That name had rattled Dan, for some reason, and now I nursed my guilt with a hot chocolate and a blanket, curled up on the sofa by myself.

But surprisingly, at around midnight, Dan came into the snug in his pyjamas. He carried a glass of water and gave me a hushed hello.

"I couldn't sleep," he said. "Too much conflict going on."

"Are you and Irene okay?"

He shook his head and sipped on his water. "I think we're done."

"Seriously? That's a shame."

"Is it?" he said. "We met two weeks ago. We weren't exactly getting married."

"I know, but, still... I'm sorry."

He ran a hand through his hair. "I get that she wanted the séance for the live stream, I get that. I was fine with being her back-up to convince everyone. But I was an asshole to Jules, I'm sorry about that." He tapped a finger-nail against the glass. I waited for him to continue. "And then she did *that*."

"What?"

"Used my sister's name."

My voice was small when I said, "What?" again, like an idiot.

"My little sister died when I was five and she was two. I told Irene about it one night and then she went and used it on the Ouija board." He placed the glass down on the coffee table with a bang. "Fucking bitch."

"Dan... I..."

"How could she? I swear she's playing mind games with us all. You know that, right? She's doing things to create tension, to up the drama for the viewers. That's why she said my sister's name. She stole Nathan's chocolate, you know."

"She did?"

"Yeah. She and him had some sort of casual thing last year. He's her ex and she wanted to mess with him, at least that's what she told me. We ate it together one night. She knew it would piss him off and it'd be good drama for the viewers." Dan shook his head. "I wonder what else she's been up to. Could be anything."

He was so agitated. I didn't know what to do. I wanted to

tell him that *I* was the one who spelt out his sister's name. But I was afraid. It was late at night, I was alone in a room with a man I didn't particularly know, who had a physical presence and was much bigger than me. I chose to keep my secret. After all, I didn't know for sure that my action had been a conscious one. Maybe Irene used Dan's sister as a way to unsettle him, to get a reaction out of him after our séance had been such a let-down. It pained me to admit it, but I believed Irene was capable of exactly that kind of deception.

Dan took some ibuprofen for a headache and left. I was troubled by the new connection with his younger sister. There'd been a moment when I could have put Dan's mind at rest, but I didn't take it. I failed. Perhaps I was an awful person like the voice in my head told me.

In the early hours of the morning, around four a.m., I fell asleep. When I woke at six, I had the strange urge to read the email from Alice. I'd been avoiding it since the publication of that now infamous Akarthis story. No doubt it was another one of my former fans piling on the hate, telling me how horrible I was for killing off Maya's twin brother. My chest tightened as I opened the email. But what I read surprised me.

Dear Cath,

This is one of the hardest emails I've ever written. I want you to know that.

I didn't like what Maya did in the story you wrote, because it wasn't like her. At first, I was angry about it, but then I stopped and really thought about why she killed Stefan for the sword. And that's when I realised that you're ill. None of the plot makes sense. Read it again, Cath, and you'll notice massive plot holes that are not like you at all. At one point Maya starts hearing voices, which was scary.

Are you okay? I worry about you so isolated like that.

Can you contact me if you need me?

Please, protect yourself against the others in that house. There are things you don't see. They talk about you behind your back and say troubling things. Leave if you need to.

I know you're getting bad reviews and some of the other fans have left the group, but I want you to know that I'm always here for you, no matter what. I like to think of us as friends. I hope you do too.

Alice

There were tears in my eyes when I read the email the second time. *I like to think of us as friends.* Aside from Jules, I wasn't sure I could remember anyone saying those words to me, at least not genuinely. I'd opened the email expecting hate, but what I'd received was love. In a way, that was worse. Who would love me? Who would want to be my friend? I offered nothing to anyone. Those were the swirling thoughts in my mind.

Pathetic girl, mooning over an email. You wait, just you wait, she'll decide you're not worth it, like everyone else.

I left the laptop in the snug and went into the kitchen to make a cup of tea. The monastery was dark before sunrise, but I decided not to switch on too many lights as I made my way there. The cold air of morning dried the tears around my eyes. In the kitchen, I heard the lashing of rain. It was clear that the weather was transforming as the season changed to winter.

There was no fear in my heart that morning, nothing seemed out of place, but I did sense eyes on my back. The cameras, maybe. Those invisible eyes spread around the world. Strange usernames knowing what I looked like when I make myself a cuppa. No, I preferred the other watcher, and imagined it was Sister Maria.

I took my mug of tea back to the snug and checked the laptop. There were a few mentions of my conversation with Dan, which of course had been streamed a few hours ago. I went through and answered several questions, typing things like:

Dan and Irene's relationship is their business.
I don't know if Irene faked the Ouija board.
We're not scared of being haunted because everything is normal again.

It felt fake to say those things, to ignore my worries, the feeling of being watched and the voice in my head. Typing out lies exhausted me. I decided to go back to my room to examine the crucifix again, and perhaps continue writing the story about Maria. She was coming to the monastery now, her belly swollen, her breasts sore. The nuns were going to take care of everything. I thought about her all the way down the walkway.

Outside my door, the Ouija board burned. It took me a moment to comprehend what I was staring at. There were flames reaching up towards the door handle, shimmering in the early light. A beautiful orange glow. I was transfixed at first, hypnotised by the way they danced. Then the door began to catch fire, paint licked by flames. I immediately ran to Irene's door, pounding on the wood. Her expression was as dark as thunder when she snatched it open.

"There's a fire out here."

Bewildered, she simply said, "What?"

"Do you have a container? I need water."

She pointed to the bathroom bin. I opened the lid, tossed out the contents of the bin, and filled it with water. Despite the urgency, my eyes drifted to the rubbish on the bathroom tiles. Condom wrappers, tissues, floss, a chocolate wrapper, an empty packet of pills. But before I could examine the pill packet, the bin started to overflow.

I hurried out to the hallway and dumped the contents of it onto the fire. Irene followed, while the other doors opened one by one. We stood over the burned remains of the Ouija board and no one quite knew what to say.

CHAPTER TWENTY-FOUR

After cleaning up the remains of the board, we decided to meet in the refectory for a proper meeting. We sat hunched over the table, our body language guarded, eyes darting between each other. Because no one wanted to own up to the burning, the first thing we did was examine the CCTV from outside our rooms. Irene sped up and slowed down the footage until we figured out that fifteen minutes were missing from the recording. One minute the cloister walkway outside the rooms was empty, the next I was standing there staring at the fire.

All eyes directed to me.

"I didn't do it," I said.

Jules placed a hand on my arm. "No one is saying you did." She smiled, but it failed to reach her eyes, and I wondered whether she truly believed what she was saying.

"I don't understand how this happened," Irene said. "My personal laptop is the only one with access to the camera to turn it off. It was in my room and I always lock my room."

"What a surprise," Dan muttered.

Irene ran her fingers through her hair and tugged at the ends. "You think this was me?"

"Honestly? I don't know," Dan replied.

"Someone did this on purpose to frighten the rest of us." Nathan eyeballed each of us. "Why would any of you do this? It's sick. Don't you think there's been enough going on around here?" He sounded exhausted by it all. On his last nerve.

Irene leaned against her chair. She appeared calm and collected, which did make me wonder whether she'd planned this as a silly stunt. "Maybe there's no point in figuring this out. Maybe it's best we don't know. I think we need to put it behind us and move on."

"Is that because it was you?" Jules asked, her mouth twisting into a grimace.

"No," Irene said. She fixed Jules with a cold scowl she reserved only for her. "It's because this was an idiotic prank and there is no point arguing over it. Why don't we agree to get on with The Event? Okay?"

"In the interest of getting the fuck on with our lives, I agree," Nathan said.

"Fine," Jules agreed.

Dan lifted his hands. "I will too, but I'm getting pretty sick of these mind games. It's not what I signed up for."

"Good," Irene said. "Then we don't speak of this ever again. Also, we're going to go on a team-building exercise."

Jules groaned.

"A what?" Nathan asked. "What kind of team-building exercise?"

"Hiking," Irene said, her smile revealing those perfect teeth.

BEFORE WE LEFT FOR THE WALK, I LOGGED ONTO THE WEBSITE and noted the responses to the burned Ouija board. There was a poll. Odds had been set up. Dan was in the lead, with me second, Irene third, Jules fourth and Nathan fifth. But I was convinced that it had been Irene. She was the one who wanted to create false drama to entertain the subscribers. She was the one obsessed with numbers and money. She was the one who suggested we all move on and stop talking about it. Even though I agreed with the latter, because we were all adults and obsessing over this silly act was only going to lead to additional friction, I couldn't stop thinking about Irene and her tactics.

The empty packet of pills I saw in Irene's bathroom played on my mind. From a glance, it was similar in appearance to my anti-psychotic medication. Could Irene have stolen my medication? And if she did, why had the packet been empty? Did she dose herself with my pills? I could imagine her stealing my medication, which, in truth, left me with a sour taste of disappointment in my mouth; and I could imagine her sneaking into my room and stealing the meds as a way to create extra tension in the monastery, like the kind of cheap trick a producer might pull on a reality-TV show. The main question was: if she did steal my pills, why would she take them herself? Were there side effects I wasn't aware of? Could my pills make a healthy person high? I had no idea and there wasn't enough time to research it. Instead, I figured that Irene having her own prescribed medication made a lot more sense. Pill packets tend to be generic.

Just because you're paranoid, doesn't mean they're not after you, said the voice.

I shook it away, pulled on my hiking boots, packed a notebook and pen into a bag—leaving space for food and water—then strapped the body cam to my chest. At Irene's request, I also put the drone in my bag.

We gathered in the kitchen where Irene divvied up water and snacks. It was eleven a.m. and the weather had finally cleared after a few days of rain. Thin mist clung to the air, but nothing like the fog Nathan and I had encountered while chasing the drone. I hadn't minded the weather, it made the monastery come alive. The rain had brought out the odour of aged stone; salty clay of damp bricks and sweet decay of fallen leaves, lingering mist and dewy grass, and the earthy scent of tree bark. Nature unaltered, unchanged, until the manufactured soles of our boots trudged right through the middle of it.

Away from Sfântul Mihail, we didn't chat much. At one point Irene talked loudly, poking Nathan with little taunts. "Is this the first time you've been outdoors, Gamer Boy?"

He barely responded. There was a lot less of the jokester in him than when we first met.

We followed a footpath out through the woods, with Irene leading the way. She was surprisingly good at navigation with her paper map and compass. Once we emerged out of the opposite side, we came to a stretch of meadows.

"The footpath goes through the field," Irene noted as we stood in front of a gate. She paused for a moment and then pulled back the latch with a shrug. "I guess we can go this way. It's public."

Nathan was the last to step through, and I watched him pull the gate closed before he caught up with us. We trudged through a damp field full of horses clothed in muddy rugs. One of them lifted its head as we walked on, but aside from that they barely noticed us plodding our way through. By the time we reached a stile on the opposite side of the field, a light layer of sweat had formed along the nape of my neck. We hopped over one by one to stumble down a slope of overgrown grass towards a trickling brook. There, perched on damp rocks, stretched out on the dewy grass, we ate a lunch of protein bars and sandwiches.

Irene started to chat as we rustled packets and swigged water. "We need to talk about what happened this morning. We're halfway through The Event and we're not much of a team, are we?" She lifted her arms out wide, raised her eyebrows in animation. "We should be great friends!"

Jules jumped in first. "Let's see, shall we? Someone stole Cath's medication on the first night. We saw strange apparitions and thought we had an intruder living in the monastery with us. Nathan's chocolate was taken from his suitcase. Food went missing from the fridge. Nathan and Cath have suffered mental health breaks, and *you* controlled the doctor they saw. Then you made us mess around with a Ouija board before burning it to get us fighting with each other."

Irene sat silently and waited for Jules to finish speaking. "Is that everything?"

Jules's left eye twitched. I sensed she was holding back. She merely shrugged.

"I didn't burn the Ouija board," Irene said. "But I did take Nathan's chocolate. I'm sorry, Nathan. It was stupid. You insulted me on the first night and I was mad at you."

We all faced Nathan, expecting an outburst, but all he did was raise his eyebrows.

"You've turned this into a phoney scripted reality show," Dan said. "We came here to connect to people in a way that's never been done before. We came here to offer a wide range of skills to the world, not to provide constant drama."

Irene sighed dramatically and her hands flew up. "*This* is why I suggested the Ouija board. You are all stupid... and,

and... short sighted. You are all self-involved. Do you think people want to watch Cath writing in silence? Do they want to see you meditate *again*, Dan? Do they want to be patronised by Jules? Or hear Nathan screaming his juvenile catchphrases? No. That's not why they subscribed. They want to see us fight, and fuck, and be frightened." Her wild eyes settled on me. "Cath has three hundred thousand new followers since she was humiliated by Nathan on the first night. Dan, you have one hundred thousand more followers since we got together, and another twenty thousand since we broke up. Don't you see?"

"These are our real lives," I said. When their faces directed towards me, my gaze dropped to the muddy ground, but I resolved to say my piece. "There has to be a line. If we're not authentically ourselves, what are people watching? What are we providing, and what are we saying to the world? Maybe this was a mistake, this whole concept. Maybe we shouldn't be selling this... I don't know, this direct line to our most private moments. You keep wanting us to do what you do, to wear a mask and sell a character. I can't do that."

When I finally raised my head, Irene was staring hard at me, face red and scrunched. "Fuck. You."

"I didn't mean to offend you." My insides twisted up when I saw the tears on her cheeks. "I'm so sorry, Irene." When I moved towards her, she pulled away.

"None of you know the pressure I'm under," she said, wiping away her tears. "None of you know what it's like. I do not wear a *mask*. I've been real. Since the beginning, since the cancer. Maman—" She abruptly stopped, her teeth clicking together as she clenched them shut. "None of you know me."

Jules opened her mouth to speak, but I caught her eye and shook my head. Now wasn't the time.

"Let's keep walking," Nathan said. "I'm cold."

Well done, said the voice in my mind. *Another life you ruined. Another person who will hate you forever. Don't forget, that I know what you did to me. I know your true, hateful soul. I'm glad it's finally coming to the surface.*

CHAPTER TWENTY-FIVE

A strange thing happened that afternoon. The moment of honesty at the stream lifted the cloud-like shroud from us all. Irene was quiet, but the rest of us chatted freely as we walked. Nathan even handed out bottles of beer he'd taken from the utility room before we left.

We continued up the mountainside, stopping every now and then to use our drones to capture the beauty of the sweeping vistas. We walked for so long that the monastery became a dot beneath us, the graveyard barely even visible, but the tower reaching up. Being that far away from the building gave us all some much-needed distance from our problems. We walked in a line with Nathan at the back, who sang a Bee Gees song in falsetto and made us all laugh.

On the way down, as we approached the field with the horses, it became clear that there were others walking the same path. They appeared to be a group of campers, perhaps four or five. We were still significantly high up, with a clear view of the path before us, able to watch as they wandered from the footpath to set up a camp close to the edge of the forest.

It took us about fifteen minutes to come within reach of the camp, and by this time they were finishing up pegging the tents. I saw that they were around our age. There were three guys and two girls in the group. One of the guys—tall and bearded with a straggly topknot—waved us over.

"Are you the people in the monastery?" he asked. I realised immediately that his accent wasn't Romanian—it was harder, perhaps German.

"Guilty as charged," Nathan said, lifting his hand for a bro shake with the camper.

"Cool," the guy said, smiling. "We saw your videos." He stared right at me then. "Wolf girl!"

I nodded my head but didn't speak, blindsided by the sudden attention.

He made the universal hand gesture for okay with his finger and thumb. "Very, very cool. Would you all like to stay for a while and drink a beer?"

Nathan clapped the guy on the shoulder. "You just said the magic word, my man."

A curly-haired guy in thick-rimmed glasses passed us each a beer and then we were all introduced. The names of half the group have slipped from my memory as time goes on. I remember three of them. The man with the topknot was Lukas, the glasses wearer was Faisal, and there was a slim-hipped girl with a baby face called Lina. The other two were a couple, both dark-haired and attractive, who hung back from the rest of the group.

Faisal made a fire while we found places to sit. Some of us were given fold-up chairs to sit on, while others rested on a tarp on the ground or the trunk of an old felled tree. I sat crossed legged on the ground with Jules, every movement causing the tarp to crunch beneath us. Next to Jules was Lina, who didn't speak much English, and liked to stretch out her long legs. They were gap-year travellers from Berlin who were on a camping holiday that incorporated rock climbing in the mountain range. Lukas told us about tour groups nearby that hiked the trails.

"We went our own way," he said. "There were too many annoying people. It was too organised."

"We wanted to see what the mountains have to offer," Faisal added.

"Is it safe to camp out here at night?" Dan asked. "The wolf Cath came in contact with has been hanging around."

"Actually, there's more than one," I said. "At least I think there is." I thought about the white wolf in the forest, about its menacing presence and that taste of pennies it always gave me. I still didn't know if it was real or not, but I felt that the group should be warned just in case.

Lukas let out a high-pitched whistle through his teeth. "Wonderful. I would love to see a wolf in the wild."

"But we reported them, didn't we?" I looked to Irene.

She nodded. "Yeah." Her voice was flat. She cleared her throat and turned to the campers. "You're not afraid of wild animals?"

"We have repellents to use around the campsite." Lukas shrugged. "We put the radio on, too. The human voices keep most animals away."

"So, have you seen the live feed?" Irene asked. "Did any of you subscribe for the month?"

Faisal shook his head. "We saw the clips that made it to YouTube and Facebook. The ghost in the hall." He clapped his hands against his cheeks and opened his mouth in mock shock.

Irene laughed. "Yes, the ghost. One of the nuns, we think."

Lukas turned to me. "I heard you told a story on the first night. People are talking about it on Reddit a lot. You guessed the names of the nuns correctly. Sister Maria, right?"

My blood ran cold. I'd hoped this hike would be a break from thinking about Maria Popescu and the other nuns. Yet apparently everything I said and did on camera was still being discussed online. The fact that I hadn't seen these discussions made my skin crawl with goosebumps. What were they saying? Did they think I was mad?

"Yeah, but Maria is such a common name," I said. "It could've happened to anyone. You think of a nun and you think of Maria first." I added a laugh to try and make myself seem less tense.

Lukas flung his arms open and began to sing "The Hills Are Alive". "Ha ha! Yes. A nun is always Maria. Have you sung that song in one of these meadows yet?" He grinned, his blue eyes shining.

"I have," Nathan admitted.

Even Jules laughed while Nathan sheepishly told everyone that it was his favourite movie. "Tell me you can watch that movie and not fall in love with Maria."

I glanced guiltily at Dan, who was peeling the label from his beer, avoiding eye contact with everyone around the fire.

"Man, this place is wonderful. Don't get me wrong, I love Berlin, but it's loud and busy. The air is not fresh. Here, I can breathe." Lukas pulled in a deep breath.

Around the fire, with the crackle, the dusk, I'd never felt so connected to a group of people. I was exhausted, sure. I hadn't slept. Yet my skin tingled when I heard each tinkle of laughter. Every pop of the branches and crackle of the fire pulled me further and further away from the weight I'd been carrying for so long. I followed Lukas and I breathed deeply, letting it all go as I exhaled. He saw me and smiled.

"There's a campfire here, and we have a brilliant story-teller." Lukas nodded to me. "Would you share one with us?" He raised his hand and performed a bow, slopping beer on the grass as he bent over.

Everyone regarded me then, even the quiet couple. I licked my lips as my mind raced, trying to remember the Romanian fairy tales I'd recently read. Finally, I took a deep breath and began. "Once upon a time—"

There was a collective *ooooh* around the fire. Lukas grinned and took a swig from his beer. I waited for them to settle in, then I began.

"David wanted to be rich. It was all he prayed for. Luckily for him, one day, the Gods answered his prayer, and David became rich beyond his wildest dreams. He was so rich that he never needed to work again. So rich that he would never be able to spend all of his money within his lifetime. And there was the problem." I took a dramatic pause. "David decided that if the Gods had answered his prayers and made him rich, they would answer his prayers and make him immortal, because David now wanted to live forever with all of his riches.

"He got on his knees and he asked them for eternal life, but the years went on and the Gods did not answer. David continued to age. He was not happy about this but remained determined to find immortality. He thought that a journey might be what he needed. He packed his bags and left his wife and his hometown behind. Wherever he went, he asked the same question: Do people die here? If the answer was yes, he carried on walking. He walked and walked until eventually he came across a land where the people didn't even understand the word 'death'.

"As David was talking to one of the locals, he asked whether their town was filled with a great number of people if nobody died. Curiously, the local told David that many of the townsfolk talked of a voice they heard calling them away. Every time someone talked of the voice, a few days later they would leave the town and never come back.

"David chuckled to himself. Who would be stupid enough to follow the voice? If he ignored the voice, he would be free to live in the town for evermore, with his wealth, and, if he wanted, his wife. Which is exactly what he did. David sent word to his wife, who travelled to the town to be with him. He told her about the voice, and how she must ignore it when the time came. He stressed how important this was.

"They lived happily for years until one day, David's wife stood up and said, 'I'm coming!' Anxiously, David said to her, 'Remember. Ignore the voice or you'll die.' He blocked her path, but she fought against him, determined to follow the voice. David did everything he could to prevent her from following that voice. He grabbed her by the coat, but she shrugged it off and ran out of the door of their mansion.

"David was distraught to lose his wife, but ultimately she'd made the decision to listen to the voice when he'd explicitly told her not to. Life went on. He continued living his life, spending his money, until one day he heard the voice. He was in the barber's chair at the time, mid haircut. His barber was surprised to hear David call out, 'I won't come with you. I refuse to go with you. Leave me alone.' It went on for a while until David snatched the razor from the barber's hand and ran out of the shop, chasing an entity that no one else could see. However, the barber was determined to retrieve his razor, so he followed David. He followed him all the way to the edge of the town, where he saw David run straight over a cliff. Cautiously, the barber approached the edge, only to find a pit filled with the bodies of the townspeople who had one day stood up, left their houses and never come back.

"The barber told the rest of the town all about the pit, explaining that he finally knew where those who heard the voices went. A mob of people went to examine this deathly chasm, but when they reached the apparent cliff, there was nothing but stretching land leading to a new world. The people went back to their lives, and from that moment on, the townsfolk lived and died like every other mortal in the world."

Silence fell. No one moved for one, two moments. Then Lukas asked, "Did you make that up?"

I laughed. "No. It's a story I read in a book about Romanian fairy tales. I just gave him a different name."

"I guess you can't ignore death," Nathan said, staring hard at the fire.

CHAPTER TWENTY-SIX

L ater, I would wonder why I picked that story to tell out of the fairy tales I knew. All I know is that it brought to mind the dark apparition in the graveyard. Maria, I'd assumed. Was she the voice of death for me? Trying to tempt me away with her snippets of history, the bible and the crucifix? Or was I searching too hard for a meaning that wasn't there? My paranoid mind was working overtime every moment of the day.

We stayed at the campsite for too long, but it was because we were happy, and none of us wanted to go back to that building, where we'd argued and seen things that didn't make sense. Where the unhappiness of history slipped over us like gloves over fingers, shrouding us in long-spilled blood.

I wandered away from the camp, longing for solitude. I was the one sober person in the bunch. Dan and Irene were bickering next to the tents. Lukas and Faisal were chatting with Jules about Berlin. Nathan was telling Lina all about his YouTube channel. But I had that voice in my head whispering to me that I didn't fit in and I never would. I was an outsider looking in; a viewer, not a participant.

Afraid of getting lost, I stayed within eyeshot of the camp, finding a stump to sit on. There was a hint of pine on the air that I breathed deeply into my lungs. I knew solitude well. I had known nothing but solitude for six months, ever since... I closed my eyes and pushed the thought away.

"Hey, am I intruding?"

When I saw Jules stepping carefully over tree roots, I was surprised to find I wasn't disappointed. It didn't feel like an intrusion to have her here with me. I budged over so that she could sit with me.

"Is everything all right?" she asked.

"Yeah, yeah," I replied, nodding my head too enthusiastically.

"No, it isn't." She smiled sadly. "I know you're struggling."

Behind us, I heard music coming from a portable radio. We briefly turned to watch the others dancing around the fire singing along.

"You can talk to me, you know," she said. "I... I don't want to make you freak out and clam up again, but you can talk to me. Tell me what's on your mind."

I raised my eyes to gaze into the distance. Here the trees were thick. The night was falling. It was difficult to see anything in that dark, and yet I could see the figure watching us. A tall, dark shape the size of a man. I ignored it because I decided it wasn't real.

"There's a voice back in my head. When my pills were stolen, the gap in my medication disrupted my treatment and I've been hearing the voice ever since," I told her.

I held my breath, waiting for her to run away from me

screaming. I watched the shadow watching us, wondering who would move first.

"I'm so sorry," she said. She didn't run away. "What's it like having that voice there?"

"Confusing. Disorientating. Depressing. She says horrible things to me. That I'm worthless, that I'm alone, that no one will love me."

Jules grasped my hand, her flesh a welcome warmth against mine. "Oh my God, Cath. You should've said. You've been dealing with this alone for two weeks?"

"I thought Irene might kick me out."

Jules let out a derisive snort. "You make us money by being here. She'd never kick you out. It's money first with her."

"Yeah, I'm getting that impression too."

"You're not alone and you're not worthless. You're my friend, Cath. I care about you." Her eyes penetrated mine in the gloom of the forest. "A lot."

My mind flashed back to the email I'd received from Alice, the one telling me that the others had said horrible things about me. Did that include Jules? I'd tried to push that worry from my mind, too consumed by everything else happening in the monastery, but now I remembered. I opened my mouth to ask Jules about it, when her face gradually moved closer to mine. I realised what she was doing and gently placed a hand on her shoulder. She leaned away and let out an "oh" sound.

"I'm so sorry," I said, as gently as I could. "The thing is, I'm not gay."

"That's okay," she said, still holding my hand, which I appreciated.

"I'm not anything." I shrugged.

She regarded me in surprise. "What do you mean?"

"I guess the term is asexual. I, umm... It's hard to explain."

"You don't have to if you don't want to."

We remained sitting there by the woods, hand in hand. I don't recall the moment she placed her head on my shoulder, but I know that at one point I was aware of that comfortable weight.

"You know, I am actually attracted to you," I admitted, my heart pounding, the words coming from me because of the stars and the smell of pine on the air. "But the thing is, I wouldn't ever want to take it further."

She lifted her head from me. "Does that mean you are a virgin?"

The night covered the blush creeping up my face. "Yes."

"Have you ever thought that if you haven't tried sex, you don't know if you'd like it or not?"

"Would you suggest a gay woman have sex with a man to see if she likes it?"

"Ah, I see your point. Sorry I said that. Was it insensitive?"

I laughed. "A bit, but it's fine." I paused. "You're the first person I've ever told."

"Seriously?"

"Yeah."

"Thank you for sharing your secret with me, Cath. It means a lot to me."

She squeezed my hand. It silenced the voice in my head. We were two friends talking, sharing secrets, in a beautiful location. The voice was wrong about me—I could be loved, and I wasn't alone. I faced the silhouette with bravery in my heart, knowing that I could achieve whatever I needed to achieve. Until Jules's body went rigid next to mine, and she dropped my hand and pointed.

"We're being watched."

"You see it too?"

"Yes," she said, "I see it! There's someone there." She raised her voice. "Hey! Hey! Who are you? What do you want?"

The sound of her raised voice attracted the attention of the others at the campsite who came over to us. Jules stood, still pointing.

"What do you want? Show yourself!"

When it moved towards us, I was convinced that Maria Popescu had come back to haunt us, to haunt me. I couldn't breathe. I held the freezing cold air in my lungs. I remained sitting on the tree stump, eyes glued to the figure as it stepped out from the trees. The shape of it wasn't right. I'd expected a long tunic hanging down to her toes, the usual nun's attire, with a covered head. But it soon became clear that this shadow was in trousers, its head uncovered. Out stepped a man. He was a living, breathing man, there was no doubt about that. He was around forty years old, clean shaven, thick eyebrows pulled together in a deep frown. There was a collective gasp. Lina, Nathan and Irene took a step backward. They were not afraid of him, they were afraid of what he was carrying—a shotgun.

"What the fuck, man?" Lukas said. "Put the gun down!"

"One of you left my gate open," the man said. "I lost a horse today!"

Nathan raised his hands. "I swear, I closed the gate behind me."

"I saw you, Nathan," I said.

"We haven't been through your fucking field," Faisal shouted. "Fuck off and leave us alone! This is public land."

This only aggravated the man. He jostled the gun and

bared his teeth as he spoke. "You left open my gate. I want you gone. Get out. Go away!"

"Jesus," Lukas muttered. "Maybe we should move the campsite."

"It's dark, though," Lina said.

Lukas turned back to the farmer. "Can't we go in the morning?"

"No, now! I wait while you go."

"Guess we're going then," Faisal said. He downed the last of his beer, eyed the man, and then stomped back to the camp.

"We should go back to the monastery," Irene said, anxiously eyeing the man with the gun.

"How are we going to find our way in the dark?" Dan gestured to the woods.

"We can follow the path," she said. "I brought a torch."

"Has everyone else sobered up?" Dan asked. "'Cause I fucking have."

Lukas placed a hand on Dan's shoulder. "It was great to meet you guys. Sorry it ended like this."

"Me too, bro." Dan patted his hand.

"Keep telling stories, Cath." Lukas raised his bottle to me on his way back to the tents with Lina and the others.

The farmer stood rigidly by the tree stump watching us leave. I was sure that his eyes followed me in particular, but it could have been my imagination.

I EXPECTED THE WOODS TO FEEL OPPRESSIVE IN THE DARK, BUT once I overcame the initial fear of the unknown, I began to find it magical, enticing even. Part of me longed to be alone, to slip in and out of the trees like a wood-nymph in the old

Greek myths. But at the same time, I was grateful for the company, and for the light from Irene's torch. She had her faults, but she kept us on course, for the most part.

When we didn't talk, the woods were completely silent. We didn't even hear Lukas and his group moving away from their camp. I couldn't help but wonder whether we should've stayed with them to ensure their safety, but you don't argue with the man holding a gun.

"Do you think that farmer will follow us?" Jules said, her voice a loud whisper.

"Holy shit, Jules, I do now," Dan said.

"I think he made his point," I added. "If he'd wanted to hurt us, he would've done it there, in the middle of nowhere."

"Yeah, I guess," Jules said. I watched her eyes dart around the trees. "But there were more of us then. Now that we've split from Lukas and the others, we might be easier to attack."

Both Nathan and Dan launched into their own angry muttering at Jules's suggestion. Irene concentrated hard on the path.

"There's enough to worry about with the wolves," Nathan said. "Let's hurry up, shall we?"

"We rush, we get lost," Irene pointed out. "That means we get to the monastery even later."

My stomach rumbled. It was after eight p.m. and all I'd eaten were the sandwiches and snacks we'd brought on the walk. I scratched underneath my chest camera, looking forward to taking the thing off. I wasn't sure how much it'd captured and whether it had run out of battery. Then it hit me. Irene would want me to upload all the footage, but I'd talked to Jules about my sexuality. Everything I'd said was on her camera, too. Uploading the footage meant showing the world a side of myself I'd never shown before. Then again, what did I have to lose? There were no friends or any family to worry about, not since Mum died.

"Careful here," Irene said. "It's steep." She traversed the slope with relative ease, balanced and upright, as only Irene Jobert could. Then she stopped and gestured to me to follow her.

I stumbled down the slope, hands groping nothing in the dark. Irene moved her torch beam towards me but the sudden light blinded me so that I couldn't see my feet or where I was putting them. My heartbeat quickened when I tripped and almost fell, running with my unbalanced weight thrown forward for the last of it.

"You all right?" she asked, when I reached the bottom. Breathlessly, I told her I was fine.

Irene moved the beam higher to help the others down the slope. Jules daintily traversed the damp ground, her arms out wide for balance. Nathan followed, using the same path as Jules. As Dan made his way down, the torch cut out. I lost sight of everything, including Dan. The trees blocked the moon and the world went black. Next to me, Irene swore under her breath. I heard the sound of her hitting the side of the torch. Dan let out a cry, there was a dull thud, and the light flashed on for barely a second before going out again. He was on the ground, rolling forward. The light came on a second time and this time it remained on, illuminating Dan's crumpled form on the ground. He was at the bottom of the slope, covered in mud, clutching his left ankle and panting like a panicked dog. We rushed over to help him, a cold vice-like grip clutching my lungs.

"I twisted my ankle," he said, groaning with the pain. "Or sprained it, I don't know."

Irene asked him if he could put weight on it while we

helped him to his feet. "I'm so sorry," she said. "I don't know why the torch went out. I put fresh batteries in."

Dan didn't say a word to acknowledge her apology. He wrapped an arm around Nathan's shoulder, and began to hobble forward.

What I didn't tell anyone was that when the light had flickered on for that moment, I had seen a pale shape in the trees. Then, when Irene's torch had resumed, it was no longer there. It didn't matter, though. It was simply my mind playing tricks on me again.

That's right, said the voice, *you're crazy*.

CHAPTER TWENTY-SEVEN

Beneath the fashionable chandelier, Irene dumped a bag of frozen peas on Dan's ankle and he let out a low moan. We were back in the monastery, still wearing our coats because the heating had gone off during the day. Despite the cold, I knew we were lucky to have made it back in, almost, one piece, considering the angry farmers and hungry wolves we knew lived in the mountains.

"How is it?" Irene asked.

"Pretty swollen. Don't think it's broken though."

"Good." She disappeared into the kitchen.

"Anyone want a hot drink?" I asked.

Tired heads nodded.

"Good work on the team building, Irene." Nathan rolled his eyes and leaned back in his chair.

I made my way into the kitchen and fixed five mugs of tea. While I was stirring in milk and sugar, Irene strode through to the utility room and back to the kitchen. Then she folded her arms defensively and stood underneath the archway leading into the refectory.

"The electricity is working fine," she said. "It looks like

the temperature had been turned right down. Weird, huh? Perhaps whoever did it should own up, because it wasn't me."

"None of us did it," Dan said. I heard the tension in his jaw, his gritted teeth. "Like we didn't steal Cath's medication, or the food from the fridge, or burn the Ouija board."

I had to squeeze past Irene as she was shaking her head. Flashing her an apologetic smile, I spilled tea on the floor tiles and hurried over to the table, dolling out the hot drinks.

A moment later, Irene dumped her laptop on the dining-room table. "It wasn't me, Dan. Perhaps it was the fucking ghost. Forget the heating. Everyone needs to give me the memory cards from your cameras. The subscribers haven't had content all day."

"I've been posting photos every now and then," Jules said.

Irene's lip curled up. "What do you want? A medal?" There was also no thank you for me when I placed a hot cup of tea next to her.

When it came to Jules's camera, Irene held out her hand waiting, but Jules glanced at me first.

"Are you happy for us to upload the footage, Cath?"

My cheeks flushed with embarrassment when her words caught the attention of the others. They knew that Jules and I had slipped away from the camp for a while, but what they didn't know was what happened while we were alone. Now they were curious.

In an attempt to make the moment less awkward, I tried to shrug nonchalantly, which I'm sure came across as completely fake. "Sure. Why would I mind?" Then I added on a short-lived smile.

As the others left the room to shower and change, I

motioned for Irene to talk to me. Quickly, I told her about the comments on The Event live stream about her make-up. But she shrugged.

"Don't worry about it. I have a big target on my back but I'm a big girl. It's jealousy. The make-up is fine." She stretched out her arms. "I'm taking a shower. See you in ten."

While the group were away I boiled up spaghetti, chopped onions and tomatoes and whipped up a quick meal. Irene returned to the kitchen first, tutting and complaining about the time it was taking to upload the files. When the others came back, Nathan took his bowl of pasta into his room. Dan sat in the refectory, his foot resting on a chair. He didn't say a word as he ate. Irene barely touched her food as she worked on the laptop. Jules and I made polite conversation but felt strange chatting in the frosty atmosphere. The team building had failed to bring us together. The longer we stayed in the monastery, the more we came to dislike each other. Perhaps I should have seen what was to come, but a naïve desire to see the good in others blinded me from the truth.

EVERYONE WAS IN THEIR BEDROOM BY TEN P.M. WHEN I showered, the water was tepid, and the pressure was terrible, and yet it was still one of the best showers I'd ever had in my life. After getting dry, I climbed into bed and checked my social media accounts. There weren't any messages about my conversation with Jules, but it would take hours for the subscribers to catch up with the hike.

That night, I slept deeply. There were no dreams, simply the elimination of time. One moment, my head was on the pillow and I was putting my phone on the bedside table, the next, a hand was rocking me awake.

My body went rigid in shock. The first thing I thought was that Maria had come to me in my bedroom. She was here and she was waking me up to tell me her story. I sat upright in bed. I turned to face the intruder, but a bright light shone in my eyes. *Shhhh*, they said, before I heard a whispered, *sorry*.

"Jules?" I asked.

She moved the torch away from my face and her features came into view. She was wearing the hoody I leant her over pyjama bottoms.

"Sorry, I held the torch too close. Can I talk to you?"

"Yeah, okay." I wiped sleep from my eyes and budged up so that she could sit with me on the bed.

"When we were in the woods earlier, you told me a deeply personal secret." She placed the phone on her knee, with the light shining up. It was so eerie, and I hadn't recovered from my fright yet, that I switched on the lamp to fill the room with light. She switched off the torch on her phone and tucked a lock of hair behind her ear. "I want to tell you something. The thing is... I don't want to do it here." Her eyes darted around the room, reminding me of her doing the same in the forest. Why would she be as afraid here as she was in the dark forest?

"Why can't you tell me now?" I asked. I wondered whether it had something to do with what the others had been saying about me. I wasn't sure I wanted to know, then. Perhaps it was better not to know how cruel others could be.

She shrugged. "Call it a hunch. Want to go for a walk at lunch? We could take sandwiches out to the graveyard or the old infirmary."

"Okay," I said.

She smiled. "See you then."

It took me a while to get back to sleep. There was wind outside, the faint call of a wolf, and a pressing feeling of worry creeping over me.

THE MIST WAS BACK. VAPOUR LINGERED IN THE TREES. BEFORE my walk with Jules, I went up the tower and took photographs of the infirmary ruins covered in low-lying fog. While I was there I looked out at the graveyard. There were no figures. No silhouettes standing by the graves. But the memory of it made me cold anyway.

While the others were having lunch—plus arguing over what to put into the next food order—Jules and I left the house to walk through the cold miasma. It clung to us like metal filings on a magnet. Her puffa jacket swished and swooshed with every step. I heard my quick, tremulous breaths in the quiet. I desperately wanted to know what she was about to tell me, which hurried my footsteps towards the graveyard.

Yet, I also didn't want to go. The back of my neck was cold. Firstly, I was afraid of what she was going to say. Did the others hate me? Did they want me gone? *Yes, of course they do*, said the voice inside my head. I concentrated hard to shut her up.

Secondly, we were heading back to the graveyard and all I could think about was the dark figure I'd seen there. I thought of it standing with its back to me, covered from head to toe in black. An apparition that could have been born from my sick mind, or an apparition that was choosing me as its target to haunt. An apparition that meant me harm? I couldn't say. The voice in my head told me I was a narcissist because I assumed everything was about me. I thought to myself that I was crazy, that nothing was real, that I should be quiet and get it over with.

"I'm sorry for frightening you last night," Jules said. "Don't know why I didn't send you a WhatsApp. Not sure why I got so dramatic." She laughed. "I just needed to see your face."

"I'm starting to get used to people coming into my room."

"Oh yeah, I forgot about Nathan. Well, at least he's better behaved these days. Do you think the doctor prescribed him drugs?"

"I have no idea," I said.

We walked around the edge of the graves, an appropriate act as we skirted around the reason for our walk.

"Did you get a good vibe from the doctor? Did he seem legit?" she asked.

"He was… fine, I think. Though he did say there was nothing he could do about the psychological issues I've had since we arrived here. He figured it was because I had a gap in taking my medication but…" I trailed off, not sure how to explain myself.

Jules caught my eye, waiting.

"But what I've experienced here is inconsistent with my illness. I've never *seen* things before, but I have here. My schizophrenia has always been about voices. One voice in particular. These new… hallucinations are messing with me, making me doubt myself."

"Wait, what did you see?"

I pulled the sleeves of my jacket over my cold fingers. "I saw a figure down here standing right there." I stood facing the mountain, pointing up to the edge of the graveyard where the forest began. "And I saw the shape of a wolf over there." I directed Jules's gaze towards the birch trees in the distance. "It was while I was standing at the top of the tower."

"What if they were real?" Jules said, pulling her eyes back to me. "We met an angry farmer last night, and you rescued a wolf two weeks ago. What if the figure you saw was the farmer and the wolf was the one you rescued?"

I shook my head. "No. They didn't look the same as either of those things. The figure was dressed in black, like a... "

"Nun," she finished.

I exhaled as I said, "Yes." I paused to lick my lips. "The day I rescued the wolf, I saw a different one in the distance. A big, fully grown thing standing staring at me. But that isn't the weird part. The weird part was the feeling I got from it. Like badness, all the badness in the world moulded and shaped into one, big killing machine. Evil. Pure evil."

"What about the nun?"

"No, I never got that feeling from the nun. The fear came because my eyes shouldn't be seeing it, her, because I knew it wasn't there."

Jules stared out at the tower, pulling her lower lip between her teeth. "I've sensed evil here, too. I've never seen the wolf, but I have dreamt about one."

"What about the nun?"

She shook her head. "The shadow on the camera but nothing else. There are times when I feel cold. The church gave me the creeps. There was a bad smell about it. The whole place was wrong. Is that what you felt?"

"Not exactly but close. It made me cold." I wrapped my arms around my chest. I didn't want to talk about it anymore. "Are the others saying horrible things about me?

Have you said nasty things about me? About how crazy I am?"

Jules sighed. "What? Why would you ask?"

"One of my readers sent me an email. She said not to trust any of you."

"Cath, no. I didn't... I..." She squeezed my forearm. "Look, there's been bitchiness, I won't deny it. Everyone here has gossiped and bitched about everyone here. I don't remember what people said."

"You don't?"

She shrugged. "I guess Irene or Dan or someone said you were a little uptight, but that's it."

"Right." It wasn't as bad as what I'd been expecting, but I still felt disappointment spread through me.

"We can get into it another time if you like. I'll try and remember everything, but it isn't why I wanted to come here."

"Okay," I said. "Why are we here?"

"I'm not even sure I know where to start," she said.

"The beginning?" I suggested.

The side of her mouth pulled up, but the smile didn't touch her eyes at all. "This is hard to say because I'm pretty sure you're going to hate me by the time I've finished."

I was surprised, both by her words and the way her skin had taken on a faded ashen colour. There was genuine fear on her face, and it scared me.

"I haven't been honest about who I am," she said, and as she kept talking, her eyes moved from mine to a spot in the distance, as though she was avoiding my eye contact. "Most of all, I haven't been honest about why I'm here."

CHAPTER TWENTY-EIGHT

"You've probably noticed that I'm not Irene Jobert's biggest fan, and there's a reason for that. When my blog took off, I got the opportunity to write a few articles for certain media sites like *Huffington Post* and *Jezebel*. I've even written the odd piece for the *New York Times* and *The Cut*. I think that's why they reached out to me rather than any of you guys."

"They?"

"The *New York Times*. There have been rumours flying around under the radar that Irene Jobert's make-up business isn't legit, that it's a multi-level marketing scam."

"Oh," I said, shocked, but steadily realising that what she was saying made a lot of sense.

"You see, what Irene does is sell starter packs to young women who then have to sell the products to friends and family. The thing is, the products are low quality, and the company targets vulnerable women, such as single mothers, those in low-paying jobs, people who have been laid off... You get the picture. Young women who idolise Irene and are desperate to make money. They spend about a hundred dollars on the starter pack. Only five per cent of those women make their money back."

My jaw dropped. "Five per cent?"

"That's right. Five fucking per cent. I did a lot of research before I came out here. The *New York Times* simply told me the rumours and I did all the investigation with the intention of learning more about Irene once we were here." She sighed. "Cath, please don't hate me."

"Why would I hate you?" I asked.

"Because once you know all the underhand shit I've done, you might feel differently."

"It can't be that bad."

She raised her eyebrows. "I've been in her room. That night when you guys played with the Ouija board, Irene forgot to lock her door. She always does locks her door, but I think the arguing distracted her. I went into her room, I went on her computer and I opened her files."

"How—"

"She was uploading video content at the time and her screen hadn't timed out," Jules said. "I got lucky."

"What did you find in her files?"

"Conversations between her and her parents." Jules closed her eyes, leaned over and rubbed her temples. "Cath, you don't even know how deep it all goes. It's been... it's been such a disgusting secret to keep."

"What do you mean?"

"I found out that Irene and her mother faked her leukaemia when she was a child."

"What?"

"Irene also lied about being the daughter of a rich business mogul. Her father keeps asking her for money and I think she pays him regularly."

Disappointment hit me then. It was as if the fog had

cleared to allow me to see all of those lies for what they were. When I'd been younger and my mother was drunk and I had no friends, Irene's videos had brightened my day. Seeing her positivity in light of her suffering had always given me the strength to carry on. I ran my fingers through my hair, trying to process everything.

"She lied about everything?"

"Well," Jules said, "she was a kid at the time. I think a lot of blame is on her parents. But she's not a kid any longer, and I think it's safe to say she's still capitalising on those lies. She could've stopped it at any moment, but she didn't. She could've owned up and apologised, but she hasn't."

Jules reached out, taking hold of my arms, her eyes wide. "Cath, you have no idea how hard it's been to keep this secret. You've no idea how much I've been bursting to tell you, especially when you went outside searching for the drone. I wanted to tell you that it was me. I'd been using the drone to try to spy on Irene, but I couldn't work the stupid thing, and I ended up frightening you instead."

I pulled away from her. "What?"

"I'm sorry I didn't tell you sooner."

I saw the pain on her face, the welling of tears in the corners of her eyes, and the contortion of her mouth as she gritted her teeth. I saw how hard she was trying not to cry. It moved me, it truly did, but I had to admit that I was hurt, shocked even, that not one, but two people in the monastery had been lying to me and everyone else. Both Jules and Irene had been deceiving everyone about who they were. What secrets were Nathan and Dan hiding?

What about your own secrets? said the voice.

"You're mad at me," Jules said.

"No—" I started.

"Yes, you are, and I don't blame you."

What she didn't know, was that I'd done things here that I was ashamed of, too. I hadn't told Dan that it was me who'd spelt out the name Maria, for instance. Or about how I blamed Nathan for taking my medication without having any proof.

"I'm not, I promise. How did you get into her room without the cameras picking it up?"

"I deleted the footage of me doing that from her laptop," she said.

"Did you delete the footage from the walkway camera?"

"Yeah."

"The bit where someone burned the Ouija board?"

"No, not that bit. That happened later when I was in bed. I deleted footage while you were all playing with the board. I don't know who burned the Ouija board. My bet is Irene, though. She's clearly trying to manipulate us into providing drama."

"What are you going to do about everything you know?"

She shrugged. "Wait until the end of The Event and write it all up as an exposé, I guess."

"You're going to stay living here with Irene knowing what she's done."

"I have to," she said.

"You don't."

Jules blinked. Her body was tense but her expression impassive. I was sure that she was grappling with the fact she'd made up her mind. She was staying. "It could be important to stay and learn about what she's been doing."

I stared sadly at Maria Popescu's gravestone. "What more is there to find? Haven't you got enough info already?"

"There were files on her computer," Jules said. "They were password protected. I want to know what's in those files."

She was determined. Afraid, but determined. Now that she'd shared her secret, a little colour came back to her cheeks, and the tears faded away. But the fact that she was determined frightened me. Now that I knew what Irene was capable of, I realised that she wasn't the harmless self-involved woman I'd thought she was. Irene was actually dangerous. Irene had a lot to lose.

"I don't think we should stay," I said.

"Are you going to leave?"

"If I do, will you come with me?"

Jules shook her head. "I can't do that. Sorry, but I can't."

"The others, though. They deserve to know what kind of person Irene is. Dan is already suspicious, and Nathan has been through so much since we got here. If we outed her now, it would end The Event early and we'd all get to go home."

"They'd lose their money," Jules said. "We'll break our contracts and Loup, or Irene, or whoever the fuck is paying us will refuse to send us what they owe. I think the best thing to do is wait it out. It's less than two weeks, now. Then we'll get our money and I can write the article."

I raised my eyebrows. "Jules, after everything you've learned about Irene, do you honestly believe she's still going to pay us?"

ICY RAIN WASHED DOWN THAT AFTERNOON, REMINDING US that winter had arrived and we were in an isolated area. The monastery was freezing cold and we were all layered up with coats and scarves, bumping into each other in the kitchen while making hot drinks. Irene maintained a sunny disposition, cheerfully telling us that the heating was having teething problems, but that the electric heaters in our rooms should be working just fine. Whenever I was in my bedroom, I crawled under the duvet and used the warmth of my laptop. At one point I saw Nathan taking a bottle of brandy into his room.

Maria's story flowed well. She was here, at the monastery, about to give birth. The mother superior had taken Maria under her wing for now, but the character building in my mind kept turning into a villain. She wasn't who she said she was. I typed and typed until my wrists ached, sure that this was the best writing of my life.

When I took a short break from Maria's story, I read through the comments on the uploaded videos of the hike. The cameras had caught everything up to the man with the gun appearing in the woods. My footage cut off as Jules and I were discussing the figure in the woods. It was the ultimate cliff-hanger. Viewers had been left waiting for hours until Irene wrote a short statement about how a local man had asked them to leave because of the open gate. That reminded me, who left the gate open? I'd seen Nathan close the gate and Lukas claimed that they hadn't walked through the field. He could've been lying to save face, or there could have been another group of walkers we hadn't seen. Or maybe the farmer was lying, though I wasn't sure what he'd gain from that. Perhaps he had been stalking us. Maybe he had a problem with us being in Sfântul Mihail.

I skim read the comments, but there were too many to take in.

Cheezemonkeys: Cath really IS a virgin. The Yorkie called it!
Lu98: That was brave. I'm still shipping Cath and Jules.
Motherofcats: the man was watching them for ages…
Draak: Nathan will murder Cath.

Draak: I will give Nathan one million dollars to murder Cath.
Burgerboi: Surprised no one died in those woods. Anyone else think it was going to go Blair Witch?

Halfway through reading the comments, there was a hammering on my door, the kind of urgent bashing that pulls you out of your thoughts and makes you sit up straight. I hurried over and pulled it open, letting cold air into my room. Nathan was standing there, breathing brandy into my face, his fingernails tapping the door frame.

"Guess what?" he said.

I shook my head, indicating I had no idea what he was going to say. Which I didn't.

"We were supposed to be getting a food delivery tomorrow, but it's been cancelled. There's a storm coming. Have you seen the weather forecast?"

"No..."

"Snow, Cath. There's going to be a blizzard, and we have no food and the heating keeps going on the blink." He turned as if to hurry away, his hands balled into fists.

"Are you sure?" I said. "I know it's been chilly, but we've just had a bit of fog, no sleet or hail or anything."

"That's what it says on my phone. We're having a meeting. Come on."

I clenched my jaw, my mind already flooded with worry, anxiously chewing on everything and anything that could go wrong. As I entered the room, I avoided Irene's gaze.

"Right, now Nathan and Cath are here, I want to make my announcement," Dan said. "I'm leaving."

He made his statement before I could even sit down. In the awkward silence that followed I pulled out a chair and took a place at the table.

"Don't be ridiculous," Irene said. "It's a weather forecast

for God's sake. The snow might not even come and then you'll look stupid."

"I've made up my mind," Dan said. "I've booked a taxi to pick me up, I've packed, and I'm going. My ankle is sore, I'm sick of you, Irene, and I don't even care if you pay me."

"*I*?" Irene made a scoffing sound. "It's not *me* paying you, it's Loup. They won't, by the way. You'll be breaching your contract."

"I don't care," he said. "I've had enough. I'm going to go and get ready."

"Are you sure, Dan?" I asked quietly as he stood up and limped out of the room.

He didn't hear me, or he ignored me, I'm not sure which. It turned out he was the first to reach his limit.

CHAPTER TWENTY-NINE

There was this secret, burning inside of me, making my skin red hot. After Dan stormed out of the kitchen, I went to my room and I prayed to Maria's crucifix. I prayed that I wouldn't ruin Jules's plans by blurting out the things I wasn't supposed to say, and I prayed that not saying those things wouldn't have a consequence.

I'm not sure how long I prayed for, but I could hear Nathan playing his games in the next room. I don't know where Jules and Irene were. After I prayed, I carried on writing my story, and while I was hunched over the laptop, Dan left. I never heard the car that collected him, and he never came to say goodbye. One moment he was here, the next he wasn't, and I missed it all.

In my story, Maria had her baby and the mother superior wrenched the child from her arms. A tiny, wriggling, red body was wrapped in linen and taken out of the room while Maria was held back by two of the sisters. It was a little girl. Once I finished writing the scene, I was emotionally spent. It was dark outside. A wolf howled. I hadn't eaten all day, but I wasn't hungry in the slightest.

Eventually, Irene checked on me and asked what I was doing locked away in my room all day. I found no answer to her question, but I knew that my wrists and fingers were sore from mashing the keys on my laptop. She called me into the snug where two other sullen people sat. I stayed standing.

"The world has not ended." Irene waved a hand. "Dan left because of his hurt ankle, that's all. There's no need for these long faces."

"We need to decide what we're going to do about food if this snowstorm arrives," Jules said. "If the delivery doesn't come, we're screwed."

"Follow me." Irene walked past me to the door. When Nathan and Jules remained still, she beckoned them impatiently.

I saw the tense set of Jules's jaw as we followed Irene through to the kitchen. There was no one who hated Irene more than Jules.

Irene threw open two cupboards and gestured to the cans lining the shelves. "Soup, beans, canned fruit and vegetables, stews." She moved on to the second cupboard. "Rice, lentils, pasta. Shall I go on?"

Jules placed her hands on her hips. "No."

"You think perhaps you can survive without steak and salad for two weeks?" Irene smirked and lifted her left eyebrow. Jules said nothing, but her lip twitched, almost snarled. The nasty flavour of satisfaction on Irene's face made me nauseous.

It was Nathan who spoke up next. "Yeah, all right, we can live on tomato soup for two weeks, but if this snowstorm hits and one of us falls ill or hurts themselves, what's going to happen then?"

"We're not as cut off as you think we are. The Butnari

villagers live and thrive in this part of the world and we can too. There are rescue teams we can contact. They have snowmobiles and helicopters. You all need to calm down. We have access to the internet and there are thousands of people around the world watching us. If anything bad happens, the authorities will be under pressure to help."

"What if the internet goes down? What if we lose electricity? What if the water supply freezes? Have you thought about any of these things?" Jules demanded.

A guttural sound came from Irene's throat. "We have back-up generators, signal boosters, and constant communication with Loup. Will you stop panicking. The storm won't even come. I was told it doesn't snow in the Carpathians until January."

THE SNOW CAME THE NEXT MORNING. SOFTLY, IT STARTED, A wet covering of sodden flakes. But as time went on the flakes grew bigger, drier, covering the tower, the solar panels, the tops of the trees and the grass below; the peak of the mountain, the snow line and the base, where the land briefly flattened before it dipped and soared again. The snow came and it brought with it silence. There was no wind howling through the casements anymore. We found ourselves tiptoeing through the monastery, afraid to destroy the majesty of it, both in awe and doused in anxiety because the world felt different; the world felt wrong.

Our isolation had never been so obvious as it was when the snow fell. At first, we were intoxicated by the beauty of it, each one of us glued to the windows. A few hours in, after a blanket had formed all around the monastery, we put on coats, gloves and hats, strapped on a camera, and headed out. The crunch of our boots on the untouched snow made us giggle. Our misunderstandings, secrets and lies all faded away. We threw snowballs and made snow-men. Jules and Nathan lay on the ground and waved their arms to create snow angels. We were children without adult supervision. We regressed because the alternative was too much to bear.

Whatever aerial Loup built for the monastery worked well enough that our connection to the outside world endured. The viewers enjoyed our childish displays in the snow. They created gifs out of our grinning faces to share on Facebook. And while that was happening, we heated up left-over fresh food to eat before it perished, all seated around the table with the chandelier flickering above us.

None of us paid much attention to the lights flickering. I remember Jules noticed it, but we weren't concerned. It was, however, the first indication that things could go wrong. It was the first crack in what had otherwise been a perfect day. I ate stale vegetables and thought about praying to Maria's crucifix.

AFTER LUNCH, JULES AND I WENT TO THE BELFRY, PRETENDING we were going to get drone footage of the snowy mountain-side. While we did get the footage, we also talked freely about Irene and the lies she had been telling us.

"Does Loup exist?" I asked. "We've never had any communication with them whatsoever. Everything comes from Irene."

"The renovation of this building would have cost a lot of money," Jules said. "I can't imagine Irene spending all that cash. But at the same time, something isn't right. I think she controls more of The Event than she lets on. I need to get onto her computer. I need to know."

I could see, even then, that Jules's determination was a force to be reckoned with. Just as I was obsessed with writing down what I imagined Sister Maria's story to be, Jules wanted—no, needed—to uncover the lies Irene had told her fans and followers. Trying to talk her out of any of it wouldn't work.

"Then we need to tell Nathan," I said.

"No."

I held up a palm. "Hear me out for a minute. Nathan deserves to know what he's got himself into. He's now the last person in the monastery who doesn't know about Irene's lies. That isn't fair. Also, he's into tech. He could potentially help us."

Jules stared out at the snow-covered gravestones below the tower. "I don't know, he's unpredictable and emotional. He's..." Jules flashed me a guilty smile before returning her gaze to the graveyard.

For once I indulged the indignation that heated my skin. "Crazy? Unhinged? Weren't you the one telling me you believe in ghosts? You told me you thought the monastery had a bad vibe."

"It does," she said.

"Yeah, and many people would say that that's crazy."

She sighed. "I know. Sorry. Maybe you're right, maybe we should bring Nathan into this. God, Cath, I'm so scared about what we're doing."

"Then maybe we don't do it at all. Maybe we wait for the snow to clear and get out of this place so Nathan and I can get on with our lives. Maybe you write that piece without knowing what's in Irene's password-protected files."

But Jules wouldn't listen.

This moment haunted me the most out of everything that followed. Could I have convinced Jules to drop her crusade against Irene? Should I have stormed back into the kitchen and confronted Irene that night, before we uncovered the secrets contained within the elusive files? If I'd managed to do either of those things, I don't believe events would have transpired in the way they did. There's no denying that I had the power to alter history, and yet, I failed. All I did was direct the drone back into the tower before descending the steps and making my way to the west wing. Then we all ate at the refectory table together, pretending that everything was fine. When I went back to my room, I opened Maria's bible. It was the beginning of the end.

CHAPTER THIRTY

I was reading the bible.

Reading Maria's bible. The seventy-odd-year-old foreign-language book that had been annotated in Romanian. I was reading all of it. I saw Maria's scribbles and I knew exactly what she'd written.

We invited the monster in. Mother Mary help us, save our souls, we are cursed here on the mountains. Our Father has cursed us. We are in your hands now Mother. Help us! Help us!

The room was dark, but I could read the words just fine. Everything was in English, and everything was visible. In fact, the words floated from the page, gilded bright, burning in the darkness. I watched in awe as I had earlier gazed at the falling snow.

There was one difference between these words and the snow: the snow had been silent. My room was not silent, it was breathing. I inhaled and exhaled along with it, becoming one with the entity inside my room. I breathed her in, exhaled out myself. Yes, I wanted to be Maria more than I wanted to be Cath. I was ready to be inhabited by anyone other than myself. Get out, I thought, get out of me, Cath. Take the voice with you. Take everything out of me, all the paranoia, the humiliation, the contrition. Take that paranoid rambling voice in my head.

Maria was as damaged as I was. She'd been betrayed like I had—I could feel it. Someone had hurt her in the same way I'd been hurt. As I inhaled and exhaled, I saw the drunk woman standing over me, berating me, slapping my arms and legs. A wail emitted from my throat. I was young, barely six years old, and she was my mother.

As I lay on my bed, I forced the memory out, exhaling Cath, inhaling Maria. I closed my eyes and pictured Maria's ghost, shrouded in black cloth, her pale face floating amid dark contours. There was one thing I could be sure of, Maria was the strong one, she was everything I was not.

"Let me be you," I uttered into the dark.

"I am not who you think I am," the dark replied.

I realised then that I could not move my arms. In fact, I could not move my body, not even my head. An invisible force was pushing me down into the mattress. It was like being pinned by a heavier person, their body, every part of it, touching every part of mine. I squirmed against the weight, but it made no difference. The room continued to breathe, but now it wasn't in unison with me, it was against it. The breath was cold at my neck and rasping. It repulsed me. I felt a sharp object pressing against my throat. I screamed. I think I screamed. I don't know if I screamed, but I wanted to scream. No one rushed into my room, no one came to my aid, all I could do was lie there, too afraid to open my eyes. This was not Maria, it couldn't be. Could it?

"Mum?" I whimpered.

The breathing stopped. My arms were released, and I sat up, opening my eyes, chest heaving up and down.

It had been a dream, hadn't it?

The bible was where I'd left it on top of the duvet. I could no longer understand the words, they were in Romanian and I could not speak it. Yet, still I thought of what had come to me in my dream as the truth. *We invited the monster in*. What if we'd done the same? I thought of the white wolf out there in the woods. It had been two days since Dan had left. What if he'd been replaced by evil?

I skipped breakfast that morning. My clothes were loose as I pulled them over my smaller frame. It was an unusual feeling for a person who'd always been chubbier than average. It wasn't a triumph to me, it was a failure, because it provided concrete evidence of my declining mental health. With the others, I managed to keep my faculties together, but alone, I was consumed by my writing, and as obsessed with Maria as always.

Today was the day we were going to tell Nathan about Irene's deception. Even without the nightmare I would've been on edge. But seeing as I'd woken up sweating and panting, I knew it was going to take an emotional toll on me. For a while I sat alone in the kitchen with my shoulders slumped, wanting to be anywhere but in the monastery with those people. At least I was alone. Irene often slept in. Nathan wasn't out of his room yet, which was unlike him. He tended to be an early riser who then wandered the halls eating snacks.

When Jules entered, I noticed that her hair was greasy, and she had a few spots breaking out on her chin. With

water and electricity becoming an issue, we weren't show-
ering as often. I also noticed that she'd layered her clothes
over her pyjamas. She rubbed her eyes and asked me if I
was ready.

"Yep. Not sure how we're going to do this, though. We
need to take him for a walk outside, but it's snowing again."

She combed her hair with her fingers. "I was up most of
the night doing live videos. Fuck those fuckers. Most of
them kept telling me how rough I looked."

"When the snow clears, I'm going home," I said. "Maybe
I'll even leave before then. Maybe I can hike to Butnari and
ask for a snowmobile."

She laughed. "Or a sled."

Still shaken from the nightmare, I could barely manage
a smile. We drank tea and waited for Nathan, who, when he
arrived, seemed bemused by the idea of walking in the
freezing cold weather. But he was surprisingly acquiescent
and somewhat distant. Luckily, Irene stayed in her room
during the conversation so that we didn't have to make an
excuse to exclude her.

"Wait a moment while I get my body cam," Nathan said.

"No camera," Jules replied. Her gaze contained so much
steel that Nathan simply nodded, and pulled on his coat.
There was no sarcastic comment. No inappropriate joke. No
reaction at all, and it concerned me.

By this point, none of us were at our best. Along with her
greasy hair, there were blue bruises of tiredness beneath
Jules's eyes. Yesterday I'd noticed that Irene had developed
the habit of anxiously waving her hands around as she
spoke. I knew I had the haggard appearance of a much older
person, with hair both oily and dry, skin that was flaking
across my forehead but breaking out along my jawline, and
my body at its thinnest. But Nathan's appearance definitely

shocked me. His skin was still that strange waxy texture, and his pointed chin made him appear gaunt. I wondered whether he was sleeping because he rubbed his eyes almost every minute. He didn't seem to be washing himself, because there was such a build-up of grime beneath his fingernails.

Outside, the snow was gathering in drifts up the walls facing the mountain peak. If the snow continued at the same rate, those drifts would be taller than us in no time. It was picturesque but terrifying. Inside my long sleeves, my fingers were trembling, half from fear, half from the cold.

Nathan's pale-blue eyes scanned the landscape. "We're screwed up here, aren't we? Dan had the right idea leaving before the storm. Is that what you wanted to talk about? Do you want to convince Irene to have us rescued?"

"Not exactly," Jules said.

"Or was it the news?" Nathan said. "About the travellers we met on the footpath the other day."

"Why what happened?" I asked.

"They've been reported missing," Nathan said. "They were supposed to meet people in Brasov two days after we saw them. But they didn't arrive, and their friends can't get hold of them."

"They'll freeze to death!" Jules exclaimed.

"Most likely," Nathan said, not giving away much emotion. "Fuck."

"Maybe we should go for a walk and see if we can find them," I said. "It's not exactly tropic conditions in the monastery, but they could bunk with us until the snow clears."

"Yeah," Nathan said. "Okay, let's do that. Wait, what did you want to talk about then?"

Jules and I exchanged a glance, but ultimately, it was up

to her to tell the story. We were halfway around the side of the monastery and the cold had seeped into my bones already.

"It's Irene," Jules said. "She's been lying to us."

Nathan didn't particularly react to this statement, perhaps he'd suspected it too.

"I'm writing a piece of investigative journalism on Irene because her business is a multi-level marketing scam."

Nathan shrugged. "MLMs aren't illegal as far as I know. My girlfriend gets messages from those annoying girl bosses and their essential oils all the time."

"I know they're not illegal," Jules said. "But Irene's company is preying on the weak to peddle her bad-quality merchandise."

"Okay," he said. "That is bad. But it doesn't necessarily affect us, right?"

"Maybe not, but I think she also lied about having cancer when she was a kid, and Cath and I are suspicious about Loup. Cath doesn't think we're going to get paid."

This made Nathan stop in his tracks. "She lied about having cancer? Jesus." He pushed his hands deep into his pockets and shrugged his shoulders. "Wait, are you sure? She was a kid. How could she fake it? Everyone saw the pictures of her when she was ill."

"It was her parents," Jules said. "I believe they orchestrated it. They must be grifters or something. But Irene knows and she hasn't corrected anything since. All she's done is use that as a springboard to getting rich and famous. Now she cons people into buying her make-up."

Nathan raised his eyebrows. "That's fucked up. What's all this about Loup?"

"Does it even exist?" Jules said. "There's no evidence it does. I'm the one who went into her room. I know, I know, it's bad, but I did it and I poked around on her computer. There are files on there that I think we should view. If Irene has lied about all those things, don't you think she might be lying to us? And if she's lying to us, don't you think we need to know the extent of those lies?"

"Or we could get the fuck out of here. We should've gone before the snow came. Speaking of which, how long have you known about all of this?" Nathan's eyes flicked from me to Jules and back. "*Both* of you? Did Dan know? Is that why he left?"

"No," Jules said. "Dan left for his own reasons. I've known about the rumours since before I arrived, but I didn't know for sure until last week. Cath only found out a few days ago."

"What?" Nathan backed away as though we'd thrown water in his face. "You kept this from me and Dan? We've been under the same roof for two and a half weeks. Don't you think I had a right to know who I was living with?" He shook his head sadly. "This place has made me ill and I've stuck it out because I didn't want to let anyone down. All this time you've kept this secret to yourself. We could've left before the snowstorm but neither of you spoke up. Shame on you both."

His words made me wince. Disgrace crept in like a virus infiltrating the body. It seeped into my bloodstream. Even Jules swallowed nervously.

"I did what I thought was best," Jules said. "It was Cath who persuaded me to tell you, so don't blame her. She wanted me to tell everyone and get things out in the open."

"This whole situation is royally fucked." Nathan folded his arms tightly around his body. He was quiet for a moment before he began to speak again. "No, enough is enough. If you manage to get those files, I'll help you open them, but

I'm not sneaking around this building in the dark like some fucking Scooby Doo character. It's Irene's turn to stay up late and chat with subscribers tonight. Do with that what you will."

"All right," Jules said. "I'll keep that in mind."

"I noticed that she doesn't lock her door when she gets drunk," Nathan said. "And that is as much as I'm going to help you."

Jules chewed on her bottom lip. "Okay, we drink tonight, then. She'll be happy if we're joining in because she's so obsessed with entertaining the viewers."

"We should search for those hikers," I said, changing a subject that still made my stomach ache with shame. "It's stopped snowing and we might have a few hours before lunch."

"Fine, I'll help with that, too," Nathan said. I sensed the begrudging tone, but was happy to see that he'd do the right thing when pressed. I hoped he'd be an ally for us if we needed him.

We walked around the monastery as a taciturn group, too afraid to call out the names of the people we'd met, for fear of causing an avalanche. Instead we checked for footprints, tents, items of clothing, anything that could lead us to the missing group. Mostly the snow was fresh. It was us who disturbed the crisp white blanket.

After an hour or so we all began to slow as the cold infiltrated our joints, and made any exposed skin feel like ice. I didn't know what the others were thinking about, but my thoughts lingered on Irene and Jules and the complicated web I was trapped in. Jules was my friend, and I didn't want to let her down, but the secret she'd shared with me burned hot in my abdomen. Nathan was right. If we'd brought everything out into the open the other day we could've called an end to The Event and left before the snow. Had I done the right thing by siding with Jules? We'd bonded over the course of the weeks, but maybe I needed to remind myself that I didn't know her all that well. I didn't know any of them. *You need to look after number one*, said the voice in my head. *Don't trust anyone.*

We carried on for a short while longer, but we were freezing, and Jules was hungry. When we saw a set of fresh paw prints, we hurried back to the monastery.

CHAPTER THIRTY-ONE

Irene was dancing in the kitchen. Pointed toes, short pyjama bottoms, her hair loose, tendrils of blonde flying back and forth as she shook her head to the beat. She wasn't a wild or free dancer; she was neat and composed. She was dancing for other people, not herself. I wanted to know her. Why had she lied for all these years? Had it been for her parents or for herself? As I stood in the entrance to the kitchen, watching her, I tried to remember the original photograph that had launched her fame. That pure portrayal of unfair suffering that she'd represented all those years ago.

There was a picture in my mind of a young bald girl with a breathing tube taped to her nose. She had been twelve and it was about twelve years ago, when Facebook was more about following friends and less about politics, and Twitter was more about politics and less about bullying. I'd been young myself, thirteen, and I remember thinking if Irene could smile through cancer treatment, I could get through my own issues, like having no dad and a perpetually drunk mother who blamed me for all her problems. None of those things compared to Irene and her life and death situation.

There was no way that kind of post would go viral without due investigation now. Firstly, a well-meaning person would set up a Go Fund Me page for Irene, which would then annoy an angry keyboard warrior to the point where they'd track down every small detail about Irene and her mother to debunk the story. It'd be all over Reddit. Then the news would latch on. *Huffington Post*, BBC News, the *New York Times*. *The Cut* or the *New Yorker* would do a deep-dive article about Irene and her mother, which would be optioned for a movie.

Jules and Nathan shuffled around me to get into the kitchen. I'd been standing there for God knows how long, watching Irene dancing, lost to the past. Embarrassed, I shed my coat and boots, and brushed out my hair. Irene smiled and offered us a coffee, but Jules and Nathan left. I took up her suggestion, while at the same time the realisation hit me that Jules would be the one who wrote the article that would lead to the movie.

"I forgot if you take sugar," Irene said, tapping a teaspoon against the canister.

"Two please," I replied.

She passed me the cup before pulling out a stool. "Did you get any good footage?"

Of course, Irene's first instinct at every turn. Content. Money. Had these things been drilled into her?

"We didn't wear our cameras, sorry. Did you know that the hikers we bumped into the other day went missing?"

"They did? That's terrible. Is anyone searching for them?" She flipped her hair over one shoulder and regarded me with large, beautiful eyes. There was little genuine concern, but, to be fair, we'd spent a bare few hours in their company.

"I think so," I said.

"Hmm," she said. "There must be a rescue team out there."

"We should get in touch with the authorities and tell them where we last saw them."

She seemed distant, uninterested. "Yeah. I'll do that if you want."

I thought about leaving then, but I was intrigued by her. I wanted to know more about who she was. I wanted to marry up the two Irenes I knew—the little bald girl in the photograph, and the woman who lies. "What was it like, when you were young?"

"You mean the cancer?" She shrugged. "It was hard, but my maman helped me stay positive."

"Still, all those hospital appointments. The tests, the needles, the side effects from the medication. Must've been awful."

She stretched out her arms and caressed the skin from wrist to elbow. "I was black and blue, always. Bruises everywhere."

I bobbed my head to encourage her. "You'd recently moved to America from Paris, right?"

"I spent most of my life in California, people don't remember that. They think of me as this French girl." She laughs. "But I'm a Cali girl." A mega-watt smile stretched across her face.

It was undeniable that her beauty could light up any room, but to me, in that moment, it repulsed me.

"Do you keep in touch with any of the doctors and nurses you met?" I asked.

"I think Maman does, but I was a child, so, no." She

pulled at a thread on the strap of her top, avoiding eye contact.

Even though I wanted to ask her outright, to catch the reaction on her face, I didn't. Instead I left her in the kitchen humming along to the music.

———

I HADN'T OPENED MY EMAILS FOR A FEW DAYS OR CHECKED into my reader group. When I finally did that afternoon, what I'd expected was for my inbox and Facebook group to be dead. What I found were several concerned messages, and questions about whether I would be writing any more stories in the Arkathis world. Despite the good intentions, I couldn't bring myself to answer any of the messages, instead choosing to write my story about Maria Popescu.

We invited the monster in. But who was the monster? That was the part I couldn't grasp. Everything I'd written so far suggested that the mother superior was the monster, and yet, that wasn't right, she was already inside the monastery. Whenever I thought back to my story about the tall man and the deaths, the air would go cold. *Wrong track*, said the voice in my head.

Nevertheless, I continued to write about the mysterious deaths. Maria was a nun now, resolute in her beliefs. She blocked out thoughts of her baby by praying.

I forgot to eat that day, and later, I would come to realise that I hadn't showered for at least three days, though I had no idea at the time. If I wasn't talking to one of the others or writing, the voice in my head was constant. Writing happened to be the one habit keeping the voice at bay.

Later that day Nathan knocked on my door. His hair was mussed, and he yawned.

"I was taking a nap," he said. "But you woke me up with all that muttering."

"What muttering?"

"You've been talking constantly for over an hour," he said. "Fuck's sake, Cath, admit it. Are you on Instagram Live or something?"

"No," I said. "I swear, I had no idea I was talking out loud. Maybe I was reading as I was typing, I don't know. Sorry I woke you up."

Nathan shrugged.

When he left, I regarded my empty room, and then checked the time. I'd been writing for five hours without stopping. No bathroom break, no lunch break, nothing. Had I been talking to myself? Or was Nathan hearing voices? Outside the room, the snow began to fall again. A pain spread from my chest to my arm. I felt dizzy, and I had to put my head between my knees in order to be able to breathe. I was having a panic attack. While I thought I'd always understood the implications of being here in the Carpathians, seeing the snow drifts gather, and knowing that Lukas and the others were missing, the severity of our situation seemed insurmountable. There was no one I could trust in this house, and we were completely sequestered. No, we weren't quite cut off from the world, because we still had the internet, but, realistically, how long would it take help to arrive if we needed it? I thought about Alexandru passing me his card when he dropped me off two and a half weeks ago. What use was that now? A car couldn't come up those winding roads.

I sat there for a time with my head between my knees, trying to breathe, filling my lungs as deeply as I could.

This is how you die, said the voice. *You die out here because no one cares about you and no one will come if you're in trouble.*

Didn't I tell you this would happen? I always told you that if you insisted on going out in the world one day something terrible would happen and you'd die. Didn't I say? I always said, listen to your mother. Listen to her and maybe you won't end up a failure with nothing good happening to you and no friends and no love life, sad and fat and pathetic and miserable because you pissed everything away with those stupid ambitions of yours that we both know you'll never, ever, ever realise and instead go on and go on and go on as the worthless piece of shit that both of us know you are...

The wall shook. I fell down onto the floor as a voice boomed out.

"You're doing it again! Shut up, Cath!"

CHAPTER THIRTY-TWO

As I was curled in a ball on the floor of my room, my thoughts drifted back to my nightmare, particularly the weight I'd felt pinning me down. The force of it, a tangible weight, as though a person had been lying on top of me. I'd had night terrors before, but nothing like that. I knew that sleep paralysis existed, but the nagging voice in my head told me that what I'd experienced was an evil entity holding me down, and that the same evil entity was still here in my room.

That was why I'd curled up in a ball, because I didn't want to face the fact that I was finally losing my mind. The doctor could've prescribed me tic tacs for all I knew, and that voice, that malicious Wormtongue would not leave me be. But I'd agreed to help Jules, and for that reason, I had to try. Jules, who still had my hoody, who had lied to me, who said we were friends, who wanted to be more. Jules, who I'd sat with, hand in hand, one head resting on one shoulder, like sisters, like soulmates, until the man with the gun had emerged from the trees.

She doesn't care about you, the voice said.

"You're dead," I said out loud. "I watched you die."

What does that have to do with anything?

It was dark outside. There was no sunshine brightening my room, illuminating the coloured glass in the old window. There was nothing shining on my wall.

I crawled over to the door in time to hear the knock.

Go on. Pretend.

My pale fingers gripped the edge of the desk and helped me onto shaking legs. I opened the door and smiled.

"Hey," Jules said. Her gaze trailed me up and down. "Are you all right?"

"Yeah, fine."

"Have you been drinking?"

"No!"

She glanced over her shoulder and then came into the room, shutting the door. "I was thinking of trying out... you know..." She lowered her voice. "Irene is taking the shift tonight which gives us a good opportunity. We just need to get her tipsy."

"Okay, cool."

Her eyes narrowed. "Are you sure you still want to do this? You don't seem yourself."

She has no idea who you are, said the voice. *But I do.*

"We could take a bottle of wine to her room," I suggested.

"We've still got Prosecco," Jules said. "That could work. I'll go and get it. She keeps her laptop on at all times to monitor the webcam. If we're in her room, we could lift the files while she's distracted. Here, take this thumb drive."

"Thanks," I said, pocketing the USB stick.

"Maybe you should freshen up. What've you been doing all day?"

"Writing."

"I didn't see you in the kitchen. Have you eaten? Irene made us do a yoga class and film it. I'm surprised she didn't ask you."

"She knows I'm terrible at it."

Jules disappeared and I went to the bathroom to wash my face. Every muscle in my body seemed disconnected to the other. It was hard to filter through a jumble of incoherent thoughts, but I picked out the ones that mattered. There were facts hidden in there, like the fact that I needed to get changed and go to meet Jules with the wine. The fact that we needed to find out once and for all what Irene was up to. The fact that we were going to pretend to drink with her until she was easy to distract. That was it. Nothing scary about that.

Unless Irene catches you.

But at this point, what did it matter? I recalled my original invitation to The Event. The handwritten message and the assertion that my life would change. It was one of the first things she said to me when I'd arrived at the monastery. She'd told me that she was going to make me rich and famous, and wasn't that why I came? If I truly searched inside, wasn't that the main reason for me coming all this way?

No.

No, it wasn't.

You came to get away from me. But then you realised that you could never run away from me. I'll always be here.

A hand gently touched my shoulder.

"You didn't pull me away from the wolf?"

No, I didn't.

"You are the wolf."

Yes.

"It doesn't matter what you do or say to me," I said. "Maria will protect me."

Are you sure about that?

Around six months ago I'd been at home alone with Mum. It was a usual Wednesday night and she'd returned with sour breath and acidic words. She'd told me her daily truths, about who I am and what I'd amount to. About how I'd ruined her life and robbed her of her youth. She spewed it all to me as she had many nights before. I did what I always did, ignored her and went to my room. I'd booted my computer and checked my reader group. In there, the words were warm, cosy, comforting. They told me I had worth, that Maya's complicated relationship with the queen spoke to those who had difficult relationships with mothers and aunts and sisters. I checked my sales and I wondered why I hadn't moved out yet. I wondered why I stayed there, listening to those words. I didn't know.

Then I heard a thud. Even though I knew that noise couldn't be good, I stayed where I was for several minutes, reading my reviews. I answered a few questions.

By the time I found her, she was choking. A terrible spluttering sound came from her throat. Bubbles of vomit burst from her mouth.

Mum was unconscious and slowly dying. There was no way she even knew that I was there and yet I was convinced she saw everything. Her eyes were closed, but I was convinced that she saw me, right down to the core of who I am.

IT WAS BLARING POP MUSIC, FLOWING BUBBLY WINE AND beautiful people dancing. It was giggles and singing and makeovers. It was feminine and cliché and it was all completely fake. We were spies.

The snug was freezing and we'd run out of logs for the fire, which made it easy to convince Irene to stay in her room. In fact, she loved the idea. We set up some extra webcams to record our fun, opened the wine and created a playlist on Spotify. It was my first time in Irene's room, and the one thing that stood out to me, was a picture of her and her mother on the desk. I leaned over to get a better view. Irene's mother had the same high cheekbones, striking blue eyes and full lips as her daughter. It was a recent photo, taken on what appeared to be a yacht. Both were in bikinis, smiling, glasses of champagne gripped by slender fingers.

I'd never had a drop of alcohol in my life, including that night, and yet I felt completely intoxicated. My stomach churned, my tongue was coated in fuzz, and my vision blurred as I watched the others sing and dance.

Two empty Prosecco bottles rolled around Irene's floor as she jumped up and down singing Katy Perry on the karaoke app.

"This is amazing!" she shouted. "This is exactly how I wanted it to be."

"What?" Jules said with a grin.

But Irene continued singing about fireworks. I was the closest person to the laptop, and I heard the *ding ding ding* of the messages coming in. Not just messages, but donations from patrons, too.

Lu98: Cath looks awful. Like a vampire.

Yorkiefan: Where's Nathan? He needs to get in on this karaoke action!

Incelious: Reenneee send nudes. Plzzzzz.

Jojobert: [heartemoji]

AliceAkarthis: Cath, u ok?

Volk: There's a face at the window.

Motherofcats: [heartemoji]

AliceAkarthis: There's nothing at the window...

Cheezemonkeys: Which window?

Volk: It's a wolf.

Lu98: I saw something too!

Cheezemonkeys: The figure from the video?

I manoeuvred myself over to Irene's window and peered out through the dark. A cold sensation washed over me. All I saw was my reflection. A blank, pale, round moon of a face. I retracted in disgust.

By this point, Irene was so distracted by her fun that I simply sat down at her desk, took out the USB stick, and copied the password-protected files onto it. Through Irene's laptop webcam, the viewers watched me; at least, I assumed they did. Because the files were so large, it took a while for them to save on the memory stick. While Jules and Irene picked a new song to sing, I replied to the messages filtering in.

Me: I didn't see anything outside the window. It's too dark.

Volk: The wolves are at the door.

AliceAkarthis: Is it him again? The one who keeps saying someone is going to die?

Forkie: [angryemoji]

As soon as the files were saved, I pocketed the memory stick. Despite the cold weather, and the dodgy heating, a cold sweat broke out on the small of my back. I had the files and all we had to do was go, but at the same time, I was sure, absolutely positive, that I was being obvious about the endeavour, and that Irene was about to demand for me to empty my pockets right in front of her. I gestured for Jules to leave and made up an excuse about making supper.

Still dancing up and down, Irene barely acknowledged our departure. She was too intoxicated to care what we were doing. We stepped out into the cloister, where I was convinced that my heart was going to beat out of my chest. I pulled Jules towards Nathan's room.

"I copied the files. Do you want to take them to Nathan?"

"Yes. I want this over."

Like two boarding school kids in a children's book, we waited for Nathan to answer our knock on his door. It took a long time for it to open. A long moment where my scalp prickled, and a ripple of repulsion spread over my body. It feels strange to admit how my perspective had shifted over the weeks, from sceptical of the supernatural, to now convinced that as soon as we figured out how to open those files, something awful was going to happen.

CHAPTER THIRTY-THREE

When Nathan answered the door, he was utterly changed from the person who had told me to be quiet a few hours earlier. There are times when I consider whether I'm remembering the physical differences correctly, or whether my memory is flawed. Jules didn't react, but I wanted to flee.

He seemed bloodless. He was thinner than before, though that was impossible. Perhaps it was the clothes he was wearing, or the fact that he'd been smoking weed again, I don't know. The yellow tinge to his waxy skin repulsed me in the same way mould on food makes my stomach turn.

"What?" he said.

He didn't open the door particularly wide. Instead, he filled the gap with his body. From within the room, I heard the sound of rapid fire from one of his games.

"We got the files," Jules said in a hushed whisper. "Can you help us?"

To my surprise, he let us in right away.

The smell that emanated from his room was vile. This time, Jules did react. It became clear that Nathan had been eating most of his meals here and leaving the dirty plates all over the floor. The rotting stench caught the back of my throat, as sour as my mother's final vomit, as rancid as the filled bins she wouldn't empty when I was a child, and the corpse of a mouse I'd once found underneath our fridge. That smell reminded me of my mother and of the childhood I'd had, and yet again I wanted to turn around and escape this place. Freezing to death, or being eaten by the wolf, or shot by the farmer, seemed viable alternatives to standing in the centre of all that filth. If it hadn't been for Jules, and for the voice in my head telling me that if I did run away, I'd be pathetic, I truly would have left that moment for a hike down the side of the mountain.

Jules visibly cringed but gingerly made her way around the dirty plates to get to Nathan's computer. He shut off his game while she inserted the memory stick in the USB port.

It all feels surreal to think about now. Me standing there, watching them. This moment always reminds me of how young we were. It had been a game to Jules, getting Irene drunk, copying the files, recruiting Nathan into the whole thing. In other circumstances it might have been harmless, or at least justified given Irene's deceptions, but in Sfântul Mihail, with its bloody history and isolated location, in a building that had seeped into our psychology and infected our minds, it was dangerous. Thinking about it now fills me with regret that I didn't act at this moment. I could scream at myself for not taking charge right then and there in order to alter history.

Sadly, I did not, and the events that occurred next will always be what they were.

"If these files are encrypted, I might not be able to open them," Nathan warned. "All I can do is use a brute force programme that systematically works its way through thousands of passwords. It could take a long time."

"We could try and guess her password," Jules suggested. "What's her favourite colour? Pet name? Anyone? Her mom's birthday?"

"She doesn't have a pet," Nathan replied. He ran his tongue over his teeth. The action reminded me how dirty we all were, rotting away in this monastery for weeks, reverting back to a primitive cave person mentality.

"What's going on?"

The three of us rotated slowly to see Irene standing at the back of the room. The contrast between our appearances and hers was stark. She still cared. Her hair was styled, her make-up fresh.

None of us spoke for a few seconds. Irene walked over to Nathan's computer, grimacing at the mess on the floor, and peered at the computer screen. She let out a long, tired sigh and took a step away.

"She made me," Irene said. Her chest heaved once, twice, and her hand lifted to her neck. "You have to understand that she made me do it all."

"Who?" Jules said.

"Do what?" Nathan said.

Irene staggered out of the room, but Nathan was on his feet and in pursuit within an instant. Jules followed, but I was slightly slower to react. In the hallway, I heard a yelp, followed by a string of angry French. When Nathan re-emerged, he did so dragging Irene by the hair.

"Is that necessary?" I asked, grabbing one of Nathan's hands in an attempt to prise him away from her.

"Open the files," Nathan grunted.

I looked to Jules for support because what was happening scared me. Nathan's eyes had gone blank, like all the emotion and empathy had drained from his being. Jules, however, was fixated on the computer, transfixed by the possibility that she would finally get what she wanted: answers.

Irene leaned closer to the keyboard making whimpering sounds. Finally, Nathan loosened his grip on her. She typed in the password with trembling fingers.

"I need to extract the files," she said. "It might take a while."

"Video files," Nathan said. "Why have you password-protected video files?"

"Are we overreacting?" I said. "Surely the CCTV around the monastery makes back-ups and Irene didn't want her computer to be hacked and the files stolen. Is that what happened?" I glanced at Irene willing her to agree with me.

But Irene shook her head. There were tears falling down her face. "She said that if I didn't do it, she'd release the pictures of me."

My stomach sank down to my knees. I didn't know what this was building to, but a sense of dread weighed heavy. I knew from Nathan's empty eyes, the grim line of Jules's determined mouth and the heavy atmosphere in that room that what would come next would not be good. As the weight settled around my shoulders, I sensed Maria's presence. It's too late to run, I thought. Now I had to stay and see it for myself.

"Who, Irene?" Jules asked.

But Irene didn't answer.

The first video downloaded. I held my breath as Nathan opened the file.

Initially, a sense of vindication washed over me because the video was simply of me in my bedroom, brushing my hair in the mirror above the cabinet. Then it dawned on me, starting with the prickling of my hairline and ending with a numb sensation in my toes, this recording was coming from *my bedroom*. Watching the smaller version of me on that screen was like disconnecting from my body, floating above everything, seeing it acted out like a play. It took me a few moments to adjust, to realise that the person on that screen wasn't an actor, but me. When the actor began undressing, at first, I thought it was okay, because they were in a play. But it was *me* taking off my clothes, sliding out of my underwear, putting on my pyjamas.

No one stopped the recording, not even me. I watched myself naked, in front of all those people. My legs were like jelly. I couldn't comprehend why. The recording skipped and came to me changing again. The boring parts had been edited out. Finally, I found my voice.

"Make it stop. Make it stop. Make it STOP!"

Irene closed the video.

"What's on the others?" Nathan asked. He didn't sound like himself. There was anger in his voice, a quivering rage. He sounded like the monster we hear but don't see in a film.

Irene didn't move, but Nathan opened a second video file. This one was of him, masturbating on the edge of his bed. I quickly redirected my gaze, catching Jules's dropped jaw before I shifted my eyes.

From behind me, I heard Jules say in a low voice, "What have you done? How many videos are there like this?"

"All of your rooms have cameras," Irene admitted. "All of them. From the beginning."

Nowhere had been safe. There'd been watchers at all times. Any illusion of privacy stolen.

"What have you done with these videos?" Jules asked.

Irene's voice was shaking and barely audible when she answered. "Sold them."

I faced Irene then. The woman who had tricked us into this event, secretly taped us and sold the footage. Other people had seen my naked body. All this time, I'd thought my room was the one safe space in the monastery with no one watching me. But it hadn't been safe. Nowhere had been safe.

Why would they want to look at you? I heard riotous laughter in my mind. *Why would anyone want to see that blubber?*

"Who did you sell them to?" Jules asked. Her voice vibrated in the stillness of the room.

Nathan's fingers remained entwined in Irene's hair. Jules stood ramrod straight with her arms folded tightly across her chest. I could barely breathe so much dread was coursing through me. When I blinked, I thought I saw Maria standing in the corner, watching, but another blink and she was gone.

"Rich people," Irene said.

"You said *she* made you do it. Who?" Jules demanded.

Irene tried to lean over her hands and sob, but Nathan held her head upright. "I used to... she used to take photographs of me, sexual ones, and sell them to rich men who wanted to see me naked. Every man had to sign an NDA. It was always a risk, but we made so much money. She came up with this whole idea. The live-streaming, everything. We ploughed so much of our own money into this place, renovating it, getting it ready for The Event. We needed to make a profit." She paused to wipe her nose with the back of her hand. "She was the one who came up with tiered membership. Regular subscribers get the live feed from the communal areas. VIPs get the same but with extra footage we filmed separately, and direct messages etcetera. Then..."

"Go on," Jules prompted.

"The top tier, we called it the God Tier, get nude videos of you all." She sniffed. "The funny thing is, when we were setting up The Event, we reached out to the rich men first, and we polled them on who they wanted to come. They could have chosen models, but they didn't want models. We had thousands of applications and we sent all of them to our clients. They chose you." She shrugged. "The lovable fitness fanatic. The uptight New York feminist. The loud-mouth gamer." Her eyes found mine. "The obvious virgin."

A shiver of shame and disgust made its way up my spine.

"Why us?" Jules asked.

"I guess you'd be the most fun to violate," she answered, and I wished she hadn't.

CHAPTER THIRTY-FOUR

W e were four people isolated on a mountain with at least two of us mentally ill, and one of us a criminal. Everything we did was being recorded. Despite the stench of Nathan's room, I pulled in a deep breath through my nose before staring out the window at the dark.

"We need to lock her up," Nathan said. "She's under house arrest from now on."

Irene lifted her palms up as though pleading with us. "I was forced to do this! Those bastards have my nudes, too. I swear!"

"You need to give us answers," Jules said. "First, tell us who forced you."

Irene's eyes dropped down to the desk. "I can't."

"Why?"

"I just can't."

"Is it Loup? Is *she* Loup?" Jules asked.

"Yes," Irene said. "We both are."

Jules's eyes narrowed. "Were you really sick as a child?"

"No," Irene whispered. "But I thought I was at the time."

"So you've been lying about that your whole life?" Jules walked over to the door and paused there for a moment. "I don't know how to process this."

It was then that I decided I needed to try and de-escalate what was happening. Fear compelled me. Maria's presence wanted me to calm down the room. "We should call the police and let them handle it. We can't imprison someone, because that's also illegal." I sensed that no one was listening to me. *Of course, they're not. No one listens to you.* "Guys, please. Irene must have a contact number for emergencies. Let's contact them and they can handle it."

"Yes," Irene said. "I do have a contact number for the police in Brasov. They could get here in the snow. I know they could."

Nathan pulled Irene's head back by her hair until she cried out in pain. I tried to grasp hold of his fingers, but he pushed me away with his free hand. "No. We're dealing with this alone."

Desperate to stop what was happening, I turned to Jules. "We can't."

"I don't know what to do," Jules said. "I feel so dirty. I want this over."

"I know, I feel the same. But we have to think clearly. We need to call the police. Perhaps Irene could agree to stay in her room until this is over."

"No," Nathan said. "That's not happening."

I was afraid of him. The rubber band keeping him together had finally snapped. He was no longer himself. Perhaps it was the stress of The Event, or the disgusting truth of what was going on, or perhaps it went deeper. The monastery itself, all that bloody history, seeping into his veins. I even considered the notion that Nathan was possessed, by either the white wolf or the tall man or one of the nuns or some other vengeful spirit.

The evil is in you, too, said my mother. That voice, that constant presence. If I could dig it out of my brain, I would.

Nathan pulled Irene from the chair and walked her out of the room. While he was busy, I logged onto the message boards using Nathan's computer, firing off a panicked comment.

This is Cath. Send the emergency services to Sfântul Mihail monastery near Butnari village. We are in danger.

"Are you coming?" Jules asked, standing in the doorway.

I jumped up from the chair, crossed the room and grabbed her hands. "We need to stop this. Can't you feel it?"

"What?"

"The sense of... dread."

Her eyes glazed over. Perhaps it was shock. "We deserve answers, Cath."

"I know, but—"

She pulled her hands from mine and made her way towards the snug. Once we were there, I saw Nathan shove Irene onto one of the sofas, pull a chair into the centre of the room and sit down.

"Tell us the names of every person you sent the footage to."

Irene shook her head. "I can't. I don't know."

"Then tell us who set you up to this," Jules demanded.

"No," Irene said. "I can't."

"Why would you want to protect this person?" Jules reached over and yanked at Irene's right ear. "You filmed us naked and sold those videos to the highest bidders. You're disgusting! You lied about having cancer. You have no morals. You're a monster! Tell us the name of the other monsters involved."

A monster just like you, said my mother.

As the smiling picture of Irene, bald from her fake cancer treatment, popped into my mind I knew the answer.

"It's her mother," I said. "Her mother is the one behind everything. Isn't that right? She made you pretend to be sick in order to get attention online. Then she forced this persona on you until you became a global star. But all the time she was selling you. She sold your body. She sold your brand when she set up the multi-level marketing scheme under your name. And then she forced you into this situation by spending the money you'd earned to renovate this building. It's your mother."

Irene broke down then and I went to her. I wrapped my arms around her, and I allowed her tears to fall on my shoulders.

We'd forgotten, you see, that the world was watching. We'd forgotten to disconnect the live-stream, and now those watching knew the truth. I'd certainly forgotten when I continued to speak.

"I know, I know. I understand what it's like to have someone in your life who should protect you but doesn't. She didn't protect me, either, my mother."

I made you the person you are today and don't you forget it.

As Irene's body heaved with sobs, rippling through her, mine did too. Her fingernails dug into my shoulders, but I didn't feel it. I was too busy letting a few things go myself.

"Don't make me go back," she whispered to me.

"It's okay." As I stroked her hair, a sense of release washed over me. I'd been holding onto hate for too long.

Irene sniffed deeply and whispered into my ear. "I'm so sorry I took your pills. She made me do it."

I leaned away. "What? Why?"

With sad eyes and a twisted mouth, she said, "She thought you'd get more views if you went crazy."

"The doctor?"

"He was real," Irene said. "But the new medication wasn't." She wiped her nose with her sleeve. "I put placebos inside the correct packaging."

A strong hand gripped my shoulder and wrenched me away from the wolf's cub. I fell onto my backside in shock, with Nathan looming over me. Then he kicked me until I scrabbled away.

"It all has to stop," he said, snatching up the poker from the fireplace.

Seeing what he was about to do, I attempted to throw myself towards him, but I couldn't move fast enough. Irene put her hands up to protect her face, but Nathan beat them away, her screams ripping through the room. He lifted the iron rod and thrashed it down on her, smashing her face, her hands, forearms, shoulders. I saw her nose explode, the bones crunching, her jaw dislocate, her head meet the smack of his fury. My hands wrapped around his ankle, clawing at him to come away. He was leaning over her as she sank down on the sofa screaming, her blood coating the beige fabric.

It was primal. Watching it happen, time dragged, and it was as though it lasted hours. The relentless thudding and panting and screaming of savagery. In reality it must have been less than a minute. She was unrecognisable by the time I managed to get on my feet and throw myself on Nathan's back. Jules stood there doing nothing as I struggled against him. My weight tipped him off balance and together we collapsed forward. I slid onto the floor in a heap, winded and afraid. Meanwhile, Nathan straightened himself, and stood there gawking at Irene's mutilated face and body. In the rush to protect her, I hadn't noticed that Irene had stopped screaming. She laid still on the sofa. The bottom half of her body resembled a beautiful woman in repose, the kind of subject for a renaissance portrait. From the shoulders up, she was broken.

My fingers groped beneath her jawline for a pulse. There wasn't one.

I lifted my gaze to Nathan's pale, thin face, seeing nothing. Merely a blank expression.

"We invited the monster in," he said.

Slowly, I edged away from him as he lifted the poker and pointed it towards me. I scrambled to my feet, staggering.

"We invited the monster in," he repeated.

Adrenaline began to kick in. I reached out to grab Jules's hand, yanking her harshly out of the room.

"We have to run!" I yelled at her unresponsive expression. The slackness of shock made her skin droopy, her mind had shutdown. But I didn't have time—*we* didn't have time for her to have a breakdown, we had to get away from Nathan.

"WE INVITED THE MONSTER IN!" he bellowed, and then laughed and laughed and laughed.

Jules's footsteps stumbled behind me, tripping on the flagstones as we lurched through the monastery. The corridor was dark and empty. I pulled Jules towards the entrance, found the cabinet, and fumbled with the drawer as I tried to find the key to let us out. In the distance, Nathan banged the poker against the stones. His rattling, unnerving laugh carried through the cloister, echoed around the walkways. Was he even Nathan anymore?

I jammed the key into the lock, sure that we were about to die, that this was it for us. How were we going to find help high up a mountain in rural Romania? Who was going to help us? Even if we managed to escape from Nathan, we were surely going to die out there in the elements.

"Do you know who the monster is?" Nathan shouted. He was close now, around the corner, I estimated, and I could barely breathe with the terror of that realisation.

I grabbed two coats and two pairs of shoes before I shoved Jules out into the cold. I threw everything down on the step to allow me to shut the door with both hands. As I was pulling it closed, Nathan came barrelling around the corner, his tall, slim frame huge to me now that he'd shed all of his humanity. He came running towards us, his yellow teeth gritted together, darkness in his eyes. I slammed the door closed, pushed the key into the lock and turned it.

"DO YOU KNOW WHO THE MONSTER IS?" he repeated. I heard the sound of his fists beating against the wood. The door rattled in its hinges, but it held. I staggered back and scooped up the coats and shoes, trying not to think about the dozens of inky shadows I'd seen behind Nathan as he ran towards us.

Forkie: Please tell me that was a joke…

Lu98: WTAF?

Cheezemonkeys: This along with Cath's message…

Forkie: Did we watch someone die?

Lu98: Irene. We watched Irene die.

AliceAkarthis: I'm calling the police.

Yorkiefan: Guys, it's obviously special effects.

Reneeleanie: I can't breathe. I feel sick.

Jojobert: IRENE PLS GET UP!!!!!

Twix: Fuck. This can't be real.

Serra: HAS ANYONE CALLED THE POLICE???

AliceAkarthis: I'm trying. I can't find the number on Google.

Lu98: I'll help.

CHAPTER THIRTY-FIVE

Half-dragging Jules, a bundle of coats and shoes in one arm, we ran. In the dark, through ice-cold drifts of snow, socked feet soaking wet, we ran until we came to a copse of trees to hide between. Jules's eyes were glazed over, her body limp. I had to prop her against a tree and push her feet into the shoes. Her arms were like jelly as I shoved them into a coat. My fingers fumbled against the zipper. As I worked, I tried not to meet her eyes, because what I saw frightened me. I needed her to be the smart, focused Jules that I knew, not this shell.

"We're okay," I said, finally regarding her blue-tinged face in the dim moonlight. "We're going to be okay."

But all the time, the voice in my head said otherwise. *You're going to die. You're going to die. And then you'll be with me again. You're going to die. You're going to die. And then you'll be with me again.*

When I crouched down to put on my shoes, Jules slid to the ground, her mouth wide open in a silent scream. As I was pulling on my coat, I heard the smashing of glass. My breath caught in my throat. Nathan was coming for us through one of the windows. We needed to go. Even though we were miles away from civilisation, we needed to run. Away. Anywhere but here. I made the choice because Jules couldn't. I decided that the best thing we could do was try to walk towards Butnari. The other alternative was begging the mercy of the man who lived at the farm with the horses. It was closer to us than the village, but the man had threatened us with a shotgun.

"Come on," I whispered, taking Jules by the elbow and pulling her up to standing position. "We're going to find the road and follow it to Butnari. That's what we're going to do." Saying it out loud helped me focus. I glanced towards the monastery, but I couldn't see which window had broken. Had Nathan forced his way out already?

You won't get to the road. You'll die first. It's dark, you'll never find it. Your frozen bodies will be found tomorrow, half-eaten by wolves.

Jules was compliant enough to walk next to me. Gently, but firmly, I led us through the trees, following the boundary of the monastery and all too aware of the tracks we were leaving behind in the snow. There was nothing I could do about that. Covering them would take too much time, and I wasn't convinced of my capability to cover them well anyway. I decided speed was the best way to stay alive, as well as to keep us warm.

"Cath?"

I'd become so accustomed to her silence, that Jules's quiet voice almost made me scream. There was no time to stop, but I glanced at her quickly, enough time to see a flicker of recognition on her face.

"Cath, what's going on?"

"We're getting away from Nathan," I said.

"Why? What did he do?"

She was obviously still in shock, but there wasn't enough time to address it. "Walk next to me and try to keep up. Have you got a phone with you?"

Jules patted her jeans pockets and shook her head. "It must be in the monastery."

"Mine too. There's no signal here anyway."

We practically tumbled down the steep mountainside to the winding road. I remembered Alexandru negotiating those hairpin bends, the headlights gracefully uncovering the steep drops around each corner. I remembered how my fingers had wrapped around the arm rest, my body clenched with fear. The road would be covered in snow by now, but at least I'd see the barriers and know where we were. And when—or if—we found the road, we had to ensure we didn't slip down the perilous drop into the pit of darkness below.

But for the moment I focused on one foot in front of the other. My fingers stayed on Jules's elbow, ensuring she didn't wander away. We moved more slowly than I'd have liked, but I had hope that squeezing through one of those tiny windows was going to cause Nathan some problems.

Sure enough, about five or six minutes later, we stumbled out of the forest onto an untouched carpet of snow. There was a curve to the edge of the trees that had to be the road winding up the mountain. It gave me confidence to believe putting one foot in front of the other could save us. I grabbed Jules's hand and strode onto the winding path. There was no sign of Nathan.

At the back of my mind, I remained conscious of the cliff, so I kept us closer to the trees to make sure we wouldn't meander over to the edge. There were barriers, but not everywhere, and I didn't want to risk the possibility of tripping on the uneven ground and plummeting down below.

Jules continued to be easily led, but she was panting, and I could tell she was afraid.

"I'm sorry, Cath." Jules's words came out ragged between her breaths. I heard the cold creeping into her voice. "This is all my fault. I never wanted it to end this way."

In a way, she was right, though I didn't hold her accountable for what Nathan had done. But I was still confused by everything that'd happened, and I wanted answers. "Why didn't you help me? We could have stopped him before he killed her. You didn't back me up."

"I... I don't know. I don't remember. I think it's that place, Cath. The evil seeps in, don't you think?"

But I didn't know what to say because I wasn't sure I believed it. I'd had so many strange experiences in that building, from the supernatural to the psychological and everything in between, and yet I'd still tried to stop Nathan. Even after my nightmares, the visitations from the white wolf, the spectral visions I believed were Maria Popescu, a murdered nun, I'd still thrown myself at Nathan and tried to stop him from killing Irene.

You never tried to stop me though, said the voice.

"Shut up."

Jules inhaled a sharp breath. "I'm sorry, I will."

"I wasn't talking to—" I stopped dead in my tracks.

This is your time now. You're coming home, Catherine.

It was dark, yes, and visibility was bad, but even still, standing there, I knew we were not alone. I saw the same faceless figure dressed in black that I had continued to see since arriving at the monastery. My breath caught in my throat. I sensed Jules staring at me, but I didn't know how to explain. Out of the corner of my eye I noticed her move her head in the direction of my gaze, before turning back.

"You don't see it, do you?" I asked.

"No," she said. "But that doesn't mean it isn't real."

The apparition dissolved into the woods and I hurried over to where I'd seen that lonely, lurking entity. In the silent world around us, I was sure that my beating heart was like thunder, as loud as the blood pumping in my ears. Our feet were unsure in the snow but we had to climb up a bank to reach the spot where I saw that... thing... hallucination, ghost, trick of the eye, whatever it was. I stumbled forward, then tripped and fell. Jules put out her hand to help me up before we directed our attention to what I'd tripped over.

My foot had disturbed the top layer of snow, revealing a piece of bright turquoise fabric underneath. Jules's hand reached out and clutched my coat. She sucked in a sharp breath and I let out a gasp. I believe we both recognised that half-frozen garment at the same time. I don't know which of us dropped to our knees first, but we were both down on the ground, freezing cold hands scooping away snow. It didn't take long, perhaps two or three minutes. After we'd uncovered the body, we both stood silently for a long moment. Jules vomited, but I didn't.

It was Dan. He'd never made it back to Brasov before the storm came. His eyes were open, still, frozen like the forest around him. He stared up at the stars, which was a minor comfort, I hoped they'd been the last thing he'd seen in this world. There was no comfort in the sight of the rest of him. His throat had been ripped open. His clothes were in shreds. I'd never seen a person mauled to death by a large, vicious animal, but that was what immediately came to mind.

A large, vicious animal, like a wolf.

"We need to go, Cath."

I nodded. We backed away from Dan's torn body, almost too afraid to face our destination. Eventually, we did, and both of us started to run.

CHAPTER THIRTY-SIX

Did Maria lead us to Dan's body? At the time I believed so. In fact, I was sure that she was warning us of the coming threat.

We ran down the dark road following the twists along the side of the mountain. We let out small, panicked breaths, our coats rustled, and our feet constantly slipped, slid and tripped. Both of us tumbled over two or three times, and each time it happened, I was convinced that if I looked over my shoulder I'd see Nathan standing behind us, the poker raised and ready to strike.

Eventually Jules slowed down to a stop. Bracing forward, she placed shaking hands on her knees and pulled in a long, shuddering breath. "I can't do this."

"It's okay. We'll walk."

"We're going to die out here, Cath. If the wolf that ripped Dan apart doesn't kills us, then Nathan or the cold will."

I reached out for her hand, but she refused to take it. "We're going to be found. I swear it. I left a message on the boards asking for someone to call the police. There'll be rescuers, I know there will."

Her eyes were shrouded in darkness, but I saw her shake her head. "No. We're going to die."

She's right. You're bad at this, Catherine. You're obviously going to die out here. You don't even know where you are.

"No, we're going to survive. Now take my hand, and let's keep going."

She took my hand. I hardly felt it, I was so numb. As we walked, I kept glancing over my shoulder, half-expecting Dan's torn body to be in pursuit. Feet dragging through the snow, a dislocated and skeletal jaw hanging from his face. There was nothing. Not even the shadow, or Nathan. Nothing. In some ways, that was worse. Danger loomed, like the clouds above us, a terrible sense of anticipation. Deep down inside, I couldn't shake the conviction that I was the one responsible for Jules's life, and her well-being would forever be on my conscience. Every choice I made, every wrong turn, every failure was all my fault. First, I'd failed Irene, now I had to make sure that Jules got through this alive. I had to. There was no other choice.

"I'm so cold," she said.

We huddled closer. I rubbed her fingers with my own, wishing I'd been able to grab gloves along with the coats. It started to snow again, and I swore under my breath. Beautiful, thick, fast, snow, covering our footsteps, but at the same time blocking our view. The flurries took away the moonlight, finally plunging us into the deepest, darkest night.

"We need to get off the road," I said.

"What?" Jules shivered next to me.

"We can't see. We could veer off the cliff and fall. If we go right and climb up the bank back into the woods, we'll be away from that danger." What I didn't say, was that we also probably wouldn't be able to find Butnari. At least being on a mountain meant that we could ensure we walked down instead of up, and not circle back to the monastery.

The climb was steep. My feet struggled to find purchase on the slippery ground. We fell into each other two or three times, but the snow provided a cushion. Once we reached the forest, the problem became the trees. We couldn't see in front of our faces.

"Wait," I said. "Slow down. We're going to hurt ourselves. Keep one hand out in front of your body."

"Okay," Jules said.

We held on to each other as we groped our way through the trees. Snowflakes soaked my hair, stung my eyes, created a layer of white on my shoulders. Each step was a gamble. We tested the ground with the toes of our shoes, checking for sudden drops. I don't know how long we walked like that, or for how far, I only know the shuddering, all-consuming weight of that anticipation, that one wrong move could plunge us down the side of the mountain. That at any moment we could come face to face with Nathan and his poker. That Maria's ghost, or worse, the wolf, could be hiding behind that tree right in front of us. I know we walked until my joints were stiff and I couldn't feel my feet at all. The snow stopped falling but we continued to walk. The snow stopped falling and our tracks were no longer covered. The snow stopped falling and the clouds shifted away from the moon and I saw other tracks ahead of our own. Not boot prints, paw prints.

Wolf tracks, my mother said. *They have to be. The white wolf is here. Remember the evil emanating from it? Remember the menace? The wolf is here and it's going to rip you open like it ripped Dan open. Your throat will be torn, your blood will be drank, and you will die on this cold, cold ground.*

"We need to move faster," I said, quickening my pace while dragging Jules along. "Come on."

She stumbled. Her hand lost its grip on mine. I watched in horror as Jules lost her footing, then her balance, and began to tumble down the slope. I called her name as I rushed towards her, feet flying until I landed on my back. All the air left my lungs. Winded and flattened, it took a while to get myself back into a sitting position.

Perhaps if I hadn't taken that moment to collect myself, things would've been different. But I did, and that's the way the past is written, one choice leading to a consequence.

Back on my feet, I chased her down the slope to the very bottom, finding her crumpled by the fall. She was whimpering, from injuries, or from the cold, I'm not sure which, but I soothed her then, like a mother would, telling her that everything was going to be okay, and that we were going to find help. I took her in my arms, and I tried to lift her.

Then the beast growled.

A strong force tugged Jules in the opposite direction. It all happened quickly after that. She screamed. I saw the wolf's jaw wrapped around her wrist, hind legs bent, its body leaning away like a dog playing with a toy.

I didn't know what to do.

I used my own weight. I threw myself back as Jules screamed. Her fingers slipped from mine. The wolf was the stronger animal. In the middle of us both, Jules fell to the ground screaming. There was no hesitation from the wolf. It pounced on her immediately, its teeth gnashing at her chest. Jules squirmed and wriggled beneath it. I panicked and threw myself at the animal, knocking it back. It regrouped, snarled, and caught Jules's ankle as she crawled away.

I plunged my frozen hands into the deep snow in search of anything I could use as a weapon. A thick branch or stone perhaps, but all I found was frozen undergrowth. The wolf had Jules pinned to the ground with paws on her back and its teeth at her neck. I kicked it as hard as I could. It stopped long enough to fix me with those pale eyes. In the darkness, I thought I saw blood dripping from its mouth. Jules's blood.

I saw then that it was the young wolf, the one I had saved from the wire. The one I had fed when I thought it was hungry. There was no recognition in its eyes. I was dinner. The wolf was done with Jules, now it wanted me. There was one last thing I could do, and that was to run. At least I'd managed to distract it from Jules, but whether I'd saved her life, I didn't know. She was silent on the frozen ground, her screams had ceased.

I managed three strides through the snow before I felt it behind me.

Now is the time, she said. *Come on, Catherine. Give up.*

A sense of peace washed over me as I realised this was it, that I could finally stop fighting. The days where getting out of bed was a chore, the weeks when I didn't leave the house or speak face to face with another person, the tar pit of loneliness I often found myself stuck in. The shame, of not being well, of not having friends, of not wanting a relationship. It would all end. Finally.

Or so I thought.

I fell to the ground and the wolf's jaw opened to snap around my leg. Before it could, there was a crack. A loud, thunderous crack that made my ears ring. At first, I thought the change in my hearing occurred because I was dead, but I was alive. The beast was dead. Its tongue lolled out of its bloody jaw. I sat up and stared down at its glassy eyes, almost saddened by its untimely demise.

"Hurt?" asked a gruff voice.

He stood above me, a shotgun in his arms. The farmer.

"No," I said. "But Jules…"

He walked over to her and crouched, pressing two fingers to her throat.

"She's dead," he said.

Two words, simple sounding, spoken to me as if they were nothing. *She's dead.*

CHAPTER THIRTY-SEVEN

A s the farmer dragged me away by the elbow, I saw the shape in the woods, and at least knew that Jules wouldn't be alone. Maria was with her. I don't know whether it was my illness making the illogical logical, or whether I truly did breathe Maria's essence into my body, but I was sure, and comforted, by my certainty that Jules would not lie in the frozen wood alone. I stopped resisting the farmer and walked alongside him. The rest of that walk, I cannot remember.

By the time we reached the farmhouse I was being half-carried, barely conscious after everything that had happened inside and outside of the monastery. His wife stripped my body of wet clothes, ran me a bath, and probably saved my fingers and toes from frostbite. Once out of the bath, she placed a hot mug of stew into my hands and piled me with blankets while the sun rose over the mountain.

In broken English, I learned that the farmer with the gun was called Sorin, his wife Anastasia. Sorin told me that he had been searching for the hikers during the day but had gone home without finding them. That evening, the video of Irene's death went viral, which Anastasia saw on her phone. She persuaded him to check on us at the monastery, but by the time he arrived, one of the refectory windows was smashed, and there was no sign of anyone. He took a lap of the woods, but again found no one. It was on his walk back to his house that he heard Jules screaming.

The rest you know.

"The curse is real," he told me. "We have been concerned since you arrived."

Anastasia, a short woman with luscious wavy hair the same colour as her freckles, spoke to him in Romanian. I waited for Sorin to translate.

"Her grandmother and mother lived through the murders. Few come out of Sfântul Mihail alive. The ghosts are real."

Anastasia nodded her head.

"The ghost wasn't the problem," I said. "Maria Popescu kept trying to help me. She pulled me away from the wolf, showed me where to find her crucifix, and showed me where Dan's body is. It was... I don't know. It doesn't make sense. I think it was the building itself."

"Do you know what happened to the nuns?" Sorin asked.

"All I know is that they were killed. But I don't know how."

Anastasia began speaking again, and Sorin translated her words.

"She says that the police did not tell us the truth, but her great-aunt worked at the station in Butnari. She was..." he paused, and then mimed a pen moving along a piece of paper.

"A transcriber?" I asked.

"She took notes," he said. "Anastasia says this story has been passed on from generation to generation. She says it is the story told from Maria Popescu's diary, and the confession made by the abbess."

"Abbess, is that a mother superior?"

He paused, listened to his wife, and then began to speak again. "Yes, it is." He listened to Anastasia again, and then began the story. "It all started when the local priest changed. The village priest was old and died of a heart attack. Father Lovas came from Hungary. He was young, attractive and the girls in Butnari liked him a lot. He was charming. Spoke well in church. He would often take trips to the monastery and check on the nuns there. That became a problem.

"Father Lovas was not a good man. He had been asked to leave his position in Hungary after several complaints about his connections with criminals. There were rumours that he had convinced young girls in his flock to sleep with these criminals for money."

"He was a pimp?"

"He was no priest," Sorin continued. "He was not holy, and things got worse for Butnari after he came. Lovas continued his friendship with one of the criminals he knew. A rich man." Sorin paused and asked his wife a question. "Anastasia does not remember his name. But she says this man would go to the monastery once or twice a year, and every time he visited, one of the nuns would die."

"How did this man have access to the monastery?"

"Anastasia says that this rich man explained himself as... as..." Sorin frowned. "He gave money to them. For food and clothes."

"Donations?"

"Yes. In return, Lovas gave him a tour each year to see the food and clothes he gave. The nuns acted grateful. But

Lovas would hide the man in the abbess's quarters after the tour. At night, one nun would be delivered to the man and she would be murdered."

Fear ran through my body like an electric shock.

Sorin listened to his wife before he continued. "According to Maria Popescu's diary, the first nun was found at the bottom of the tower."

My story had included a death at the bottom of those stairs.

"The strange deaths went on. A hanging. A wolf attack. A fall on icy ground. One body was found down a well, another at the bottom of a cliff. It was three or four years until Maria realised that these deaths occurred the morning after their rich visitor. One night after one of his visits she stayed awake. She saw the priest walking along the cloister with one of the nuns at his side. The next morning, that nun was dead."

If part of Maria was inside my body, her sadness became my sadness. The ache of remorse, that she hadn't managed to save her sister. Or perhaps it was my own regret for not being able to save Jules.

"Maria went to the abbess, who told her that her ideas were ridiculous and blasphemous. She was not listened to. She had no idea that the mother superior would later confess that she had allowed these deaths to happen to receive her cut of the money."

Sorin sighed and took a break. Anastasia placed a hand on his shoulder, a tear dripping from her chin. My own cheeks were wet. I almost opened my mouth to tell him to stop. I had a feeling that I knew what was coming. I knew the ending.

"The rich man knew that suspicions were raised. He stayed away from the monastery for two years, and Maria began to believe that his reign of terror was over. That was until he came back. This time, he did not pretend to take the tour. He murdered them all. He cut their throats with a knife, splattering the blood up the walls of that sacred place. He had been starved of his addiction, all the time knowing that he could not go on living a lie. He was unleashed, at long last. A beast in a man's body."

"They invited him in," I mumbled. "And he betrayed them."

"Only the abbess survived. She confronted the man. Beat him to death with a poker taken from the fireplace."

The air froze in my lungs.

"At the police station, she told her version of the story. Maria's diary confirmed that this man had been slaughtering women for many years. The mother superior cracked. Confessed it all. She'd needed the money to send to a daughter born in secret before she arrived at Sfântul Mihail." He entwined his fingers.

"What about Lovas?"

"He was killed along with the nuns."

I let out a shaky breath. "They were sold by their Father and Mother. Like lambs to the slaughter."

"Yes. Still the shame hangs over Butnari. We do not speak of it. The monastery should never have been sold."

I nodded my head in agreement. My half-eaten stew was cold. My appetite had left my body. All I could think about was Nathan hitting Irene over and over again. I placed the food on the table and hugged the blanket tightly. "Why the rumours about vampires? If the truth was out there...?"

"It was a scandal, of course! A priest behaving like that. An *abbess*! The police and the church covered this great shame by revealing no details to us. They told us an outsider came into the monastery, committed the crime and killed himself."

"What about the abbess?"

"She was never seen again."

Anastasia cleared away the mug of stew and brought me a glass of water. She sat on the chair next to mine and placed her hand on my arm. I turned to her then, and I asked her a question I knew she wouldn't understand.

"Do you think the sins committed by those three people are still being felt today?"

Sorin translated.

She squeezed my arm and spoke to me in her language. I didn't need the translation because I saw the pain in her eyes.

"Yes," Sorin said. "Butnari is still in pain."

In my mind I saw agonised tendrils snaking over the walls, black vines against the stone. I saw the bricks squeezed, overtaken by menace. I thought of Nathan, blank-eyed and vicious, out of his mind with rage. "Do you think that pain still lingers inside the monastery?"

"She says they should knock it down."

CHAPTER THIRTY-EIGHT

The police came for me on snowmobiles about two hours after sunrise. I'd slept a while, eaten a hunk of bread, and drunk a cup of rich coffee. Empty inside and numb all over, but at least I hadn't heard my mother's voice since Jules had died.

Sorin came with us to find Jules's body. She was prostrate, which spared me the sight of her face. Our conversation about souls popped into my head. I'd never believed in souls, or ghosts, or an afterlife before arriving at Sfântul Mihail, but everything I'd seen since then had challenged those views. Perhaps Jules's soul was at rest now.

I gave them a description of where we'd found Dan's body. A smaller party split off to collect his remains while I was taken to the police station in Brasov. I was wearing Anastasia's clothes. I felt awkward in them, as if I was in costume. I was taken to an interview room and a paper cup of water was placed in front of me.

The police officers both spoke English. One had a smattering of grey stubble on his chin, partly covering the loose skin on his neck. He had drooping, swollen eyebags beneath grey eyes. His partner was slender, blond, with a thin face that reminded me of Nathan's.

Their names I forgot as soon as I heard them. I was still in a state of stupor, clinging on to a scrap of reality.

"Explain what happened last night," said the older officer.

Before I started, I sipped the water, and then I told them the story about how we found the files on Irene's computer. How she lied to us and sold us online. I told them about Nathan's precarious mental state that built up to his violent outburst. I told them about tripping over Dan's body, and the wolf in the woods.

"Have you found him?" I asked. "Nathan?"

"Yes," replied the young officer.

"Where is he?"

"The morgue," he replied.

My hand flew to my mouth. "How?"

The older officer cleared his throat before he started speaking. "The wolf, we think. He was mauled. Perhaps the wolf got to him before you."

"What about the missing hikers?"

"Those idiots? They're fine. They were rescued this morning. They were lucky the same wolf didn't find them."

The younger officer added, "What happened is strange. There have been no wolf attacks for many years because they are usually afraid of people. They don't attack, they stay away. And now"—he shrugged—"three attacks in one week. Very strange indeed."

"One wolf?" I asked.

"We believe so," said the younger officer. "Perhaps this wolf was more aggressive than the others. We don't know."

"Could I show you something online?" I asked. "Do you have a phone or a laptop?"

The younger officer pulled a smartphone from his pocket. I searched YouTube for the video of my rescuing the wolf from the wire. "This wolf?"

The officers watched wild eyed. "It could be."

"I'm the one taking the video. It's from two weeks ago. It doesn't seem like an aggressive wolf to me."

Neither appeared concerned. "It's still a wild animal. You don't know when a wild animal will strike."

THREE DAYS LATER, MY BELONGINGS WERE GIVEN TO ME IN plastic bags. Dirty underwear, stained tops, notebooks, my laptop, my phone, my passport. There was nothing else I could do to help the case, because the attack had already been streamed to the world. Nathan and the others were dead. I could go back to my empty house in England now.

The news of Irene's death had travelled across the globe. In fact, many had seen her die, and many more would watch the footage because one of our viewers saved it to their hard drive.

Before I packed my suitcase, I opened my laptop and logged into the hotel Wi-Fi. When I checked our website for The Event, Irene's murder video had been removed, as had the live-stream message boards. The police must have forced Adele, Irene's mother, to remove them. In my inbox, I found twenty or so emails from members of my reader group, as well as hundreds of messages in the Facebook group. They sounded so worried, so genuine, that I began to cry for the first time since Jules had died. I cried until I couldn't see the laptop screen for my tears.

After pulling myself together, I filtered through the emails and comments to reply and let people know that I was safe. Mixed in with the well-wishes, were emails from reporters wanting the scoop on the monastery murder. I ignored them, closed that tab and loaded YouTube. There I found the arrest video of Adele Jobert. I watched her being pushed into a police car under a sunny Los Angeles sky. She had smudged eye make-up, acrylic nails and bare feet in flip flops. There was no expression on her face. No anger. No fear. No desperation. I couldn't stand the sight of her. I closed YouTube and began reading my story about Maria Popescu.

It was a rambling mess.

I remembered, distinctly, sitting on my bed in the monastery, believing that everything I was typing about Maria was my best work to date by far. I'd believed it with my whole heart. Now I read it, and I found run-on sentences, paragraphs about nothing, page-long descriptions of the monastery, characters that disappeared from the text. I read three chapters before I gave up and closed the computer. It hit home, then, how fragile my mental health had been. In that moment I knew I couldn't trust any of the supernatural experiences I'd had at Sfântul Mihail. Anastasia was right, the place should be pulled down. Whatever historical blight tainted those walls had also messed with our minds. I never wanted to go back there.

For the rest of the day, I packed and ate room service. I was back on my real medication, which helped me deal with the stress of the events around me. In the hotel, I was in a bubble. I was sheltered by it while the world went crazy over Adele Jobert, the woman who sold her daughter, who believed the world was made up of the strong and the weak. Wolves and sheep.

I slept well despite everything, waking up early for my flight. A familiar face greeted me in the hotel lobby.

"Alexandru!" I said.

To my great surprise he pulled me into a bear hug. "I saw the news. It is a relief to see you well. I have been worried ever since driving you to that place." He mumbled what I suspected was a prayer beneath his breath.

"I wish I'd taken your warning more seriously."

He dragged my suitcases out of the hotel and opened the boot of the taxi. This time he didn't complain when he lifted the heavy cases into the car. "I'm sorry about your friends. No one thought anything like that would happen."

"Thank you."

"You must be ready to leave Romania now, yes? Ready to go home?"

I said I was, but inside I knew I was merely replacing new ghosts with old ones. To brighten the mood, I added, "Why don't I show you how to sew on your own buttons now?"

He laughed and shook his head.

———

It was on the flight that I took my laptop out of my hand luggage and opened the story about Maria. Slowly I worked through the first chapter and began editing. Weeding out chunks of clunky descriptions, shortening the sentences, developing Maria's character. It was difficult to describe her because every time I thought of her, I saw the faceless figure dressed in black. But I continued to be drawn back to her. There was no logical explanation for it, but I was convinced that she'd given up a baby.

I came home, unpacked, dusted and edited. I worked almost as intensely as I had in the monastery. There were over fifty thousand words to wade through and decipher.

Usually I hated editing, but for the first time I enjoyed it. The drive was there, but I had to manage it. I couldn't let myself obsess over Maria's story again.

In the weeks that followed, I also reread my last Akarthis story, realised where I'd gone wrong, unpublished it, and promised fans that I'd upload a new version of the story with corrections. Then I contacted Jules's parents to talk to them about their daughter. Over the phone, they thanked me for calling them, and tearfully invited me to the funeral in New York. I was her last friend, they told me. She'd mentioned me in her emails to them. She cared about me.

For three days I agonised about whether to fly to New York. I thought about Jules wearing my hoody. Jules in the woods, holding my hand. Jules telling me about Irene's deception. In the end, I couldn't do it. I wasn't ready. Instead, on the day of her funeral, I sat alone in the cold, wintery park, bundled up in a thick coat, watching dog walkers go by. She would've called me an idiot for sitting out there, but I thought about her the whole time. It was easy, in the cold, because we'd spent so much of our time freezing in the Carpathian forest. The colder I was, the easier it was to see her face.

In the first weeks back in the UK, I had nightmares every single night. Nathan's thin features peering through the darkness, mouth twisted into a scream. Irene's broken face as she laid lifeless on the sofa. Dan's mangled body half-frozen and covered in snow, a dark apparition standing over him. Jules prostrate on the forest floor, a wolf's jaw around her ankle. Whenever I woke, I edited a few chapters of Maria's story, and that usually calmed me down.

After about three weeks, I had a pretty good grip on Maria's story. It was time to test my theory. I didn't know how I was going to do it, but I decided I was going to find out if Maria did in fact give up a child.

I contacted Sorin first, who was willing to help. He checked public records, asked for favours from local police, managed to get them to open old case files on the mother superior, and found notes made by her about Maria's new-born baby. It took about a month, but Sorin came through for me. I was at home writing when he emailed me a name. Maria's baby boy. But it had been seventy-eight years and the baby had been a man who passed away in 2015.

There was a grandchild. A girl born in 1967. With Sorin's help, we tracked her down to a coastal Romanian town called Constanța. It was Sorin who called her and explained the strange and wonderful circumstances of my task. I don't know how he managed to convince her to meet me, but she agreed.

It was January, after a lonely Christmas, that I flew to Bucharest once again. There I took a train to Constanța and arrived at an apartment block near the shores of the Black Sea. Travelling was not something I did often. I found the experience stressful, but empowering. However, standing in front of that apartment door was perhaps the most nerve-wracking part of the entire trip. My heart beat a quick tattoo against my ribcage, and a hot flush crept up my neck. It took me a moment to bring up the courage to knock.

When she opened the door, I was sure that this woman resembled the Maria in my story. Her name was Crina, she was fifty-three, and she had grey hair that fell straight to her shoulders. Our greeting was in silence because she didn't speak English and my Romanian language skills were limited to asking where the public toilet was. We'd exchanged emails using translation software, but now we were face to face and I shyly uttered *buna* in a bad accent. She smiled politely and waved me into her home.

Before arriving at Constanța, I'd finished Maria's story, and then hired a Romanian translator to translate it so that Crina could read it. Crina was in the process of reclaiming her grandmother's diary from the police in Brasov, but I'd wanted her to read my story. I had the laptop in my sweaty hands, holding it awkwardly as she made us coffee. She used an app on her smartphone to ask if I needed sugar. We giggled at the robotic voice coming out through the speaker. I knew right away that she was kind. I liked her.

After coffee and pleasantries spoken through our phones, I opened the laptop and allowed her to read the story. Now my heart was pounding even harder and the coffee wasn't helping my anxiety. I placed it back on the table, rubbed sweaty palms on my jeans, and waited for her reaction.

Halfway through, she stood up to fetch tissues. Then she settled back down in her chair and I waited in silence for her to finish reading. She dabbed her eyes and looked at me. I hastily typed a message to translate:

I don't know if this is how it happened. But I think it is.

Crina typed back.

I think you're right.

CHAPTER THIRTY-NINE

There was, I felt, the sense of a task still incomplete. My nightmares were different every night. One night I dreamt of Nathan screaming about the monster. The next it was Dan, running for his life. The next it was Irene sobbing on my shoulder, the smell of her coconut shampoo in my nostrils. Then Jules, being dragged by the wolf, her hands reaching out to me, eyes begging me to make it stop. Finally, Maria. Even after meeting Crina, Maria had no face in my dreams. She was the same smudged outline of a human being, facing off against the white wolf on the mountainside.

I hadn't followed much of Adele's trial, but there was one thing I knew. She was releasing the names, bit by bit, one by one. The names of rich, powerful people dropped. Five men and one woman so far. I skimmed headlines, trying not to see the names or faces, wanting to keep those viewers as a non-entity, like Maria's faceless presence. If I knew who had seen me, my naked body, my private moments... I could hardly bear it.

In February, I contacted Nathan's family and told them all about their son's last weeks. I told them that Nathan hadn't been himself, that he'd suffered a psychological break, or at least been under extreme stress, and that there had been times when he was kind to me. I told them all about the way we searched for the drone in the mist together, him helping me even when he didn't need to. They were kind, too, and invited me to Leeds for a memorial in the summer. To them, he was always a son first, but to the rest of the world he was a murderer. I accepted their invitation.

There was an uncomfortable part of these events that I hadn't quite accepted. It was the fact that I had become recognisable to people. I was the girl who survived. They called me the Final Girl. People came up to me on the street and asked me how I was. It made it even harder for me to leave the house. But then whenever I was home, I was reminded too much of the past, and it would reach the point where I had to get out.

A week after my call with Nathan's family, I contacted Dan's parents and talked to them about his sunrise yoga classes, the ambitions he'd had about his business, and the love he'd shown for his sister Maria. This call was the worst. They'd lost both of their children—what do you say? How do you console that kind of pain? They told me more about Dan's death as we talked on the phone, which helped me fill in some of the gaps. The Brasov police service figured out that the taxi driver had called Dan to tell him he wouldn't be able to collect him due to the imminent bad weather, but Dan's phone had no battery by the time the call was made. Dan had walked to the road hoping to find the taxi. Instead, he found the wolf and was dragged into the woods. Dan's mother sobbed as she told me. I shed tears with her and felt like a wet sponge by the time she was done. I was exhausted, and I needed a break.

Two weeks sped by as I redecorated the living room listening to true crime podcasts. For a while, I was content. The nightmares ceased for almost a week. Then they came back.

I thought about sending Irene's mother a letter. But what could I say? She wasn't the person I wanted to talk to. I wanted to talk to Irene, to tell her that I understood her. I didn't condone what she did, but I understood what it was like to live with a person who cared nothing for your well-being, who saw you as either a burden or an opportunity to be used for personal gain. It was abhorrent to think that she'd used her fraudulent past to rise to stardom, but I'd forgiven her already. I'd even forgiven her for stealing my medication. Whether I could forgive her mother was another story.

As you can imagine, Irene and Adele's story was a juicy one. Various publications like the *New Yorker* and *Vanity Fair* published in-depth articles about the Joberts' deceptions. About the poison Adele bought to make Irene appear sicklier while pretending she was dying. The hospital staff they duped into posing with them. The men they'd seduced. The dodgy make-up they sold. Irene's father crept out from beneath a rock and cried on television shows, but I remembered how Jules found messages from him begging for money. He told everyone how Adele liked to refer to herself as Maman Loup. Mother wolf. Loup, the name of the investment company she'd set up. In the end I stopped reading because it nauseated me, but I saw that Adele's list of the powerful continued to be drip-fed for maximum exposure.

The internet called for the arrest of these people. Every outraged young internet warrior had a pitchfork for justice.

Every day I found several emails in my inbox asking me to support the cause, but I didn't have the fight in me to respond. There had been arrests, warnings and slaps on the wrist, but not enough for the vengeance mob.

In early March I met Alice for the first time. We met in Birmingham, because it was part way between our homes. My stomach buzzed with butterflies as I entered the quirky book café we'd found on Google maps. Would I be a disappointment to her after all these years? Was she a fan or a friend? But from the first smile and wave, the awkwardness disappeared.

"I sat next to a woman cutting her fingernails on the train," she told me as she settled into her seat. "I'm still frazzled."

I laughed. She was exactly as I'd imagined her. Small, with a pixie haircut, dressed in a jumper dress, leggings and Doc Martens.

"The guy across from me was eating cheese and onion crisps," I said.

"Those should be made illegal in public."

We ordered and chatted about the Akarthis world for a time, which I enjoyed. Alice told me her favourite stories and characters. We lost track of time talking about them all and there was a smile on my face that hadn't been there for a long time. A different kind of contented smile I wasn't used to. Being appreciated felt good.

During the second pot of tea she began to tell me about that night in the monastery. Several of the other subscribers had been interviewed on the news, but this was my first experience hearing Alice's perspective. Because I'd been avoiding much of the news, many of those experiences were a surprise to me.

"A couple of the others thought it was special effects at

first. They couldn't believe their eyes." She shook her head. "I feel strange when I think about it even now. My mind doesn't want to believe it was real. It took me a long time to finally stop seeing her face when I closed my eyes."

"I dream of her," I said. "I dream of what he did to her."

She nodded. "So do I. But my therapist is helping. What about you?"

"I haven't got one."

"Cath, why? You've been through serious fucking trauma."

I shrugged. "I don't know. I've been putting it off."

She raised her eyebrows as she spoke, and I took that to mean how earnest she was about this. "If I need therapy, maybe you do too. What you went through at that place was far, *far* worse than seeing it online. Cath, you have to get help."

I focused on a tea stain in the centre of the table, not trusting myself to talk, tears burning.

"It's okay," she said. "You're safe now."

Another sip of tea pulled me back together. "There was that strange account that kept offering money for one of us to commit murder. How sick is that considering what happened?"

Alice leaned towards me. "You don't know, do you?"

"Know what?"

She lowered her voice. "With this legal stuff I'm never sure what I can say and what I can't, but, well... After Irene died, there was a rush to contact the police in Romania. *Hundreds* of us were trying to help. Even when we'd finally contacted the police, we stayed online discussing what we'd seen. That was when we started talking about Lupo, or Volk, or whoever, and their nasty comments. A group of us decided to try and track them down for the police. We all thought it was weird that they'd been offering money for..." Her body vibrated, an exaggerated shiver. I knew what she meant. Murder. "We couldn't track them at all at first, because of VPNs or whatever those private servers are called, but apparently, there was one occasion where they messed up and used an IP address in California."

All the pieces fell together at last. "It was her mother."

A grim smile spread across Alice's lips. "It was her mother. You know what else? Every one of her sock accounts was a word meaning wolf in a different language. Cheeze-monkeys figured that out in the end."

"Loup is French for wolf," I said. "And it's also a fake investment company she set up to finance The Event. She was Loup. She was Volk. And Lupo. Jesus. She wanted to play so many games with us."

"I don't understand a person like that," Alice said. "It sounds like she was a complete control freak. Anyway, we've passed on all that information to the police and it'll be used at her trial. I guess she'll go to prison for a long time. I hope they get the names of the people buying the nudes." When Alice saw my reaction, she added, "Sorry, maybe I shouldn't have brought that up."

"It's fine. In the long run I guess some rich pervert seeing my tits isn't so bad. At least I'm here. At least I survived."

Alice reached across the table and squeezed my hand. It was such a Jules thing to do that I almost burst into tears.

"God, what happened in that monastery," I said. "Am I insane to think that place is evil?"

"No," she said. "Absolutely not."

"There are times when I think it was the building, and times when I think we were simply too broken to stay in a place like that. Do you think it was fate that brought us together?"

"Maybe," she said.

I sighed. "I never believed in fate before."

"You know what I think?" Alice said. "It doesn't matter. You're home and safe, and you never need to go back there again."

It was good to hear her say that.

"Did any of you see who burned the Ouija board?" I asked, suddenly remembering that night.

Alice shook her head. "No. Didn't you ever find out."

"I guess it was Irene. We realised she'd been stirring things up for a while."

"Did she take your medication?" Alice asked.

"Yes. It was the last thing she told me. Maybe the mics didn't pick up her voice. She whispered it to me."

"Why would she do that?"

I shrugged. "She said her mother told her to." And then I shivered, remembering the nuns, remembering the story Sorin had told me in his farmhouse kitchen. "I think Adele Jobert wanted people to die. She wanted to capture our deaths on camera."

Alice was pale. "So she could sell it?"

We swiftly changed the subject, but even after my fingers stopped shaking, and we exchanged a few light-hearted jokes about life, it was as though I wasn't there. I couldn't stop thinking that I had brought a piece of Sfântul Mihail back with me, and that I would never be able to rid myself of it. But Alice was so kind, and there was spring sunshine outside. We talked about brighter things before walking back to the train station, meandering in a few bookshops along the way. We arranged another meet up. She suggested I visit her in Oxford and meet her wife. I told her I'd bring signed books next time.

She reminded me that I'm not alone.

Now I had three places to visit. Oxford in April, to make a new friend. Leeds in the summer, to say goodbye to Nathan. New York in the autumn to say goodbye to Jules.

But there was one place that still made me uneasy. Home.

SILENCE GREETED ME INSIDE, YET THAT SILENCE REFUSED TO last.

I told you that I'll never go away. I told you that I'm here to stay, Catherine.

I ignored her. Instead, I left my bags by the door, and slowly made my way through the house. I passed the living room, where once I would come after school and watch television while she slept upstairs with one of her headaches. I passed the bathroom where she saw me putting on make-up and told me no amount of slap would make me beautiful. Heavy legs made their way up the stairs, but I did not go in my bedroom. I went to the one room in the house that I hadn't set foot in for a long time. I finally unlocked the door and stepped in.

In my mind, I saw the surge of fluorescent jackets as the paramedics rushed into the room. They were too late, as I knew they would be.

Of course, they were.

After they removed the body, I'd cleaned the room, changed the sheets on the bed, sprayed cleaner into the carpet until nothing smelt like vomit anymore. I'd removed the empty bottles, cans and food wrappers. I'd hoovered the carpet and dusted the drawers. Then I'd closed the door and never gone in there again. A week later, I attended a rainy funeral. The one person in this world who watched my mother's coffin lowered into the ground. And at that point, I'd promised myself that when I died, I'd have friends to mourn me, that I wouldn't be the unloved body lowered into the cold, lonely ground.

You're kidding yourself.

There was a mirror above the bed. In the reflection, I saw the dark, featureless shape of Maria. An empty space where a face should be. It was okay, I wasn't afraid, because I knew she'd be there.

"It's time, isn't it?" I said to her.

She didn't need to nod.

It's time for you to join me. Otherwise you'll have to face up to what you did.

But my mother was wrong about that. I spoke the words out loud as I stared at Maria's reflection. "I found her lying on her back, choking on her own vomit. She was *still* choking."

Murderer.

"When I saw her, the first thought that popped into my head, was that she was dying. Her skin was turning blue. I knew she couldn't breathe."

Murderer.

"I could've stopped it. I could have saved her life. But I didn't. I stood there and I watched."

Murderer.

"What I did was wrong. But it was my first opportunity to get out. I... She never let me leave. For all those years I'd listened to her tell me I was worthless, and I'd believed her. I didn't know how to walk out of the door on my own two feet. Her weight pressed me down until I couldn't stand tall. But then I saw her lying there and the future seemed clearer than ever. I saw a new life. I saw a way out, and I didn't have to do anything. Perhaps it was what you deserved, Mum, but I still shouldn't have done it. I should've left years ago."

Bitch.

"What I didn't know, was that you would refuse to go. No, you couldn't leave me alone, you had to stay, whispering in my ear until I almost lost my mind. Chipping away at whatever self-esteem I'd clawed back for myself when you died. I hated you more after you died. And now..." I sighed. "I don't hate you now."

Quietly, I walked over to her bedside table and picked up an old, metal-based lamp that had belonged to my mother for many years. I walked back to the mirror.

"Maria, it's time for you to go, and it's time to take her with you."

No.

"It's time to go, Mum. I have a life to live."

I gazed into the mirror and saw nothing but my face. That too round, too plain, too expressionless face. With one, hard strike, I smashed it into pieces.

If you asked me now, whether ghosts exist, I don't know what I'd say. I'd say there's no answer. The one thing I do know, is that I threw away my medication the next day, and I never heard my mother's voice ever again.

THE END

ABOUT THE AUTHOR

Sarah A. Denzil is a British suspense writer from Derbyshire. Her books include SILENT CHILD, which has topped the kindle charts in the UK, US, and Australia. SAVING APRIL and THE BROKEN ONES are both top thirty bestsellers in the US and UK Amazon charts.

Combined, her self-published and published books, along with audiobooks and foreign translations, have sold over one million copies worldwide.

Sarah lives in Yorkshire with her husband, enjoying the scenic countryside and rather unpredictable weather. She loves to write moody, psychological books with plenty of twists and turns.

To stay updated, join the mailing list for new release announcements and special offers by going to my website www.sarahdenzil.com.

Find me on Facebook, Twitter and Instagram.